"**GROSS AND UNLIKEABLE** made me feel the way I felt as a kid reading scary stories with a flashlight in the dark. These tales hit at something primitive and true, something beyond fear. Then and now, I felt almost giddy as I read, the way one might when the footsteps are getting closer and the only thing left to do is scream."

LINDSAY HUNTER
Author of *Ugly Girls*

"Deeply inappropriate, unbelievably disturbing, these are some brave and real stories of love, sex, family and other horrors."

CHARLIE JANE ANDERS
Author of *All the Birds in the Sky*

"I've long thought that the most interesting work being done in a genre is being done on its fringes, by the people who those at the center fail to acknowledge: those marginalized writers haven't drunk the Kool Aid yet. *Black Candies: Gross and Unlikeable* is about what happens when women take over Horror, invert its tropes, turn them on their head, and make Horror do things that you didn't know it could. An important and razor-sharp anthology that will leave you breathless and bleeding."

BRIAN EVENSON
Author of *A Collapse of Horses*

"The writers in this anthology breathe life into characters and conflagrations that are frightening and fearful, cagey and forthright, familiar and unknowable, repulsive and endearing, vulnerable and indomitable, befuddling and unmistakable, gross and unlikeable, yes, i.e. human. Together, they churn up a vital miasma of horror's sub-genres to create something heedless and lasting. Reading this book is like being drawn and quartered by a stampede of half-decayed, red-eyed horses."

ADRIAN VAN YOUNG
Author of *Shadows in Summerland*

Book design: Carolyn Ramos
Executive Director: Justin Hudnall

ISBN: 978-0-9979499-0-2

So Say We All (SSWA) is a San Diego-based 501(c)3 non-profit
organization that provides arts education to populations
without access and supports local artists through showcase
opportunities and peer-to-peer counseling.

sosayweallonline.com
blackcandies.sosayweallonline.com
info@sosayweallonline.com

GROSS AND UNLIKEABLE

GUEST EDITED BY NATANYA ANN PULLEY

FOREWORD

Steaming viscera. Menstruation as omen. The sharp blade of a returned violence. When I agreed to guest edit for the all-female issue of *Black Candies*, I thought the call for Gross and Unlikeable would result in tales of gore, abjection, and pain. And it has. And it is here. But what surprised me was the similarity in the ways these stories made meaning or expressed these themes. I noticed something beyond content and narrative style or form. Women were telling stories of the gross and unlikeable, the horrid and repulsive, the haunted and darkly sad, of course. But their words were more than windows or a stage—more than mirrors of our reality even. At root, each story in this collection knows that it contends with an expectation of images, tropes, and textures coded female and of a male-dominated genre and canon. I learned quickly that editing this journal would be as much an act of listening as of coordinating and proofing. What I heard was a wail; what I saw was myself and us. What I knew was I had no armor (nor could anyone) for what was to come. In terms of content,

I wasn't prepared for the dead babies or the re-enactment of violence marked on female bodies in the submissions we received. But there was something else to these pieces for which I wasn't prepared: the wish within each narrative to split open all the stories sold to women—stories we are forced to swallow, digest, and let grow inside us. Here all the fruit was laid out on the ground and stomped on. Juices running. Coaxing spoil and rot.

The horror women want to talk about, want to write about couldn't be wrangled or pinned down into one theme or aesthetic. I had to just listen.

And I've had my share of editors who did not listen, as have my female writer friends. This is not simply to say that writers have disagreed with editors' revisions and suggestions and cuts, but that in the age of a thousand outlets—of journals and anthologies and books and readings and video-readings and text sites and conferences, the writer's voice is easily lost to that of the editor's. Editors hold the line and sculpt and create. I, too, sculpted in this issue. Trimmed and fussed as one does when there's a larger project at work (more so than I want to admit). But in my tinkering I knew I was doing more than working through a story with someone. I was feeling out the space of their voice—where it had been and where it wanted to go (as I want to believe editors do). I followed as best I could. Lines and paragraphs I suggested be cut were tendrils, not excess. I second/third/fourth-guessed all amputations. Unlike editing for other projects though, when I felt myself scrutinizing, re-imagining, and word-wavering, I tried to remember—to keep it at the forefront of me as mantra, as reality, as various truths—that this open textual landscape was unknowable, untamable, unspeakable at times. While tightening images, wording, and pacing was one thing, what these voices demanded was room for ideas to sprawl. Legs and mouth open, chest flayed back and ribcage exposed. Messy and without your permission. Musings, notions, dreamspeak, and intonations. Conjuring, reporting, weighing, declaring. I learned the difference between editing towards filling a defined spaced—one polished and tuned to an invisible marker given to me daily—and editing with trust and curiosity towards an expanse or a threshold or an oblivion.

I believe writing stories (like all art) is a political act. Whose story we tell, whose we share, and how we expect them to be handed to us is an engagement with truths. These truths can be filtered, dove-tailed, hedged, and, at times, erased by narrative structures and voices that seek to solidify a phallocentric reality. This collection doesn't just give women a space to tell vile stories, it grapples with notions of story and reality handed to women through things dark and dangerous. In form, in content and in its claim of things weird, rancid, and gruesome. This means, for me and this issue, "gross and unlikeable" is not an aesthetic. These adjectives do not make concrete a known, they do not qualify a reality for a non-female audience. "Gross and Unlikeable" is not just a theme either, the checkbox of content. Some of these stories are beautiful and sad, some are light, and some silly even.

Gross and unlikeable is reality. When women tackle the stories that are handed down to them, or muck about in the narratives bodies share, or live in the liminal as they do in this collection, they aren't evoking a theme but destroying the lie of women tamed, of women just so. They speak of violence and they dole it out again. And the future they hold can be just as vulnerable as it is dark—not sexy and defiant dark, not dark for your pleasure. If I've learned anything working on horror with all women writers it is this: The pleasure is ours.

Natanya Ann Pulley
2016

BLACK CANDIES

GROSS AND UNLIKEABLE

VILE GIFTS AND WHAT THE BODY SECRETS

IN THIS BREATH, A VIOLENCE

CHEWING BEDLAM AND THE BITE OF BECOMING

POSTLUDE

PRELUDE

SECOND SKIN

STORY BY RACHEL MARSTON • ART BY CHRISTINE HAMM

Sarah decided, when she had decided after all, to quit this life, that she would do so in a way fitting such a grave decision. No razors at the wrist, no pills for her. She first drugged her neighbor's dog, that giant beast, whose barks had kept her awake during the night for six months now. This dog, the size perhaps of a small bear cub, bounded eagerly toward her offer, her home-baked dog treats held high in the palm of her right hand.

The dog licked and slobbered vigorously, eating every crumb, and gazing at her with a look of such stupid friendliness that Sarah knew she'd made the right decision. The owners, her neighbors of six years, smiled and looked on with the same stupid friendliness, while saying to the dog "well, isn't that nice for the puppy, some yummy treats from the pretty lady." The dog returned to them, and, as they scratched behind his ears, they looked rather pleased with themselves.

She dragged his sleeping body from their porch at three-thirty in the morning and heaved him into her truck.

She arrived at the spot, this nice high glade of aspens in the Uintas, just as the sun began to pinken the sky.

She pulled his heavy body from the trunk to the ground and over to two close trees, fine white-trunked beauties. She stretched those great limbs and paws of his between the trees, securing him with rope and nails and netting. She whispered into his ear, "Good puppy" then she slit him from groin to neck with one sharp motion of a hunting knife. The knife slid in so easily, that metal blade through fur and skin, and the inside slid out so easily, the bladder, the bowels, the kidneys, all reds and browns and purples, just piling up at her feet.

She took a sledgehammer to the ribcage, cracked the sternum, making space. Then she picked up her needle, a heavy gauge industrial one, threaded with fishing wire, and stepped into the dog's embrace. His skin was slick from the inside out. She turned herself around, so that they faced the same direction and let his giant head, heavier than she realized, rest on her shoulder. Her shoes slipped as she turned. She bent low and pulled the skin of his stomach together at her knees, pushing back into the warm stickiness of the remaining organs and blood until she felt his spine against hers.

His skin slipped from her fingers and she wiped the needle, every so often, against her shirt, but eventually, she stitched herself in tight, right inside that dog skin. Her feet stood on his entrails and as she shifted, she jarred his tongue loose, and it lay smooth and wet against her cheek.

She sighed for this smell, this strangely clean scent of flesh and blood. She closed her eyes, her arms tucked in at her chest, wrapped in this slick blanket, so warm on this cool morning and waited for the sun to rise. For the smell to rise. For the insects and the birds to arrive. For their small teeth and claws to begin their work. For those small pricks at her flesh and then the burrowing. For her to be eaten from the outside in, but to be safe, for this moment, in this other skin.

BEDTIME TALES
UNEARTHED

A HORSE'S CROWN

STORY BY LILY HOANG • ART BY MADELINE GOBBO

Once, there is a princess, her handmaid, and a talking horse. The handmaid rides a horse as well, but it is old and ugly. They are on the way to a great prince's castle; this road is long and arduous. This is the wedding procession.

Suddenly, the handmaid says, "Stop," and they all stop. They don't freeze in place or anything—this isn't a children's game—but they halt all the same. The handmaid says, "Get off your stupid talking horse. I want to ride it now."

"Well what shall I ride then?" the princess asks. "All my life I have only ridden one horse. Barney is my only companion in life, I cannot let you ride him."

The handmaid gets off her horse and pushes the princess into a mud puddle. When she rises, it is not graceful. When she mounts the old and ugly horse, she is not lithe. No, she is soaked with goop and slides all over the place.

•

So a princess, her handmaid, and a talking horse walk into a bar.

"Three beers, please."

They order another round, and then they go to sleep.

•

Later, when they reach the castle, the prince meets them at the palace door. The handmaid gets off the fancy horse and curtsies all the way down to the prince's knees. But the handmaid is not a lady. She looks like a jester, except that the rouge on her cheeks is more subdued.

When she lowers her head in a bow, the prince can see chiggers cling onto her matted hair, lest they fall into gravity.

Yet—this is the way of arranged marriages. And so they married, the handmaid and the prince.

The king is unhappy. His queen is dead, but still, she mourns and flowers pipe out from her grave. Her tears fertilize them. The prince is unhappy. All day long he pouts. The real princess is banished to servitude. Even the talking horse is appalled. Someone is satisfied, though: can you guess who?

•

There was once a princess who would adorn Barney's

8

neck with a string of thick pearls and braid ruby flowers in his mane.

·

After the ceremony, the crown princess tells the prince to cut off Barney's head and mount it on the wall of the kitchen, such that her handmaid may have a companion when she sleeps by the oven for warmth.

·

In the name of altruism.

·

For purposes of clarity, the old princess is now the handmaid; the handmaid is now the princess. Their identities have not changed. Their personalities have not swapped. This is an exchange in title alone.

·

Except title *is* identity. Or, it can be. There is a relationship there, and it is not tenuous.

·

Time moves, but patiently.

One day, the handmaid mourns to her horse head, says, "Oh Barney!"

And Barney says, "Your mother would be so disappointed. Her heart will unravel its chambers."

The blood has dried around the horse's neck. Nails adhere his skin to lacquered wood. When she pets Barney's desiccating mane, her hand is a milky stream of elegance. Barney leans his horse face into her smell, and a nail pops out of its hole. Barney bleeds and he bleeds and they both think this is the end. Everything is hopeless.

But—because they live inside magic, the handmaid picks up the nail, shoves it into an unbloody patch of skin, and the horse is healed and there isn't even a mess to clean up!

·

The princess is cruel to her handmaid because when their titles were reversed—well, reciprocation is merely an ethical suggestion, not a requirement.

·

Oh, nothing special, just some whipping and some caning.

Just audio torture and a cement floor. The handmaid does not even have a blanket to call her own.

·

Before, blankets crammed tight with goose. Now, she must braid her own hair. The water for her bath is not boiled first.

·

Starvation, too.

·

One day the king notes the goodness of the thin pretty maid-girl. He commands her as his own, not like a concubine or mistress or anything, and he is a good king, a kind one. He gives her proper chambers and simple smocks with pockets.

·

Meanwhile, the prince will not fuck his new bride. She arrived with bugs leeched everywhere.

He will not let her into his bed, but her chambers are lush so what does she care?

When the princess strikes the handmaid with an iron bar, the bruises form and then heal immediately, and so she must strike harder the next time, and the next, and the handmaid does not cry out for help. The horse watches it all, helpless.

·

When will the hero arrive and save the disguised princess? Already she is surrounded by royalty; figure it out already, please!

·

The handmaid cries to her horse, and pearls fall from her eye sockets. It is torture, and there is blood everywhere. The handmaid drops the pearls into a basin and washes them. She forces a needle and thread through. She is making Barney a new crown, but that requires many, many more tears.

·

When the handmaid cries, Barney closes his eyes and pushes his head to the side. He cannot witness such woe.

He laments, "Your mother would be so disappointed.

Her heart will unravel its chambers."

But this only causes the handmaid to weep, and the pearls become so large that they rip the tender skin beneath her eyes.

•

Hard to follow the logic, but when Barney makes her cry, her wounds do not heal. It is only when the princess torments her that the fabric of magic falls over the handmaid's body with elixir.

•

Ahoy! Who comes this way? A royal procession? Light the chandeliers and behead us some goose! Tonight, there will be a feast of welcoming!

•

The sight of her old flag from her chamber window sends the princess into a frenzy.

Insects line the floor, her miniature army.

But they will not follow her commands.

•

Of course, the handmaid does not know about her mother's arrival. She is in the kitchen, preparing for a feast. She walks by the talking horse and pets his mane. He nuzzles her face and his skin does not tear. Trumpets declare the arrival of royalty and the handmaid runs to her chambers to change her smock. Even servants must look presentable when a feast is at hand.

The handmaid disrobes and re-robes, and her beauty emits enough glow to illuminate the darkest dungeon. She grabs a box and runs back into the kitchen, says to the horse, "This is for you." She opens the box and a crown of pearls descends upon his head. And still, Barney says, "Your mother would be so disappointed. Her heart will unravel its chambers." And then, "Thank you, my princess. When your agony is washed away, only the precious remains."

•

The queen is anxious to see her daughter, who she is told is terribly ill at the moment.

The king and prince receive her. She asks if her daughter is yet with child. The prince will not look at her. He seems bored, but really, he is frightened of the revelation that he has not copulated, that he will give his father and mother-in-law no child. *How odd*, the prince thinks, *that a daughter can look so different from her mother.*

How unfair, the king himself thinks, *that a woman so fair birthed such an ugly girl.*

The king whistles for his handmaid. She carries in a carafe of wine and curtsies, first before the king, then the prince, then her mother.

And so it is, the queen's heart unravels in its chambers and the handmaid's true identity is revealed.

•

Don't call it revenge.

Call it justice.

A handmaid's head mounted next to the talking horse.

Barney never liked her anyway. He spits right in her face, and mites crawl out of her eyes. They pinch onto her flesh, lest they, too, are crushed under the weight of air.

THE REPULSIVE

STORY BY MARY CROSBIE • ART BY CARABELLA SANDS

Translated verbatim from the original 17th Century German "Die Repulzwartig."

Once upon a time there lived a couple of weirdos. I don't know how they met, but they just sat around their house all day. They never got haircuts and ate grubs with their filthy hands. They were gross weirdos, too. I didn't really want to tell you, but they both had severe back acne. Or bacne, if you prefer? They would pop each other's back zits all day long. Then they would rub corn oil into their backs to make more zits.

One day, the weirdo woman looked out the wall hole where the window used to be. She spied into her neighbor lady's yard. She liked to spy on her stupid neighbor lady who had this garden and grew all this stupid green stuff which seemed like stupid. That day, weirdo woman noticed some little red berries on a bush.

"Like little zits on the bush," thought the weirdo woman. See how weird she was? Who thinks stuff like that?

So the weirdo woman began fantasizing about getting those little bush zits in her gross mouth. She told her weirdo husband how she didn't want anything else to eat but the bush zits.

"But there's a fence!" whined the weirdo husband. He was very lazy and had pustulous legs he couldn't operate very well.

So the two weirdos cried because there was a fence. And they cried some more. Then the crying reminded the weirdo husband of something he had seen on TV.

In the middle of the night, he went to the fence and smashed it with a big hammer. Then he got into the neighbor lady's backyard. He grabbed a sweaty handful of the red bush zits and ate them. He ripped every last bush zit off the bush and swallowed them until he choked and barfed. Then he got lost in the backyard. He couldn't find the place where he had made the hole.

Eventually the neighbor lady came out and asked the weirdo husband what was going on with him. And he said, my wife is having a baby and he needed to feed her food because they had no money to buy pizza pies. And that his weirdo wife really wanted some bush zits.

Oh yeah, the weirdo lady was pregnant. They hadn't made any plans for the baby. They hoped it would just stop being a baby and come out weird like the last one and they could throw it away.

When the neighbor lady heard the weirdo's tale, she threw up in her own garden. She never wanted to hear the words "bush zits" again. The weirdo's breath smelled exactly like a plague of dead rats. He was shirtless so she could see all his bacne and his frontne.

The neighbor lady showed him how to get out of the garden and made sure he left. Then she ran inside and washed her hands for an extremely long time until she could taste antibacterial soap.

One week later, the neighbor lady went to the red berry bush and found an aggressively ugly baby beneath it. It was covered in bursty zits, and had a giant mole covering its face.

The neighbor lady picked it up—with gloves on though, because it was slicked in zit slime and was really the grossest baby you ever saw. "Repulsive," thought the neighbor lady. And that's what she ended up calling the zit baby.

Repulsive always had a wet coat of slime on her. The neighbor lady could never figure it out. It wasn't in any baby books. She didn't want to bring it to the doctor because she was sure they would exterminate it. And the neighbor lady really did feel sorry for Repulsive.

Repulsive's most disturbing feature was the mole in the center of her face. It was bulbous and bleedy. And most shocking was the long shiny hair that grew out of it. It was thick like rope and grew twenty feet long. It was coarse, like spun scabs—didn't I mention it had a crusty sediment on it? Because it did, the mole hair was somehow scabby.

The neighbor lady had to continue wearing gloves with Repulsive. She found the slime was highly toxic and would make her own skin break out in horrendous carbuncles.

Repulsive liked to dig. She dug a hole in the garden twenty feet deep. She never came out of the hole. She would sing down there and crap down there. It smelled and sounded awful.

The neighbor lady was really worried about Repulsive living in that hole. She also was worried about her coming out of that hole. The whole thing was really worrying.

When it was time for Repulsive to eat, the neighbor lady yelled:

Repulsive, Repulsive,
Send up your Long Mole Hair
That is somehow scabby and shiny...

And sure enough, the sickening mole hair would emerge from the hole. The neighbor lady would attach a whole chicken or a bag of McDonald's, her hands trembling. She never got used to it. I mean how did this happen to this nice neighbor lady? She had never hurt anyone. She went to college. Now she was three times a day sending food into a hole. What the hell message was she supposed to be getting here?

The neighbor lady would yank the mole hair twice to let Repulsive know the food was attached and the mole hair would disappear down the hole. On hungry days, the hair would reappear again fast. The neighbor lady would have to go find more food.

One day, while the neighbor lady was preparing pig feet in lard for Repulsive, the doorbell rang. The neighbor lady wasn't expecting anyone, but ran to the door, excited to see anyone that wasn't covered in slime and had a mole hair of scabs. She really was spending all her time tending to Repulsive's needs. She had stopped taking care of herself and noticed a slimy film covered her arms now too.

The neighbor lady swung open the door and nearly gagged for joy! A man with a briefcase stood there. Not any man, but the most sickening looking man. Not to be mean, but his head was all dented in and his eye was in the dent. He drooled steadily and had stubby little arms that could barely hold the briefcase.

"Would you like to buy a zit-popper?" is what he asked. The neighbor lady practically swooned. Oh, this was going to be a match made in heaven. And he had a job!

The neighbor lady wasted no time and ushered the man through the house to the backyard right to the edge of the hole. She called to Repulsive:

Repulsive, Repulsive,

Send up your Long Mole Hair

That is somehow scabby and shiny...

The mole hair came up and the neighbor lady attached it to the sickening looking man's lapel—which was caked in vomit! The neighbor lady yanked twice and the mole hair tugged the sickening man into the hole. Down he went.

There was silence for a while. The neighbor lady stood there in eager anticipation. She was already imagining the wedding, the bus tickets she would give to them to start a new life, far, far away. The emails she would send on holidays...

Finally, Repulsive yelled up: "What happened to the pig's feet?" and the mole hair appeared and touched the neighbor lady's leg. She startled at it—how she hated to be touched by the hair. But, never mind. She rushed to the kitchen and dragged out the pig's feet, and strung each greasy hoof along the mole hair, in a festive manner. Then she waited some more. Not for a thank you. She never got one of those from Repulsive. She didn't really get anything from Repulsive. Oh, one time she got rabies when Repulsive bit through her gloves.

The neighbor lady waited all night. They never came out of the hole. All the next day too, she never heard from them at all. Although it made her feel very ill, she even thought perhaps they were "honeymooning."

The neighbor lady couldn't stand the suspense any longer, so she stopped sending food down the hole. The mole hair kept poking out the top of the hole, unbidden, searching for the neighbor lady. The mole hair had grown quite long and thick with scabs. It snaked all the way into the house and found the neighbor lady while she hid in her bedroom.

The mole hair circled around her neck like a noose and dragged her down the stairs, bumping her hard on each step. The neighbor lady's arm grabbed at the railing to stop herself from falling. And although it made her completely nauseous, she clawed at the mole hair around her neck, picking away at it until scabs fell off and she was freed.

She ran to the kitchen and found a big pair of scissors. She cut the mole hair. Then she ran to the hole and cut the mole hair some more.

Repulsive, Repulsive,

I've cut your mole hair.

If you want to eat,

You have to come out of there.

It took several days, but Repulsive finally got out of the hole. She was caked in dirt with underground roots still attached to her limbs. Worms nestled in her hair. She looked like a grave; it was an improvement.

Also, Repulsive was pregnant.

But the neighbor lady showed her out of the garden, out the hole her father had made years ago that the neighbor lady never got around to fixing. She gave Repulsive some money and a few bush zits for her coming travels.

Repulsive wanted to dig herself a hole in a pig farm; somewhere sunny and smelly.

The neighbor lady waved goodbye to Repulsive.

She stared down into Repulsive's putrid hole with a flashlight. There was no man there, only bones.

BLIZZARD

STORY BY RACHEL LEE TAYLOR • ART BY CARABELLA SANDS

Let me tell you a story.

It's been snowing for hours, from late morning into the afternoon. When I got up for school it was so warm that I took off my hat as soon as I was out of the yard, so I could feel the damp breeze in my hair, even though my mother says not to. My hair is long and white blonde as corn silk, and everybody says I would be pretty like a doll with my hair and blue eyes, except for the way I have of looking so sullen.

Now all the little ones and me are gathered close around the stove. We've been getting low on wood, and with how cold it has gotten all of a sudden, Missus has left and put me in charge—I as the oldest, nearly fifteen and almost done with school anyhow. I do wish she would come back, old hag that she is.

I'm cold and tired of all the whining. It had seemed kind of a treat when it started snowing all of a sudden. The little ones like it, you know? Kept watching it fall through the window. Everybody saying it was strange, don't you think, how warm it had been for days and days and now

this? They had wanted to go out and play in it and Missus had to keep banging on the board. Nobody wants to go outside now.

I feel cold fingers pushed into my clenched up hand. It's one of the littlest girls. She has a thin string of snot running down to her pale lips. I've told nobody to cry, cause the tears might go and freeze. In truth, it makes me scared to hear them carrying on so.

"D'you want to hear the one about Snow-White and Rose-Red?" I ask them.

"Quiet it up now, if you do. So. Once upon a time there was a cottage in the woods and by the cottage door grew two big rose trees. One had roses white as that snow falling there, and t'other had roses red as blood."

"What is it you're telling about," the little girl asks.

"Hush," I say.

"Let me tell you a story."

•

Let me tell you a story about a girl who went out walking in the snow.

Hours have gone by and no one knows what to say anymore, so everyone is quiet. I could see the chilblains coming out on their fingers and the tips of their noses had started to go blue. The world is a small hushed room of cold children and falling, falling snow.

I claw my way through a wall of powder when I open the schoolhouse door. Great huge drifts of it cover the yard and the whole world around me is white. I sink in, up to my knees, then my thighs, then my waist. It gets down into my shoes and burns my ankles. My dress is soaked right through, and it chills my skin like a gown made of ice.

It is slow going. Instead of seconds it takes me long minutes to even make it to the road. At least, I thought it was the road. The snow is coming so thick and fast I can't see but a foot in front of me. My path fades soon as I make it.

No part of me is dry and the snow just falls, and falls, and falls…

•

Once upon a time there were two very good girls who lived in the woods. One of the girls was rosy, red as the tips of my fingers. And one of the girls was fair, pale as the snow in my hair. And everyone loved them, oh, so very much. Beloved they were by the birds of the air, the fish of the streams, and the beasts of the woods. Everywhere they went they held each other by the hand, and swore never to be parted, even unto their death.

But this story is not their story. This is the story of a terrible blizzard, a desperate girl, and white without end.

I am lost now, or had been all along. Nothing changes, it seems, but how hard I'm shivering. On and on I walk. My fingers are now more white than red, and swollen. The cracks in my skin from doing the wash have begun to weep and blister.

I begin to weep.

Then I start to fall. My feet are so clumsy, caked with snow, and I've long since lost all feeling of them. I trip over myself, trip over nothing.

There used to be a road here and a sun to navigate by, but now the road and the sun and the sky are all a piece. I wonder which way Missus went. I wonder if maybe we will pass each other in the snow.

I wonder if anyone will try to come for us.

•

Once there was a big house on the hill. You could fit my house in it ten times over. Probably your house too, for that matter. Huge and sprawling, with towers and arches all over the place, like fungus running riot on an old stale cube of bread. Now it is sugar-frosted white all over. It came out of the blankness like a ship through the fog. Or, how I imagine a sailing ship to be.

The front door opens like the dawn, hot light spilling out and the kind people they rush out crying "Liebchen!" with my mother's voice and I am saved.

This is how I wish the story goes.

I knocked and I knocked and I knocked on the door. I wanted to weep but my eyelashes were frozen and nobody was home.

But that's not how this story has to go.

Instead, the story goes that after the third knock a great booming chime like from a giant clock begins to sound and the door opens. I know you might think I'm curious, but really I'm not. It's only that I'm very cold and very tired and I just want to get inside.

•

I turn down one paneled hallway after another. There are mirrors all over the walls—the reflections make it look like a hundred girls are wandering in a hundred halls. The white sheen of silken wallpaper is as clean as the frost outside, though the air smells as heavy as rotting roses in summer. I am still so cold and I wish, how I do wish I was warm.

Each door I pass is closed and sporting a heavy brass knob carved in all sorts of fantastical ways. One was a great eagle claw, another the head of a bear—or is it the face of a prince in disguise? Each door has a keyhole, too. Never in my life have I seen so many locked doors. Yet I know I must not look inside. I know what happens when stupid young girls try to be clever.

Slowly the doors begin to swing open and I hear the crackling of fireplaces. I look only ahead, but I can smell coffee and cinnamon and all manner of good warm things. I hear, oh, I hear my Mama singing, and birds, golden birds, and the rain in spring. I want to cry, for they are calling me to come, they are telling me to forget the snow, to forget being the oldest who is almost done with school, to forget the others I left alone, to come and forever be their child. I want to look. I do not want to look. I do not want to be like the foolish sisters in all the old stories, the selfish sisters who cannot follow the rules. I will not look, I will run. I will go back into the cold and I will pray that God delivers me.

But when I turn, the hall behind me is not the same as it was when I began. It ends at a great golden door, the doorknob a great golden egg. And when the door opens it was not I who opened it.

•

A ballroom, all done up in red. Red carpet on the floor, red plaster on the ceiling, red damask on the walls. The only thing not red is the black fireplace. It is heaped with black, black ashes. But it is warm—as warm as I could wish. And there are so many people. How did they all get here? How did they get in through the snow? Over and over they are dancing the Quadrille. The thick red carpet sucks the sound out of their footsteps and makes everyone move quiet as cats.

My gossipy companion, how does my petticoat look when I dance?

Round and round they go. Just like a cuckoo clock, if you can imagine that, just like the little wheels of a clock.

My gossipy companion, it goes like that. Like that, like that, like the tail of the cat.

I want to shout at them. Get your fancy fur coats! Break up this fine furniture for firewood! I think my mouth has frozen shut. No flame comes from the fireplace but it throws such a light over the dancers that I cannot see the

eyes in their sleek, milk-white faces. I have to tell them about the children, the little girls whose mothers love them very much.

I just have to tell them. But around and around they go, like the tail of the cat.

Again and again.

They are calling to me, calling me to dance, calling me to come be a fine lady in a fine white gown. As sullen as I am, as poor as I am, child of the dirt and the sod as I am— still they call to me. The light dances too, cheerful over where their eyes should be, black pits like the fireplace, like the keyholes, like the icy lakes of Hell.

"Come, my dear," they sing, and the dancers part to show me my place at their table, *"a feast for lords, a feast for queens.*

Such fine goblets of silver, such fine plates of gold,
(but I try to remember, instead, my mother's old table)

salt of alabaster for the cellar to hold,
(the flour sacks, the hard packed floor)

no more wells to draw, no more floors to sweep,
(the icy mornings, and the cold, the cold, the cold)

never again to toil and weep."

And then they fall like crows upon their Devil's feast, the table laid heavy with the frozen bodies of little children.

•

Once upon a time the two little girls

they are sehr gute kleine Mädchen and nothing bad ever happened to them—or, once upon a time a little girl ran away back into the snow.
No, it was the two beautiful little girls that everyone loved once upon a time they were sleeping in the woods, when an angel woke them and

no, the dawn woke them and they found that they had been
sleeping on the edge of the cliff and would have fallen right
into the darkness if they had only gone a few paces more
but their mother
their mother she said
she told them it must have been the angel
the angel that watches over good little children.

I've often heard that bad things happen
when little girls aren't careful or don't do as they're told.
I've often heard that little girls
are rosy red or white as falling snow.
I'm not so sure
but that is the story my mother told me and that is the
story I will tell you when
when I get back and I find the good little children and
where all the children are good and
warm.

•

Do you want to hear   a story?
It's about a girl who dies in the snow.
I got lost   along the way, I went wrong   somewhere.
I see a light   up ahead, but I   know   it isn't   right.
A fairy lantern to   confuse me. I will not go.
I was trying to get   home, to find   someone   that could
help us.
But I went wrong, somehow.   I went up the hill
instead of down.
Where is the angel,   mother?
It is not fair   for my fingertips to
blacken and bleed
It is not fair
to make me   the oldest to make   me a girl in a story
To make me choose

And the light I see   belongs to the big house   on the hill.

Mother, I   am so   tired.
Your child is so   cold. It is   not fair

But I am fair

My skin is   rosy red and red as snow
                              white and white as roses
                    •

light
ahead
sailing
near
          Warmer
and
in
my   skin
crawling   whitehot

home

                    •

Out of the snow the great door opens for me. Not a ser-
vant's door this time, a door guarded by rose trees. There
are so many lordly people come to welcome me home. They
sing for me in the voice of a mother to her sleeping child,
they light the fires for me so that I may rest. They tell me
I'm beautiful as the roses clad all in snow, snow like a fine
white gown.

Tonight we will dance the Quadrille. We will dance the
tails off cats, round and round forever.

Goodnight, children. Goodnight, mother.

I will take my place at the table with you, dear friends,
and we will tell each other stories to keep us warm in the
dark.

TODAY WE GO TO NOAH'S ARK.

STORY BY KAYLA MILLER • ART BY RAYNA HERNANDEZ

Today we go to Noah's Ark. We have never been and feel spiders underneath our skin in anticipation.

After the great whites in 2020, we were more than a little giddy. We had been so scared of the water, so scared of the secretive teeth it hid. Now, we can be fearless! We can be thankful. We can have it all—the animals *and* the ocean.

Because now we have Noah's Ark. There is a place for all things, surely, and now our place can be at the bottom of the sea. We don't remember who to thank and, unfortunately, history doesn't either—it seemed a colossal think-tank amalgam, or a spontaneous ejaculation of collective unconscious. It seemed everyone's idea at once, and certainly everyone endorsed it.

After all the world's great white sharks, both those known and documented and those unknown, beached themselves in a mass suicide, we were glad. Some grieved, but we were glad to have the beaches back for good. Noah's Ark came next and we were gladder because organization is gorgeous and there is surely a place for all things.

The gates to Noah's Ark are overwhelmingly high, thick as tanks. We have never been and there is a buzz in our chests that thrums our excitement in time with the air conditioner's background belch, louder outside than inside, we hope. It is a giant thing housed far from the entrance but still so audible, working hard to cool the massive Ark in the 130 degree weather.

Well, maybe it wasn't just the great whites. There were other precursors, signs that we couldn't be responsible stewards. When we killed a beached dolphin calf by passing it around for selfies. When we found the impossibly thin bodies of starved polar bears floating on melting ice islands. When the whales died of starvation with bellies full of plastic junk.

Certainly, before the great whites there was the Household Pets Act of 2019. After Ku Klux Klan members nationwide began hanging dogs alongside the bodies of Black men, the government responded by instituting legislation to remove pets of all varieties from US households, save (select) insects (after filing the required paperwork) and pet rocks. Again, we were pretty giddy, but more secretly this first time. We feigned outrage. We mimed disgust. Public outcry did nothing to stop the removal of all household pets, however—probably because we were secretly glad. So much responsibility, so much concern that we couldn't meet.

Though millions of cats and dogs were euthanized, some two hundred were saved for the Ark. We didn't know then that they were already planning the Ark, but when we found out later, we were even gladder. A place for all things is best. We feel our heartbeats pick up passing through the gate because here we can rent dogs by the hour and get all that love without the challenges of care.

Inside, there is a world. Our eyes mirror astonishment at the world inside, so much more a world than the one outside. The entire Ark is the length of some one hundred thousand square miles or football fields or something, we can't remember exactly. It is giant and we know that much, which is enough. The Ark is compartmentalized into three main sections: The Earth, The Water, and The Air. We take off our shoes and outright rub our feet into the grass we encounter entering through The Earth. We miss grass.

Considering the significant population increase and the Significance of the Ark, we are unsurprised to find millions of other visitors here. Like any theme park, there are long lines outside each habitat, which house one to hundreds of species of animals. Entire ecosystems thrive inside.

We select our first line: the forest. We will see bears! Remember bears?

The wait is hours. Luckily, the Ark never closes to accommodate its millions of daily visitors. It is our right to see the animals here, since we can't see them anywhere else, as long as we've got the $145.50 for 24 hours of individual admission. Next quarter, the cost of admission raises to $164.99. We have thought about this and saved for it and it is tremendous and we are giddy here, now, in this line, as we wait, because the forest will be dark and cool, there will be trees, there will be deer and squirrels and bears and a stream and otters and fish. We miss these things.

The Privatization of Animals Act came later and secured the Ark for all the Earth's animals except for those raised by corporations for corporate purposes, which vary. The only animals allowed outside this Ark are in factories and labs. After the Household Pets Act, we were feeling so free and light that we tap-danced down our tarmacs. When they offered to take further weight from our shoulders, we thanked them.

We are next in line after four hours of waiting. We will enter the forest! After this, we can pet the dogs!

It is so lush and green, it is difficult to look at. We didn't realize we missed green, but now we do. The visitor pathway is fenced on all sides, but through the fence we can see small animals, darting rabbits and chipmunks. There are even birds.

Only briefly do we spot a bear in the hundreds of miles of forest outside our tight fenced path. It is too far to tell what type, grizzly or black, but not far enough to make its bloody muzzle indistinguishable. We walk two miles through the forest, then turn around and walk the two miles backwards. We want more forest and more bears; we want the distance between us closed so that we can see what the bears have been eating.

After the darkness and damp earth, we want the dogs and their lightness. We want a clipped lawn and sunshine but also air conditioning. And we will get it. We can truly have it all.

The line to visit the two hundred dogs and cats spared is two lines: dogs and cats. The dogs line is longer: six hours compared to the cats' four and a half. We are happy to wait. The line sits outside a tall cinderblock fence—on grass, we scarcely believe! The Ark is all inside, there is no outside, but it seems so outside that no one notices, not even the trees and grass. Along the roped line there are vendors selling cotton candy, donuts, lemonade, sports drinks, energy drinks, and our favorite gas station snacks, too.

We buy crunchy, salty things and soft, sweet things. We smack our lips in anticipation. Some small children in line are too expectant, we hear them; they think that maybe, just maybe, they'll see *their* dog in that one hundred.

We swirl grass blades between our toes. We love the feel of grass! And without any lawn to mow.

The exit is on the opposite end, so we can't see those leaving. We are so close to the fence. We will pet dogs soon. An attendant mentally counts heads as we enter,

then stops the crowd a few heads after we pass. Nearer now, we hear gasps, brief cries, snarling.

We see the dogs! There are no fences once inside the cinderblock gate, only close-cut green and artificial sunlight and one hundred dogs. They are running towards us! They are of all breeds; only purebred dogs were saved, we guess.

The dogs are not smiling. What is wrong with these dogs this is not dogs dogs are kind they are friend they are known to know us and we are here and they do not know us now. Now, they do not know us.

We see the whites of their teeth. Only now do we see the red muck on the ground. Only now that they're on us do we see their crazed eyes. We do not see the corporate accountant. We do not see the tremendous operating costs and even more tremendous profit margin. We do not see the attendant shutting the gate. We cannot see the sign now posted outside—Closed for Feeding.

THE FINAL GIRLS

STORY BY MARIE JOHNSON PARRISH • ART BY CARRIE ANNE HUDSON

The stories we tell around the campfire are our own.

We gather before the light is completely gone. It's easier to let the air go dark around us than it is to force our bodies to go out into night. We sit on logs that have been worn smooth on the top, and we wrap our arms around our own ribs or tuck our hands between our knees. We look at the fire. We close our eyes against the stinging smoke, but we don't move away. And we're silent. Still. Until one of us says,

He wore a mask.

You would like our stories. You've heard them before. You'd recognize the bones.

A leather mask.

A stranger in the dark.

A hook, swinging from a door handle.

We know how strange it seems to have a camp for girls like us. A *camp*, of all things. But think: if we gathered any-where, all of us—if we gathered in a café, or a hotel lobby, a farmhouse, a high school gym, a park bench, a hospital room, our mothers' homes, our childhood beds, the back seat of our boyfriends' cars—it would be just as strange.

Remind us of a place you believe is safe, and we'll tell you what happened to us there. Not all of our stories took place in the woods.

Though some of them did.

And not all of us join the circle around the fire. Some of us stay in the bunkhouses that are arranged around the fire pit like the spokes of an iris. We press our cheeks to the other side of the dusty mesh screens, and we try to hear the stories we tell to each other. Some of us stay in our beds with our hands over our ears so we can't hear anything but our own blood. And we try to pretend we can't hear anything at all.

Beyond the bunks are the other buildings—the mess house, the cabins where we have art therapy and music therapy and physical therapy. The cabin we go to when we need first aid, or to take our pills. And beyond those buildings, past the vegetable garden and the volleyball court, there is a fence that is twelve feet high and hard to climb. It's laced with curling tiers of razor wire. Designed to keep out, not in.

We aren't prisoners here. We're safe.

We are told that we are safe.

During our first weeks, we each walked along the inside edge of the fence. We found gaps—spaces just wide enough for our own bodies to slip through. We found them, or we made them. We pried links apart with our red fingers. We snipped them with tools we'd stolen. We dug until we found the buried bottom, and we scraped the mud out from under our broken fingernails before dinner. We tested them. And then we hid them. We pushed the seams back together or filled the ditches with loose dirt that could be cleared away in a hurry.

We hid them from each other.

Does that surprise you? Our selfishness? It shouldn't.

We tend them like fruit trees. We return every other day to make sure the spaces still fit the width of our shoulders and the depth of our bellies.

We come in more sizes than you think. We don't all have willowy limbs and runners' thighs.

Some of us have willowy limbs and runners' thighs.

Some of us put on weight to cushion our bones after what happened. Some of us were fat to begin with, because why wouldn't we be? Fat girls can run. Fat girls can hide. Fat girls can scream, and scream, and scream.

Some of us are the girls with big tits who, in the stories you know, were supposed to die first. The ones who dared to show flashes of pink and brown and red nipples but who lived anyway, because bare flesh isn't a death sentence.

Though sometimes it is.

We know the exact number of steps it takes us to reach our gaps in the fence from every landmark in the camp: our beds, the showers, our favorite seats in the mess hall. We count them at night to calm ourselves when we cannot sleep. And on the nights we pretend to sleep, lying still on our beds, smothering our own breaths for fear of missing the sound of a footstep hidden beneath the pulse of the cicadas, we count them to drown out the words that form in the dark.

Sometimes, we sleep.

Sometimes, we wake with our tongues swollen from panting and our throats sore.

Sometimes, we wake with the scent of blood in our noses. And we do not think, first, of our own bodies—how they open and empty, predictable as the tides. We forget that we've known this smell since the sixth grade, when we woke to a smear of it still warm beneath us. In those first conscious moments, all we can remember is the sight of blood spattered on a cement wall. All we can remember is the taste when our boyfriends, startled, coughed red into our mouths before they slid out of our arms. Or when a plume sprayed from our best friends' throats and our own tongues lapped the drops from our lips before we could think.

All we can remember is the morning we opened our eyes and saw the red, wet wrist of the girl who slept in the bunk three feet away from us, and her red, wet sheets, and the note she wrote with a half-empty marker from art therapy that said that she did this to herself.

You're safe. Still.

We do not count days. We count the number of mornings we don't wake up with our hearts shivering in our chests. We count the number of times we don't look over our shoulders. We carve notches into the fresh paint on our bedposts with the knives we're not supposed to keep under our pillows.

We do not count nights. We do not count the number of times we kneel in the doorways of the bunkhouses, straining our ears, or gather around the fire with the bitten cuffs of our sweatshirts pulled over our hands. We do not count the number of times our hearts beat in the silence before one of us says,

It was late, and there was a knock at the front door.

Here is what we do not say: the words that take shape before the story begins. The words that fill up the space before we tell the story about the door that we opened, and the stranger in the dark. Before we tell the story of the picnic blanket in the woods. Before we tell the story you want to hear. We do not say those words that are always there, in the dark.

I wish I had stopped running.
I wish I had stopped running.
I wish I had stopped running.
I wish I had stopped running.

STRANGER SELVES

DOLLHOUSE

STORY BY CAIT COLE • ART BY SARAH GIRDZIUS

I saw them in her bedroom, limbs and body parts shaking in different directions, his indistinguishable from hers. Sounds of moisture and skin smacking against each other. I only looked for a second and then kept on walking, closing the door behind me as I shut myself up in my own room. I couldn't understand what I had just seen.

•

Sara had been bragging to me about her new boyfriend for weeks but I never believed a word she said. Maybe because a little drool fell from the corner of her mouth as she spoke excitedly, or maybe because she couldn't look at me without her eyes wandering in different directions. Maybe it was terrible of me to think this way, maybe I was an awful person for not believing someone could find my sister attractive, but I had always assumed she was going to live her life alone.

I decided I should tell our parents about what was going on; I had seen Sara doing something dirty in her bed with a boy. They should know.

After doing it, and feeling satisfied with their horrified reactions, I spent the night out with my own boyfriend. As I sat on top of his lap in the front seat of his car, rough hands grasping at my breasts, his wet mouth on my neck, I started to feel sick. I opened the door and vomited all over the pavement. As I wiped at my chin, I looked down to see his hands still holding my hips. He had a glimmer in his eye and a smile on his face.

•

Instead of wailing like an infant and throwing temper tantrums as I had expected, Sara barely reacted when our parents intervened. In fact, she ignored anything they had to say on the subject. She pretended like nothing had ever happened between her and the boy.

And so I forgot about it.

Until one day after school had let out, and I had gone to meet my sister out front as I usually did to drive us home. There she sat, cross-legged on the sidewalk, crying big fat tears that spilled upon her chubby cheeks. I looked at her for a moment from a distance. I wondered if we at all looked alike. We shared a womb for nine months, had been born minutes apart, and yet we were nothing alike. People always say that we have the same smile, but I know they're just being nice.

What's wrong, I asked her as I knelt down on one knee.

She was inconsolable. I thought about calling our mother. Sometimes Sara would listen to her voice on the phone and it would make her feel better. I didn't know what else would work—if I tried to pull her arm or do anything to make her move she would definitely begin to scream. I didn't want that; there were still people around.

But as soon as I pulled out the cell phone, Sara saw me dialing and stopped crying at once. I smiled at her.

Do you want to tell me what's wrong?

She shook her head, no.

•

Mindlessly, I had sex outside in the grass that night with my boyfriend. My knees stained green, I climbed into the car when it was over and kissed him on the cheek as he buckled his seat belt to drive me home. After he dropped me off, I watched his car disappear into the dark before going inside.

•

I couldn't sleep. Dreams kept fading in and out, dreams about Sara, dreams about what I had seen in her bedroom that day weeks before. Who was it that had been on top of my sister, touching her and making her feel things? Did he love her? I tossed and turned until a light touch on my shoulder woke me.

I jerked my head to the right, eye level to where Sara's hand was still resting. She was standing before me, looking at me, but she wasn't awake. She wasn't wearing any clothes, and she had what looked like bile on her chin.

My eyes still bleary from sleep, the image of her body came into focus and I put my hand to my mouth to cover the scream creeping out of me. She was very disproportionate, lumpy all over, awkward. I used to know how my sister looked, I knew every inch of her, but as I looked at her in the dark, I began to see the unfamiliar marks that

covered her legs, her stomach, her breasts.

I jumped out of bed and took her by the arm. Carefully, I walked her back to her room and covered her with a blanket. I wiped her face, brushed her hair as she fell back asleep.

I had no doubts that the mysterious boy had caused those marks, with his nails, with his teeth, with something else, maybe. But when? Sara was never to be left unsupervised. I lay in bed until morning time with my eyes wide open.

•

As I sat in biology class the next morning, just starting to feel a little more at ease, a little more forgetful of the previous night's events, someone knocked on the door and informed the teacher that I was needed in the nurse's office. Sara had been her normal bubbly self at breakfast and had talked to me about childish things on the drive to school—what could be wrong? I quietly gathered my things, all eyes on me, and slipped out the door.

Down the hall from the nurse's office, I heard a mixture of confused noises: my sister's outrageous laughter, bellowing out of her like it was coming from deep inside her belly, and various shouts coming from both men and women.

Sara was on the floor, laughing hysterically, so much so that tears trickled out of her eyes. The nurse was crouched down beside her with a tissue, and only then did I see that Sara was bleeding from the nose. I rushed over to her.

What's happened? I asked the nurse.

She's had an outburst, said one of the teachers, a man who had his hands on his hips and a sour expression on his face.

She was out of control, said the other, a woman with deep creases on her forehead.

Sara continued to laugh, but I noticed that her fists were clenched, knuckles white.

•

She was sent home that day; my mother had to pick her up from school. We were told that Sara had lashed out at the male teacher completely out of the blue. When he

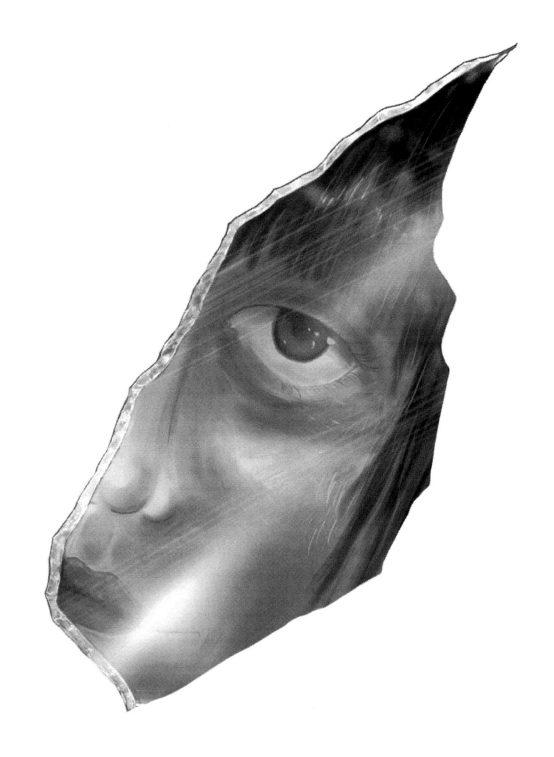

tried to calm her, she tried to hit him but wound up hurting herself. The sound of her laughter that morning rang through my head; it was as if none of us were in on her joke.

I crept into Sara's room that night before bed and begged her to tell me where she had gotten those marks on her skin, if it had anything to do with what happened at school that day. She ignored my questions and started talking about something else. She asked me if I wanted to play dolls. When I pressed her, she became upset, and I feared that she would throw another tantrum. I gave up, decided to leave her alone, and was about to leave the room when she stopped me.

I have a boyfriend just like you, Sara said to me. She sat on her bed and looked up at me through the bangs that covered her large forehead, her eyes glaring and wild.

I know, you've told me, I replied. Do you want to tell me who?

She resumed playing with her dolls and said nothing.

Don't you want to tell your sister about your boyfriend? I asked her.

Sara stared at her dolls and said to me in her girlish but gummy voice, You know who.

I certainly didn't. I had no idea.

You know who, you know who. Sara's sing-song voice filled the room.

Stop it, Sara, I said to her firmly. But she wouldn't stop.

You know who, you know who, she continued to say with laughter.

Stop it, stop it, I kept saying, but she wouldn't. Her eyes began spinning in opposite directions as she looked to the ceiling and laughed. I recoiled toward the door, crawling into my own skin.

Soon my parents had come to the door and I was yelling, I don't know what she's talking about. Please make her stop. I fled the room and locked myself in the bathroom, Sara still bellowing with laughter.

•

My mother eventually knocked on the bathroom door and asked for me to come out. My knees curled up into my chest, I sat on the floor with my back to the tub. I had become fixated on a shard of glass that was sitting on the floor, behind the toilet. I didn't respond to my mother's knocks, but they soon became frantic poundings.

When I finally came out, both my parents followed me into my bedroom and said they needed to talk with me about Sara. They asked me questions. They wanted answers.

I'm telling you, I don't know what she's talking about, I said to them.

You're responsible for her after school, they told me. So you should know who she's been with. Tell us the truth.

I swear I know nothing.

They were silent for a few moments. They looked at each other.

Sara said—, my mother began.

What.

Have you been hurting yourself?

What.

Lift up your shirt.

What? No.

Do you want your father to leave the room?

What are you talking about? No.

My head was spinning. They stared at me; my mother had tears in her eyes. Why would Sara say something like that? I became furious. I got up and ran into Sara's room, prepared to expose the hideous marks I had seen on her skin and set my parents straight.

•

Sara wasn't in her bedroom. I found her in the bathroom, where I had been just minutes before. She had found the shard of glass, knew it was there all along. She held it in her hand, turning it over and over like a stone. I wanted to scream for my parents to come quick, but words couldn't escape my mouth. She was standing, looking in the mirror. She saw my reflection and looked at it, smiling.

You know who, you know who.

I'M BETTER NOW

STORY BY DANIELLE RENINO • ART BY MELISSA GUTIERREZ

Organic apple juice. Organic peanut butter. Lean, grass fed beef. The kind they only flay from happy cows. The kind that's transported from the types of slaughterhouses that are painted cerulean blue. Slaughterhouses that are made to look like barns, with feel-good murals on the sides. Caricatures of smiling clouds, smiling farmers, smiling cows, so no one can see the blood past the bleached citrus.

That's the kind of girl I am now. Thin wrists, and sharp fingernails curved around a soymilk latte. In the office by 8:45, out by 5:15. Fifteen minutes early, fifteen minutes late, every day. Shiny heels, and gleaming silver watch. No more dollar beers down at the dive bar, or kissing boys for cigarettes. No more stick and poke tattoos of birds or crudely drawn cartoons.

Blond hair pulled back into a bun.

Martinis during lunch.

I'm a better person now.

I'm better.

I stand next to the trashcan while I wait for the elevator and take one last sip of my latte before I toss it, leaving a red film around the lip of the cup.

•

Monday morning. 8:30. The building is empty, and I get the ladies' room to myself. One of the benefits of getting in early. My mother hounds me about it, "Lucy, you're gonna work yourself to death. The stress isn't good for you. Lucy, have you been sleeping?"

She doesn't understand. I'm better now. Sleepless nights are a part of a corporate career. That's what concealer is for. Face masks with jasmine and mint. Baths with so many essential oils mixed in that if I knick myself while shaving my legs, the blood just sort of floats there, swirling with the oils. Another layer of perfume against my skin.

The ladies' room consists of smooth white marble, bright white lights, and silver faucets. The gentle hum of florescent bulbs, and the faint aroma of marigolds. Shine, on shimmer, on flowery scent.

I busy myself at the mirror, at the very edge of the marble

countertop, at the very end of the row of sinks. Foundation, mascara, blush. Gooey paste, charcoal caked onto the applicator. I'm about to start on the blush when I drop my compact. A light ping as it hits the floor, and that's when I notice the red. The blood.

Three little drops. So dark against the stark white marble. Three little drops. And flies. Two at first. In the blood. Twisting through it, thrashing against each other. Then two more. Fruit flies. I follow their movement to one of the sinks. Four more around the drain. Three more on the mirror. I keep counting and counting. Until I'm sure it's not the hum of florescent lights that breaks the silence here.

There's more red too. A faint whisper of it. So sparse it would take a trained eye to notice. Splattered up the side of the wall. Thick like syrup in the sink, curved around the mouth of the drain. Cherry syrup, thinned down oil paint, and rust. Layers on layers. Some very old. Most of it fresh, the bulk of it fresh.

"Is anyone there?" I ask, my voice cracking. The room is white. And bright. And bleeding. I can't take my eyes off the pinpricks of color. The way the dark red clings to the tile walls, how it shines like my gel manicure. The harshness of it. The violence in the tender way it's spread across the floor.

A groan escapes from one of the stalls, and the door at the far end of the bathroom hangs open.

"Come here," a voice says. It's muffled. It sounds so far away.

"I'll go get help," I say, but find myself taking small steps towards the stall. My sharp heels click, clicking, clicking.

"I'm trying so hard," the voice says. It sounds like someone speaking through a bite of hamburger. Through a mouthful of rare meat. The juices dripping out over their lips. The sloppy sound of a roadside steakhouse, or a crowded bar. A kitchen after midnight.

I stand in front of the stall, my eyes trained on the floor. There are bits of what looks like ground beef, pink and angry, littered throughout the pinpricks of red. A shudder runs through me.

I peer into the open stall.

There's a girl curled up at the base of the toilet. She can't be much older than I am. Early twenties maybe. Thin wrists, sharp nails. There's red in her blond hair, and slathered up her arms, and butterflied out over the front of her blouse.

"Since Friday," she says and grins. Her teeth are pink. Her chin is crusted over with layers of flaking red, and chunks of gray and green. "I puked a few times, I guess."

"I just need to get it out. It's been stuck in my throat since Friday," she says. Her voice is a rasp, a gurgle. Barely audible, even standing a few feet from where she sits. The smell is overpowering. Perfume mixed with sick. And blood. I never knew blood had a smell until now. It's a sharp scent. A sweetness.

There is a fly inside her mouth. It walks over her two front teeth and down over her tongue. She holds a pair of scissors to her chest.

"Oh my god..." I whimper, looking down at the mess of pink pieces scattered around her.

They're bits of her tongue.

"I just need to get it out. You understand, don't you?"

Her voice is muffled, and when she grins again I see the place where the tip of her tongue is missing. I see the pieces that she cut away. The emptiness.

She turns the scissors on herself, and slowly unhinges her jaw. The flies are drawn to the mess. They settle on her tongue, between her teeth. Her mangled teeth. The bottom two in the front are missing. A pair of pliers sits curled beneath her foot.

"There's something in my throat," she says. "I just need to get to it. I'm so close."

The sound of flesh slicing open.

The sound of flies.

The gurgle of blood, and spit, and body fluids spilling.

"There's too much in the way," she says, and it's barely audible through the harsh buzz, the slosh of the fluids, three days' worth of busy work, of self-dissection.

"How did you spend your weekend?"

I scream.

•

Back at my apartment, I sit curled up on my white leather couch and examine my fingernails. The layer of nude nail polish is marred by Angie's blood. That was her name. Angie. They told me after the stretcher was rolled out, after the police had taken down my statement. After the harsh wailing of the siren faded to a dull pulsing in my head.

She was twenty-five. They say she had a mental breakdown. They say the stress got to be too much. She didn't meet her quota and so Friday night she hid in a bathroom stall and spent the weekend carving away at herself.

But here's the thing. There's a tickle in the back of my throat. And when I shine a flashlight back there, beyond the darkness, beyond the flesh, there's a little bit of *something*. A little bit of sharpness in the side of me, on the inside of me. And here's another thing. It doesn't bother me too much yet. I soothe it with honey. I try to wash it down with chamomile. But each day it's getting worse. It's *sharper*.

I think of how cold Angie's hands were, beneath the warmth of fluids, the gloves of blood, of calcium. Of her, and her, and her. Layer on layer. And how loud the flies were, and how this sharpness in the back of my throat keeps getting worse.

But I have a pair of kitchen shears, and I have a long, thin carving knife.

My mother thinks it's stress. She keeps hounding me about it, but she doesn't understand.

I'm better now.

I'm better.

X-RAY SPECS

STORY BY JENNIFER D. CORLEY • ART BY CARRIE ANNE HUDSON

My father is a radiologist. He can see things that aren't there.

I am a girl, and I sit in my father's office, behind him, watching over his shoulder, listening, being silent, because if I make noise he has to turn off his voice recorder and start over. The one time he didn't, the lady transcriptionist teased him about his daughter saying things in the background, and he didn't want to have to go through that again. He didn't like to be teased.

So I sit still. I catch myself kicking my legs, and I stop, because they're making a noise against the aluminum legs of the Berber-upholstered chair.

My father clears his throat and rolls his eyes—a nervous tic—and begins speaking in a monotone, almost robotic way.

"Thirty-four-year-old female, Johnson, Melinda (period). Lateral left clavicular injury (period)."

He shuts off the recorder. I stand and walk up next to him. He studies the x-ray, which hangs on a double row of glowing white light boxes, and taps the microphone on his chin. He's searching for something. I can't see his eyes; the black and white image of bone reflects in his enormous square eyeglasses.

"What are you looking for?" I ask.

"See this little mark right here?" He points to a tiny line, almost indiscernible to me, on the image of the shoulder bone. "That's a break. She fell and I want to make sure it's not too serious. Looks like it's just a hairline."

"A hairline?"

"Yep. Means it's small, thin, like a hair."

"Oh."

"Ok, sit down."

I sit.

He clears his throat. Rolls his eyes. Turns on the recorder. "No evidence of serious displacement (period). Hairline fracture (period)."

Sometimes at home I'll imitate his recording voice and it makes him laugh. I like saying the word "period" to end my sentences.

"Ten-year old female, Milt, Celeste (period). Sat at breakfast table (period). Would like some orange juice

41

(period)."

I roll my eyes to imitate him too, but he doesn't laugh at that.

At school I make noise.

I like to make people laugh, especially when we're supposed to be quiet. When the teacher has her back turned, I'll kick Jason, who sits across from me, and he'll look up at me and see that I'm making my nostrils flare out really fast, in and out like a pig hunting in the mud; or I'm crossing my eyes back and forth, or sticking my tongue out to the side; and he giggles; and the teacher turns around and asks him what he wants to share with the class and he says, "She's making me laugh!" And I look at her innocently like I don't know what he's talking about; and then she warns him that he better be quiet, and he gives me a dirty look, and I shoot him another quick funny face and he forgives me.

I don't like Jason though, not LIKE like him. He's the fattest kid in the class. I like Mark, but Mark doesn't like me. I've tried shouting at him on the playground, but it doesn't work. He doesn't laugh like my dad does at the jokes I make.

I do my snort-laugh, I dance, I even dumped milk on my head once because that got a ton of laughs when I did it with orange juice at my house once, but there was only milk at the cafeteria, so I don't know if it made the difference, but nothing works with Mark.

•

Sometimes I have a problem with taking things that aren't mine. I take things from my father's office, but just little things like these neat wax pencils that unwrap with paper instead of being sharpened, and colored rubber bands, because I want to make a rubber band ball to keep in my room. I take things from school sometimes, like Misty Trujillo's pencil case—to keep the pencils from my father's office in—and a pair of scissors from craft hour, but I don't know why I took those. They're pretty useless. One time the teacher found Mark's homework in my cubby, and I was able to pass that off by saying I found it and meant to put it in his cubby and just wasn't thinking when

I put it in mine. I hated her for asking me about it in front of the class.

•

I sit in my father's office, waiting on his workday to be over so we can go home. I busy myself with a bowl of paper clips from his desk by linking them together. When I've used them all, I put the bowl back. After a few minutes, he reaches for one and pulls up the chain the way a magician reveals a length of knotted scarves.

"Dammit, Celeste! Stop playing with things!"

I didn't know he would get so angry about it; I thought it was funny.

He hands me the bowl.

"Fix them."

I take one off and hand it to him, then start taking the chain apart.

He opens his drawer and sees the rubber band ball I've made, and he sighs as he removes one to put around a stack of files.

"Catch," he says as he tosses it to me. We throw it back and forth a few times, then he tells me I need to be quiet because he's got to get back to work.

He slides a film into the light box. A leg bone is splintered, as if it had been hit with a bat, or a car, or a meteor. I ask, "What's wrong with that one?"

My father looks at me with widened eyes for a second, then lets out a small laugh. "Okay, go play outside if you need to." He knows that I like to joke.

I mime zipping my lips and throwing away the key. Then I'm bothered because I realize that you don't really lock after zippering. I should have mimicked one or the other, not both. I need to work on my comedy.

•

I talk to myself in my room the way he talks into his recorder.

"Ten-year-old female, Milt, Celeste (period). Cleaning her room (period). But not really (period). Moving crap around the room, shoving things into the closet (period). Brain is tired (period)." I make sure to put the things I've taken into the far corners of my closet. Sometimes my friends at school ask around, ask if anybody saw me take something that they're missing, but I think I'm good at hiding it. Stephanie will never know what happened, ever. Ten-year-old female, confused about where her Wet n' Wild lipstick went (period). If she finds out I'll shatter her tibia, and the femur of whoever tells her (period).

I listen to records while I clean. My father has given me ones that he doesn't want anymore—Hank Williams Jr. and Led Zeppelin. He says he's not the same anymore but I think maybe if he kept listening to them, he would be. I like them okay but they're not my favorite.

I listen to Led Zeppelin and dance in the mirror. "Eleven-year-old male, Adamson, Mark (period). Maybe eating dinner (period). Maybe out riding his bike (period). Brain is tired (period)." I look into my mirror. It is framed in white and gold, and sits on top of a matching dresser, fit for a princess. I start brushing my hair and it gets caught up in the tangles. I give up and put it in a ponytail. It doesn't look very good. My friends will tell me so tomorrow.

My father opens my door. "Did you finish cleaning your room?"

I nod. "Milt, Celeste (period). Cleaned her room (period)."

Mark walks across the basketball court outside on the playground. I sit on the giant spinning wheel that nobody else is using. I drag my feet in the dirt to keep it from turning; it makes me dizzy if it spins too much. Adamson, Mark. He's cute, cute.

"MARK! MARK!"

He looks at me. I wave. I roll my eyes the way my father does; that's funny. A couple of the boys he's walking with giggle. They think it's funny.

Mark looks away and talks to his friends.

•

At my father's office, he cuts open a package he had ordered. It's desk supplies.

"Don't play with that box cutter—it's not funny. It has a blade. Come see, I got this desk set. It has this container for paper clips that dispenses them one at a time. It uses a magnet. No more playing with my paper clips. A tray for rubber bands, so no more playing with those either." I wonder what my father used to be like, since he says he's not the same.

What will Mark be like. Will he wear glasses. Will I. Will we listen to Led Zeppelin or Hank Williams or Madonna or somebody else entirely. Will we be somebody else. Will we not be the same anymore. Will I not be quiet.

A lady's voice comes over his telephone asking him to take a look at some films.

•

Mark's hair is silky. It isn't tangled like mine. He sits a couple people away from me in class.

The lights are off in the classroom because we're supposed to be watching a movie about nature. The TV is on a big cart, and those few minutes that it always takes the teacher to get the VCR sorted out even after she thought she had it working are the best. It's dark, there's only the light of the TV. It reminds me of the light boxes in my father's office, as the teacher pushes buttons and makes grunts and "tsk" noises, and my classmates laugh at her for never figuring out the process.

I use this opportunity, sitting in the dark, with only the light that bleeds in through the blinds, to pass Mark a note. It's actually a drawing. I made a drawing of a skeleton. There's a heart behind a ribcage. I know you can't see a heart on an x-ray, but that's a technicality. It's a cute drawing. The note says: My heart will break if you don't like me. I took a chance but I thought why not be daring. I need to see things that aren't there.

I pass it, folded up a few times for safety, to Julie, and nod towards Mark. She passes it to him, nodding back in my direction. He looks at me and I smile at him. He opens it. My chest hurts. I feel like my heart really is going to break. I might need my father to look at an x-ray.

Mark is staring at it. He won't look at me. He isn't smiling. He isn't writing back on the note. He isn't doing anything. He's just looking at it.

I can feel the picture on the TV changing, flashing on me as the teacher has gotten it sorted out. The light on our faces changes from white to blue to yellow, and I hear animals, sharks and lions and hawks, tearing into otters and gazelles and mice, but I can't look away from Mark. I hear shrieking.

He keeps looking down, and he crumples up my note and throws it into his book bag. I thought it was a funny drawing.

•

I'm in the school bathroom.

I look in the mirror. It's simple; it doesn't have a frame, just plastic tabs that hold it into place against the wall. Fit for a plain girl.

I take the box cutter from my backpack.

I hold it up to my face, and I make a slice along my jaw-line, the way my father cut open the package, all the way around from ear to ear. The blood makes a red mark. Some of it starts dripping down, but it mostly looks like a red magic-marker line around my face. Mark will notice me now. I think my father will like this too. It looks *really* funny. I start to laugh. It's not too serious; it's just a hairline.

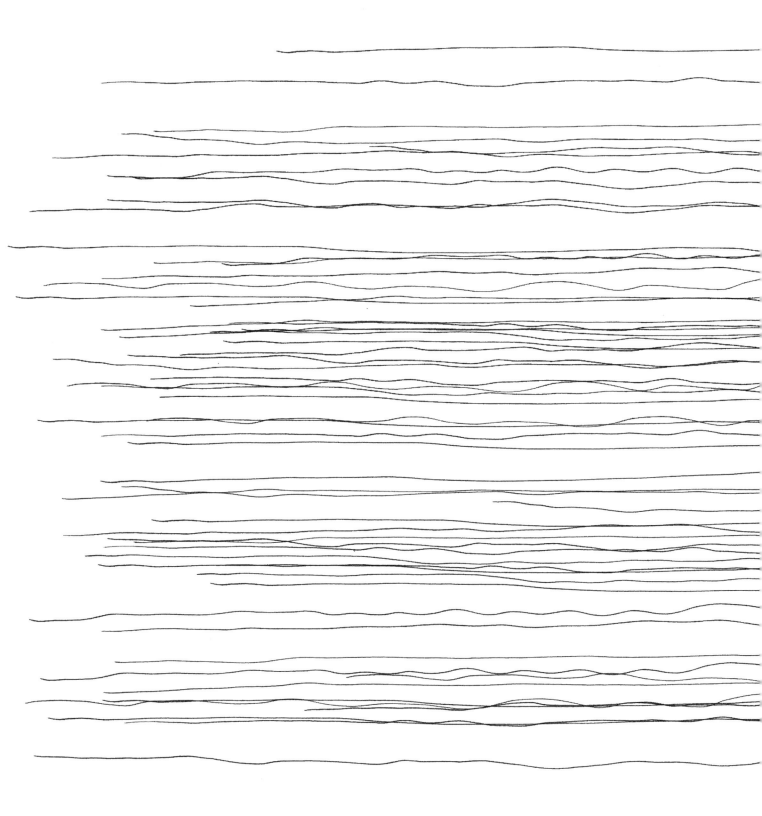

THERE'S SOMETHING UNDER THE BED

STORY BY BONNIE ALEXANDER • ART BY CHRISTINA COLLINS

Almost. You are almost certain that there is something under your bed. You can feel its presence like someone's stare from across the room. As soon as you step into the bedroom, dread itself wafts up at you from under there. You're not sure when the feeling began—slowly creeping in the back of your mind, all at once? Sleeping there this evening is a bad idea.

When she walks into the room, you say nothing. Well, actually, you say, "I'm feeling really anxious tonight," and she makes dulcet noises of sympathy and doesn't notice the weird little hop you do to prevent your feet from being too close to under the bed. She doesn't mention it, at least, and you're thankful for it. The dark feelings persist as you curl around her.

The next morning nothing is there. No feelings of deep foreboding, no certainty of old-school monsters or evil spirits anywhere in your home. Just reality, sunny and peaceful. You remind yourself once more to chill out and take deep breaths when something like that happens again. It's all in your head.

A few days later, it creeps back in. Dusk falls. And you're anxious like you're homesick. You dread going to the bedroom.

Once, in a dream, you felt the same feeling, and you crawled to your knees and looked. The wood slats were gone, the true form of the floor revealed: a fog like amorphous gray lint and brain matter that roiled around on itself, like a pot boiling in slow motion. You wanted to run but it drew you, drew something inside of you, and while you tried your hardest to back away and get out the door you found yourself squatting, then belly flush against the cold floor, neck craned as your arms began to push you under the bedframe.

•

In the morning you check under the bed, a quick, silly duck of the head. Your lover is beginning to stir, but you'd really prefer not to explain that you're checking under the bed because you had a weird feeling and you freeze, trying to make your motions nonchalant. Over the course of the next week or two you find yourself checking again, and again. The floor looks the same: hardwood slats, a little dusty. The nail in the end of one of the boards is beginning to pop out a little bit.

The fourth or fifth time you give in and check. Just as you drop to your knees and crane your neck, a whip-quick motion catches your peripheral vision. Adrenaline shoots through your legs and arms and your heart pounds hard. As you hear it echo in your ears it becomes apparent that the space under the bed is as it always is.

You've lived in this house for months: not a long time, but not so short a period that you think you just over-looked this dark presence until now. No, it's new. Part of the reason you chose it was its warmth, the domestic comfort that it exuded. Moving to a new city had never been easy, but at least you could picture your life here—summer evenings in the backyard, Sunday mornings in the large-windowed living room. You loved the coziness of the bedroom, smaller than the rest of the rooms but full of old-house character, built-in shelves and cracks running along where the walls met the ceiling. Looking back, it would have been impossible to imagine the sort of feelings you have now about this room.

You know you've never been prone to paranoia or hallucination before. Joan, your old therapist, would probably tell you that it was all a manifestation of stress, of the lack of communication between you and your girlfriend. "These things come out some way, you know," she would say at nearly every session, peering across the room at you while you stared at the elephant painting over her head. "Better to be in control of it and start the conversation."

And so you want to start the conversation, but you're fairly certain there's no way to do so without sounding crazy. One day the need grows too strong, and after a glass and a half of wine you say: "Do you ever feel like there's something under the bed?"

"Our bed, specifically?" she asks.

"Yes."

"You mean like mice?" she asks.

You feel irritated. Your face heats with embarrassment. You're not ready to give up entirely though, not quite. "Like, you know when you were little and you thought there were monsters under the bed? Maybe not even specifically monsters, you know, but something scary or evil. Like, bad things?"

You're on a dinghy, close to shore, throwing a rope with no weight on the end of it toward the dock. Her hands are outstretched, but there is no way that rope is going to do anything but smack water and splash her face with it.

She grabs your waist, tight, and pulls you to her. She smells like lilacs and her touch reminds you of the way you love her.

"I can protect you from monsters, lover."

•

But things have been stilted anyway, since the move. When you fuck, it is passionate but impersonal. You feel further and further from your body while becoming enveloped in hers. Every motion has a violence to it, which is not so strange, given how tense everything has been. You try peering into her eyes, but she's not making eye contact. She stares at the ceiling while you fuck her hard, pushing down on her stomach with your other hand. You know it will help her come if you do this. It's an act of love, of pleasure-giving, but you're also trying to hurt her, to shove her down into the mattress as far and as hard as you can. You lose yourself in the force of it, your pussy dripping onto your thighs but your mind without feelings of arousal. After she comes once she pushes your head to her cunt, hard, and you lick and suck and everything is slathered with saliva and juices. She comes again and flips you over, fucking your cunt, and then your ass. Hard. You're getting closer to coming, but the feeling stays deep in your pelvis. No excitement. Instead you feel angrier and angrier. You scream into the pillow. Your pussy contracts hard in orgasm, but your voice is all rage. You lie still for a while. She strokes your ass, your thighs, wipes her hand on the sheets. She goes to the bathroom to wash her hands. "I'm getting some

water," she tells you, and disappears into the kitchen. She doesn't come back. You lay still, the dread pooling around you. It's still underneath.

She must feel poorly about walking out later, because the next day she makes it a point to sit and talk. "I know things are really hard right now," she says. "And please don't think that I'm forgetting that this is a sacrifice for you. I appreciate it so, so much. Once I have my degree we can move again."

"You want to leave here?" You watch her.

"I mean, it seems like you do," she says. "I'm just saying that after we get through two years, we can do whatever we want to do. Move wherever it is you'd like to live. Does that sound good?"

It does sound good. The conversation quickly devolves into playful wrestling and kissing before it's time for bed. Things feel comfortable again, like they were before you uprooted yourselves. Once the lights are off, though, the presence returns.

"You know, it's the weirdest thing," she says, brushing her hair in the bathroom. "You know that lady down the street with the kids? Joyce or something?"

"The one who's always out gardening?"

"Does she talk to you?" she asks.

"Not really. Once, maybe."

"She keeps asking me about how we're doing, and how we like the house."

"That doesn't seem that weird," you say. "She's a mom. In the neighborhood watch and shit."

"Yeah," she agrees. "I guess it's just the kind of stuff she asks about. She keeps talking about our house. Keeps asking if we like living here. But she says it weird. She always asks, 'How is it in there?'" She puts on an old-lady affect for this last sentence, and you laugh appreciatively. "Maybe the basements flood around here."

"Like maybe if it rains too hard, the house will slide off the hill?" You smirk, and she laughs.

"Maybe just mold or asbestos or something. The way she talks, our landlord must be pretty shady."

"Great, so we're for sure getting cancer." You're leaning against the wall of the hallway, watching her. When she scoots by you she kisses you. You keep your cool, but now your body flutters. Maybe Joyce knows about the presence, about whatever's going on. Maybe it's frightened other tenants away. You're not crazy.

•

The next time you leave the house, you notice Joyce standing in her front garden, hoe in hand. She wears gloves and a large sunhat. You put your hand up. She waves back to you.

"Hi," you yell.

"Hey there," she shouts to you. It sounds morose. When you pull out of the driveway, you notice that Joyce still hasn't moved. She's watching you. She stares after your car all the way down the street.

•

It gets stronger. You can hear a low throbbing before you go to sleep. In the darkness you listen to its rhythm. You don't wake up nicely or happily for your girlfriend anymore, even when she brings you coffee or simply starts hugging or kissing you. Morning is the only time to get any sleep, the only time without the slow bass beat rumbling or the encroaching dread.

Eventually she stops trying to roust you, just gets ready and leaves the house. You move your work hours to accommodate late starts. You show up around noon and work long into the evening, after the office has cleared out. It is always dark when you come home, and the presence is stronger in the dark. You feel it when walking up the steps, fumbling with your key. You feel it when you swing the door open, collapse onto the couch or at the kitchen table. And most of all you feel it near the bedroom, when you pass the door in the hallway, when you enter and undress, and when you lie down to sleep, right over the epicenter of this dark thing.

•

You start to align yourself with it, in small but undeniable ways.

When you find yourself alone in the house on a Sunday afternoon, you undress and lie in bed, straining to hear the rumble, quieting all of your senses and all of your thoughts to feel the pull. When nothing happens, you begin to touch yourself—and then, as your pulse quickens, as pleasure starts to flower in you, you feel it: a quiet apprehension. You don't stop. Slowly, slowly, you rub, eyes closed, letting the feeling envelope your body. Your fingers keep moving, and the darkness spreads over you like a sheet descending from above. It rests over you, and you find that it is tranquil underneath it. It feels your pleasure, and it likes it, encourages it.

When orgasm hits, you aren't as fully unified with the feeling as you hoped you'd be. But you feel as though you are moving in it, swimming in deep, forceful currents. The dark presence is all around you now, splashing around the room.

After you come, you are full of rage. You get up, walk around the house like a drunk. You let yourself slam the cabinet doors. You're generally not one for violent displays, but it feels good, the outward ripples of frustration like you're a stone in a pond. That night you sleep for the first time in weeks.

•

"Will you come home early tonight?" your love asks you on a Wednesday. "I miss you. I'm worried about you."

"I'm right here," you tell her, smiling.

"Baby." It is a statement, one holding a trial and verdict in itself. "We haven't spent an evening together in weeks. On weekends we're both here, yeah, but you haven't been with me."

Sometimes, when it is sunny and warm and she touches you, you don't feel the pull from under the bed, and the slow beating seems like it's the farthest thing away from you. On those afternoons you wonder if you're going crazy.

•

One day, you walk into the bedroom, and find your lover, broom in hand, crouching to reach deep under the bed with it. She turns sharply when you walk in.

"What are you doing?" you ask her.

"What does it look like I'm doing? Trying to clean this fucking room out."

It sounds innocent enough, but you keep your eyes on her for the rest of the afternoon, waiting for some action or glance that will give away her communication—or even her collaboration—with the presence. That night, listening to its pulse, you watch her sleeping face. You're not sure she's really asleep. In fact, you suspect that she perhaps doesn't sleep at all. She is being nurtured by the pounding. The thing under the bed is pulling energy from you and giving it to her. She must hear the noise. She hasn't complained. It is nourishing her.

•

You begin to always take the time that she's away on Sundays to masturbate. A gentle ritual. The deep foreboding that you once felt as you approached the bed is now a quiet comfort. You never enjoy your orgasms anymore. They just happen, and all the energy and pleasure dissipates off you like steam. But you are never angry after you come, never frustrated or vengeful. You understand that this is how it needs to be; the thing under the bed needs your orgasms. A trade-off for some peace. The throbbing bass goes from disruptive to soothing.

At some point, you have the impression it no longer lives under the bed. It moves with you from room to room, unwavering in its strength or quality. It's not always with you, not constantly. But you're just as likely to feel it next to you or around your shoulders in the kitchen or the bathroom. You start to see glimpses of it in the mirrors of the house—never a full gaze, but a flash of something is in your periphery whenever you turn your head from a reflection. It doesn't seem to leave the house with you, but as soon as you cross the threshold you'll catch it in the window, in the shiny side of the toaster. At first it bothers you. But it becomes familiar very, very quickly, and the initial urge to tell your girlfriend or even call for professional help moves out of the foreground.

•

One afternoon, you sit at the table, drinking a cup of tea. You don't think about anything. These moments of blankness have grown more and more frequent. The sound of the car pulling into the drive, the familiar hum of the engine, the crank of the emergency brake. Without knowing why you're doing it, you stand up and bolt out the back door. You're moving too fast to put on shoes or a jacket. You don't want to see her, panic you once felt as a child playing hide-and-seek.

You crouch behind a small bush, in the dusk, and peer at the woman you love. You feel animal. It grows. This is how prey feels, hiding, listening to its own breath. You hide because you wanted to hide—and now that you're there, you're hiding because it would be silly, maybe downright embarrassing if she found you here, crouching, feet bare in the dark.

You watch her get out of the car. She goes to the trunk and bends to extract something. You stare at her litheness, look up and down the form of her legs—smooth, muscular, feminine.

She goes inside, flips on the lights. You know that she's wondering where you are, that she can see your mug on the table and your keys at the door. If she wants to feel the kettle, she'll find it still warm. You curse yourself for not covering your tracks better. She doesn't come to look for you, though, and you watch while she busies herself in the kitchen, her silhouette switching from one window to another. Her hair is long, her profile perfect.

This is not how prey feels at all. This is how predators feel.

A cool wind has picked up. By now your feet are almost totally numb, save the dull pressure you feel when you step on a particularly sharp stone. Every muscle in your body is increasingly heavy and you realize that you're exhausted. It doesn't make sense to procrastinate any longer; you're going to have to see your girlfriend and answer to her. You thought that you would've come up with something by now but it's becoming increasingly clear that you're a blank.

It's been a long time since your girlfriend was in the kitchen. The light is still on but her silhouette disappeared from the windows some time ago. In the darkness the windows look like television screens or still-life paintings—images of a reality. You feel surprised when you walk in and find that the kitchen is entirely just as you left it.

Your girlfriend isn't in the house. You didn't hear the car leave, but it did—it is gone, along with her keys. You've been in bed for hours by the time she joins you.

"Where were you?" You ask her sleepily.

"Out with friends, baby." She kisses your cheek and rolls over. You hear her snores in minutes.

•

Your girlfriend spends increasing amounts of time in the bathroom. Her post-workout showers are longer, and several evenings a week she soaks in the tub, reading a book or magazine.

After a run she peels her shirt off as soon as she enters the door, headed for the bathroom. You're in the living room. Your eyes follow her as she does this, arms and shining torso stretching as the shirt passes over her head. You make eye contact, briefly, and wonder what she's thinking. You can see sex written on every motion in these moments. Her sweaty body is full of energy. Once, you couldn't keep yourself off of her after a workout. You can see why, still, but every small voice in you that drove you to touch her is now silent. You stay on the couch.

You're always more alert when you hear the squeal of the shower shutting off.

You listen intently, hearing the toilet flush, the cabinet doors close. You hear her open and close the medicine cabinet not once, but twice. Your heart jumps and you tense. It's probably in the bathroom mirror. It must leave the mirror and curl around her shoulders, too. Maybe they speak to each other in ways you aren't privy to. Every inch of you aches at this thought. More minutes pass. She remains in the bathroom. You can't stand it; you get up and knock on the door.

"What?" she says.

"Uh, are you almost done in there?" You hadn't thought

about what you would say. Some part of you just believed she would confess her sins right then.

"Just come in and pee, if you need to," she tells you.

"It's okay, I'll wait," you say.

"Okay then." She sounds annoyed.

You've returned to the couch, satisfied that nothing is awry. Unless she heard something shrill in you and is only now surveying the bathroom—slowly, meticulously. She'll be scanning the surfaces, feeling for something dark wavering in the tile. Taking advantage of that closed door. She hadn't noticed a thing until you panicked and opened your mouth. You're a fucking idiot.

That's it. You stand up again and walk right into bathroom. At the noise of the door she jumps. "Jesus," she says, one leg propped on the side of the tub.

"Sorry." You plop yourself on the toilet and try your best to pee. You don't look at her directly, but you're surveying everything in the bathroom. She finishes rubbing her lotion in and kisses you perfunctorily on the forehead on her way out, while you're still sitting there trying to piss.

"You're such a weirdo, hon." She walks into the bedroom, wrapped in her towel.

You sit on the toilet. You're alone. The presence is nowhere to be found. You walk back to the living room, then the bedroom, feeling for it, listening. There is no dull throb. The only dread you feel is that you might not locate it again.

Weeks go by like this. You begin to spend as much time as possible in the house, roaming from room to room, but the dark presence is rapidly fading. You have to be sitting or lying on the bed to feel it now, and even then it's weaker. You're puzzled by your attachment to the dark force. It's like the time you broke your leg as a teenager. You spent weeks resenting the crutches and thick cast, but once it came off you missed it. It had become a piece of you, and you felt like you had lost something special when it disappeared.

•

One evening you're sitting at home, in bed. There is no dark feeling anymore, but your girlfriend walks in. She sits next to you for a long time without saying anything.

"Are you okay?" she asks you. You nod, but it's hesitant. "I've missed you, babe," she says. "I know it's my fault for being distant. But you've been distant too. I was so worried about you."

"I'm sorry," you say. You don't feel like you can explain more right now, but you're touched by her care.

"I love you," she says.

"I love you, too," you say and smile.

You're filled with warmth. She touches your arm, and you raise your eyes to meet hers in the mirror.

When you look in the mirror into the eyes of the woman you love, the dark presence is staring back at you. Your first instinct is to bolt, to get away from it. From her. Her hand must feel the twitch of your forearm, but neither of you take your eyes off of each other. Her expression is still warm and loving, but the steady malevolence in her eyes—that is unmistakable.

Slowly, without breaking the contact of your arms, you turn from the mirror to face her in person. Her face doesn't change. The eyes don't change. That familiar dread seeps into every pore of your body. Then you lean in for a kiss.

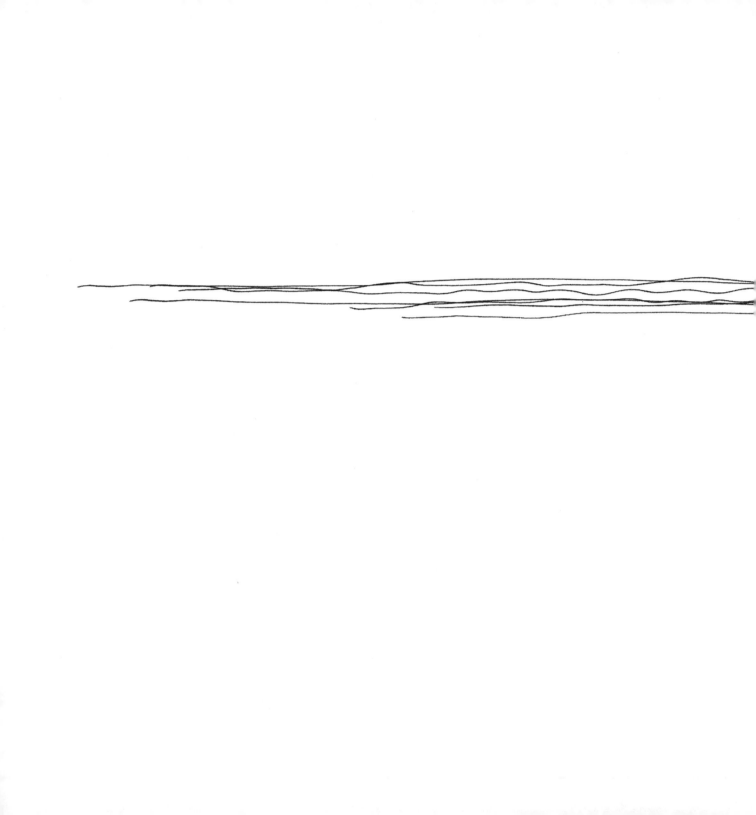

THE ECHOES OF RUPTURE

fig 1. starling

MURMURATION: A CONFUSION

STORY BY COLLEEN BURNER • ART BY JULIA DIXON EVANS

Sitting at a card table, in front of a window. The table faces southeast and the blue light of morning veils across its vinyl surface. The vinyl looks like wood grain. A terra cotta saucer sits on the table. The saucer holds a terra cotta pot, and they have a crusting of dirt and mineral accumulation in common. The terra cotta pot holds a packing of graying dirt. The dirt holds itself together. The dirt holds a plant. The plant holds its greenness.

Something over the dirt, around the plant. White. It is not milk. It is water white with paint. It is some spilt bile. It is water white with soap and dust. It is the liquid from inside the globe of an eyeball. It is this morning's breakfast milk. The whiteness pools over the dirt in the terra cotta pot, gathers around the base of the aloe plant, turns grayish next to the greenness of the plant body, which is slightly, through some trick, translucent and glowing in the morning light. The dirt under the plant does not absorb. The dirt under the plant refuses light and liquid. The dirt is dead. Am I dead?

I try to understand what has happened. This is an aftermath, an aftershock. This is a vision. This is a dream. This is the result of synapses sorting themselves out and resting from the body's senses. This is something actually happening, the milk and the plant; the not-milk and the essential greenness. This is on the table in front of me. This.

The plant is a green growing being, all one part that put itself together. There is nothing else like this plant except for other plants. There is nothing else like this plant that is not a plant already, unlike the white liquid, which comes from something else. A product, and not the thing itself. This plant is something thick and succulent with few needs. One of the Franciscan monks of Nature. Something that has healing stored inside it, which can soothe and give itself, though it refuses and doesn't need much. It never takes. Cannot. This is what I look at this morning. This is often an opposite of you.

I sit at the table, begin looking at my hands, flat in front of me, and the cool purple hue made in them by the blue light and my cold skin. They seem dead. I sit so still I feel my fingernails growing over the dirt trapped beneath them, feel the thin blond hairs on my fingers emerging, feel what moves under my skin. What I have instead of greenness. Would that I were a plant.

In front of me is white in a bowl. Milk I painted the walls with. Milk that came out of another body and went into mine and came out again. Milk I do not wish to slurp. Milk that may have ceased being milk. Used milk, through milk, tired and retired milk, refused milk, also blued in the window light. Held in a bowl that held other food that is now held inside me. Now the milk moves around the plant. When did the milk leave the bowl?

Black flapping tries to turn inside out. The closed window lets in light and keeps out the bird that wants to fly through it. The closed window glass bears prints of feathers and face made by bird grease; it is a mark of surprise; it is a sort of proof. The bird keeps trying. Does the bird see the plant, the milk?

The milk around the plant is interrupted forever by a splash of something so deeply red it leans toward blue. The new liquid plumes in, sinks through, spreads out with density, swirls through the white. A liquid blooming within liquid. An exchange of viscosities. Still refused by the dirt, by the plant, but the plant watches. I see these things, but not fully. There is a new shadow. A new blue spreading.

Perhaps the bird did not come in through the window. Perhaps glass did not fall over my hands, did not come near my face. Perhaps it was someone entering through the door, seeking that which seeks, and didn't I raise my hands? Didn't I see my hands in front of my face, at the same time seeing this other face before mine? Seeing so closely. A face like mine and where were my hands?

A separation, a separating. Body from body. I am the fat at the top of the milk. I am the sediment at the bottom of the paint. Liquid has its own life. Two sharp wedges drive themselves in and take from the left side of my face. A handful of fingers dig for a bulb. A cloud of red and light and something feels unplugged. And the void, the negative space, created by the separation, the hollow part, the new chamber, a well reaching into revealed veins: it is an open mouth, it is an open grasp, taking in new breath. New to the air.

An eye in the socket already looks like a wound: a veined, wet thing with thin peels of skin, lucid lids, as its only protection. An organ of vulnerability. And this specific eye, mine, green like the plant, surrounded by white like the plant, roots constrained like the plant. The plant lacks the black center, yet it witnessed, was unbroken. What a plant keeps inside itself.

Who poured the milk on the dirt? When you entered through the door, you tipped the liquid over the dirt so I would watch it and not you. Or I poured it over the dirt, attempting nourishment, wanting the life to be stronger, more vibrant, animated. Or I spilled it over the dirt, because something behind my eyes was already telling me how to do. Some murmuration, like starlings. Another kind of dark, surging cloud. Hundreds forming one undulating body, watching from the air.

Darling, starling, darker in the springtime but still shining like spilled oil. You with a yellow beak that gaped my eye from my head like it was a gift I'd promised; you who could not move your own eyes inside your own head. I saw your face as much as I didn't, as much as I saw another's, caught your round eye looking angry. But it was not you, brother, lying on your back in the breakfast bowl, not you with your wings spread out and your feet grasping nothing, reflexed. But this is how I saw you. But my vision couldn't be trusted. But this is the form the new sight gave you. But you came in through the door, wearing a mask with a yellow beak. But I recognized you.

The outside and the inside. Glass broken on the table. Or the fracturing of remaining sight, altering planes of matter. Broken ice on the table, not melting. Spots and pools of red on the table, beading like rain on the vinyl. Arrows of dark feathers on the table, shadows, burns, lines of dirt. A bowl on the table still wet with a thin layer of white, wetting new with a measure of red, holding a dark bird, or a breakfast uneaten, or a collection of detritus swept from the floor, or a dark bird only. An eye caught inside an esophagus. An eye glimpsing from a mouth. Beholding the plant on the table, in front of me.

I saw you through the window before it broke. You, burrowing your beak in the ground, searching. In the yard, scaring snakes and thundering the tunnelings of burrow animals. I watched and remembered you didn't have wings. I remembered us smaller, pretending to flap wings in the dirt behind the house. I saw you through the window, walking toward me, head turned, seeing two things at once. Eyes aligned. Did you see me sitting here, did you see me seeing you seeing me?

Already half-blind and you plucked my dead eye. It began as a dark spot in the center of my vision, grew outward like seeing my own pupil dilating. It was milky and thick with a veil of early cataract. It was dried out, unsatisfied by insufficient secretions. It had simply never worked. It was a dead plant rotting. Perhaps you think you did me a favor. You found what Newton probed for with his bodkin. An end. You found the treasure buried in the front of my brain. Half a sense. But it was mine. But it was not yours for the taking. But it was right in front of you, of me.

But the window broke. The bird broke it inward. Or you broke it outward. Or you broke it inward. Did you need to break it? I know the window broke because it brought in breath from outside and I realized how the air around me had been so much my own breath. My own breath was so my own I hadn't noticed it. It stayed close. My own breath feeding the plant. The plant's breath. Milk and breath and what I smelled next. Yours: morning breath, memory of breakfast breath, milk breath, soured and round smelling, death breath. Not what the window rushed in. Not that cooling green stream of breeze. I smelled these things when your bird face was in front of my face (did you see a bird face on my face?), telling me there was glass in my eye. You removed the glass. You removed the eye. My left eye. Too much shock in my blood to resist. My hands on the table. I lost sight of the plant. Of my hands. Of your

hand. Your face. How do I know this is not a memory you fed me? Because a bird, so much smaller, would not have the muscle to hold me down. Or was I so passive in this moment? Didn't I raise my hands?

The window broke and didn't upset the plant. It didn't upset the view it held. It didn't upset the table. It didn't upset the bowl. It didn't upset me. Everything was the same except the milk had glass in it. My face had glass in it. And then absence.

Now what does it see? What does eye see? Do I? Is the sight through the socket or the far away? Who did I become in that moment of dilation, when the ribbons of muscles hadn't yet realized the emptiness of their grip? In the instant I am severed, I am several at once. With the new sight I become an oracle, this new hollowness like a portal, like a second mouth for something else to speak through. Any voice sounds like it comes from the back of a cave. Not like Oedipus, not like Telephus, not like one who causes an eye to stumble. This is separate. Seeing different. The voices, that murmur, arrived immediately, trying to fill the space. Or were they there before? Is there a there for them to arrive at? I am the savage giant in the cave; I am the bald child with claw feet, appearing where you don't expect; I am the creature with horse legs and dog head, iron teeth ready to eat you alive; I am the Norse god seeking all of time's wisdom; I am the bird with one wing to match my mateless eye. A woman from thousands of years ago, who covered her own empty socket with a patch of gold, remaking her loss into a gilt sun, revered by the fully sighted who saw her. A saint who sacrificed her sight, eternally offering it on a platter. I am these things too horrible and magnificent to exist. I am joined to this race of cycloptic creatures, this divine order. The ocular turned oracle.

My blind socket is shown the future, while the right eye sees the red swimming in the white around the green, the red slowly flowing across the table. You, vanishing, ashamed. You, wearing my eye on a string around your neck, so I can see wherever you go. You, trading my eye as an object of disgust, for something else also stolen. You, swallowing my eye, and not finding internal sight. You, succumbing to lunacy, and plucking both of your own eyes.

Me, not seeking revenge, not wanting one of your eyes in exchange. Me, never getting back what you have taken. Always wanting to be whole again. Being a thankless, bitter beast, always waiting for the promise of flowing honey to match the milk. Burying this dark bird with one eye forever peeled.

SHE'LL ONLY COME OUT AT NIGHT

STORY BY JEANETTE SANCHEZ-IZENMAN • ART BY CHRISTINA COLLINS

His eyes blinked. His lips moved as if trying to wet them to speak. I looked down at his head. His eyes opened and fixed on mine for just a moment and then closed. His face spasmed and his eyes opened again. His body still strapped to the wreck of his car lay a few feet away. I looked back, not seeing at first what had caused his head to have landed at my feet on the side of the road. Still unsure, and not caring what delivered this boon, I called his name gently and reached out to touch his chin, "Steve. Steve, your time is done now." His eyelids fluttered and opened wide upon the terrors the night held for him. Then he was still.

•

I ride in cars with men. They talk to me. They confide in me. I listen. I never talk. I don't know why they feel compelled to tell me some of the worst things they've ever done, but they do. It's like I'm a priest in a confessional and they repent. Afterwards, they sigh like I've lifted some burden from them. I shiver even on the warmest nights. I don't know why.

•

"Phil, this is my little sister. Isn't she pretty?" Steve said. Phil looked at me and then at the three men crammed in the booth with us. He noticed how the other men looked at my body, but he walked away. He went to the restroom, sat at the counter when he came back out. He heard them laughing at the jokes Steve told. Jokes that no girl my age should hear. Jokes that no person should have to hear. The men laughed and laughed. Steve gripped my thigh under the table and pinched it hard enough to bruise as he told them about a prostitute sold by her john for a profit. I tried not to wince, but his rough touch made me afraid of what the night had in store.

I had left my home that morning with Steve. He met my mom at the bar last night and spent the night making her cry out both in pain and pleasure until there was silence. I knew from experience that the silence meant she'd finally been sated for the time being or that she'd passed out. Usually I tried to pretend to be deep in sleep on the couch that served as my bed in the living room of our tiny one-bedroom apartment. I'd learned that if the men hadn't finished with my mom, they'd expect me to do it for them if I was awake and sometimes even when I wasn't. I'd woken up to men removing my panties or stroking my breasts through my shirt. Once I'd felt a man sit on the edge of the couch and heard him start to stroke himself as his breathing quickened. I stayed still, almost not breathing, hoping he would finish and go away. Just as he climaxed, he shoved his dick into my face coming onto it and wiping the tip across my lips.

I had to leave.

•

Men tell me about cheating on their wives. They tell me about lovers who said no or who were passed out when they took their bodies. They tell me about the smaller indiscretions, watching pornography at work, wondering if their co-worker is good in bed, confessing that they have thought about sleeping with other men. They drive their hard-bodied cars through the night, penetrating the air around us and they talk about sex. I listen. I don't speak. I shiver and when they stop the car, I wake up somewhere else.

•

Steve lifted me into the cab of his truck while my mom still slept. The truck was warm. It smelled acidic, but also like cheap cologne. It smelled like Steve. He promised he'd drive me to Las Vegas where he assured me that his friend who owned a bar could get me work and I am pretty enough to be a showgirl he said. He said, "You shouldn't waste that beauty here. Come with me." And I did.

•

It's springtime. The trees are still silhouettes, but they have tiny budding leaves that soften them in the late afternoon light. I walk under them and look up at the branches that reach over the road. I like when I can walk in the twilight in spring under trees. I don't know when the last time I walked in the spring was, but it seems I should be able to remember it. This road is narrow. Too narrow for two cars to pass each other. It's really too small for a hitchhiker to get a ride on, but I must walk here so I walk. A car slows as it

approaches. The driver looks up from her steering wheel and sees me. Her face lights up with recognition and then, eyes wide. I touch my hair, tangled and slightly matted and look down. My jacket is still white, but a little dusty. I don't look threatening. When I look back up, she's gone. She's driven away leaving dust in the air.

•

The diner was brightly lit that night. Almost too bright. My eyes hurt after staring at the road for so long. Steve wrapped his white Members Only jacket around my shoulders as we walked to the building. He had been laughing earlier in the truck with his friends over the CB. They'd agreed to meet here. We were the first to make it. He introduced me as his little sister travelling with him on break. We'd driven all day. West. West toward my freedom. Steve kept telling me how he'd check up on me in Vegas and watch me dance. Sometimes when I woke from a nap in the truck, he'd be looking at me and would tell me how like an angel I am.

His friends arrived later. We took a corner booth. The vinyl of the seats cracked under me and the cold made me shiver. Or was it the strange way Steve's friends looked at me? They studied me. Steve leaned to my ear and whispered, "Sweetie, they're on the road and you are the loveliest little thing they've seen in weeks."

The food arrived and an older man entered the diner. He saw us there and came over, shaking hands with Steve and then excusing himself. I watched him because he had little interest in looking at me. He also furrowed his brow at Steve's introduction of me as his little sister. He said nothing. I wondered why.

•

Fall leaves swirl around my feet. I see a car on the horizon. I lift my arm in the familiar gesture, hoping this time she'll stop. She looks upset, like she's been crying when she sees me and slows down. I think she may give me a ride, but as I walk toward the car, she suddenly shakes her head and gently applies pressure to the gas, driving away from me. I can almost feel her misery in the air left behind her. I say

a little prayer that this woman makes it to her destination safely.

•

We're in the parking lot now, walking to Steve's truck with his friends. Steve has his arm wrapped around my shoulders, pulling me close to his body. I try to move away and he slides his hand down to grip mine and pull me close. We fall behind the group and he hisses in my ear, "Now, be an angel and let me and my buddies show you a good time." I flinch and he notices. His grip on me tightens as he playfully calls out to his friends, "Who goes first?"

I'm on the icy ground. Shoved to my knees. Steve has pushed my face into his crotch. The other men hold me down and laugh. My pants are wet from the snow and it's so cold. Steve's body is the only thing I can feel that is hot. So I open my mouth and try to warm up. Steve's body tightens up and he pushes me away. I look up and see the old man from the diner staring at us. Steve reaches into his truck cab and pulls out a gun. I gasp, but the smoky man has my throat and tightens his grip before—the colors start to fade. The old man pauses, shakes his head and walks away.

•

It's nighttime. I'm walking on a deserted road somewhere cold. My body is aching with the vibration of the road. I've not slept. My hair falls in tangles down my back. I draw the white cloth of the flimsy jacket in toward my body, but it does little to keep me warm. I don't remember why I'm here. I remember being in a diner. I remember my mother's face bleary with alcohol—she's driving and sees me. She doesn't see me. She drives away. I remember better times. But I don't remember how I got here. Headlights illuminate the road behind me. I turn and stick out my arm, thumb up. The driver is a woman. She is sleepy and nearly hits me as she passes and jerks awake. I see her glance in her rearview mirror.

•

It's July. I don't know what year it is. I only know it's July because it's hot, the air still smells like gun powder

and there are scraps of cardboard and fuses all around. The pavement is melting and heat waves shimmer up on the horizon. Blood sizzles as it drips onto the surface of the highway. I watch. He's older now. The Harley Davidson he'd been riding is several yards behind him on the road. As I look at his face and see it grimacing in pain, I remember how it looked when he cut into my belly and entered me there. His face looks so similar now except then he was squinting his eyes in ecstasy and there were fewer wrinkles. His face is a roadmap, only looking at it, I still can't find my way home. He sees me, eyes widen in recognition but he can't speak. I let my gaze travel from that face, down to his broken body. Road shrapnel pierces it in all the places he cut me open. A deep gash in his middle abdomen oozes blood around a piece of metal. Drip. Sizzle. Drip. Sizzle. Drip. Sizzle.

•

I ride in cars with men.

I shiver even on the warmest nights. I don't know why.

I don't speak. I shiver and when they stop the car, I wake up somewhere else.

The trees are still silhouettes, but they have tiny budding leaves that soften them in the late afternoon light.

I don't know when the last time I walked in the spring was, but it seems I should be able to remember it. This road is narrow.

•

It's a balmy night. I'm somewhere with high humidity and lots of green shrubs and undergrowth. Some trees. I walk to the car that is now wrapped around a sturdy tree just off the side of the road. It's dark, but I can see by the glow of the night sky. I see a man crushed in the driver's seat. He's too young to be gasping for air the way he is. If I look hard enough, I swear I can see the cancer growing inside his wasted smoky lungs. I smell a hint of bourbon and stale cigarettes as I approach. He sees me. His lips move, but I can't tell what he's trying to say. There isn't enough air passing through to make sound. His eyes bulge in his head and he twitches, then lies still. I watch the life leave his eyes. In his lap a cigarette burns its way through his pants and into the flesh between his legs. I remember this man burning my skin that night. I watch.

•

I see a car on the horizon. I lift my arm in the familiar gesture, hoping this time she'll stop.

I feel her misery in the air left behind her. I say a little prayer.

I remember being in a diner. Headlights illuminate the road behind me.

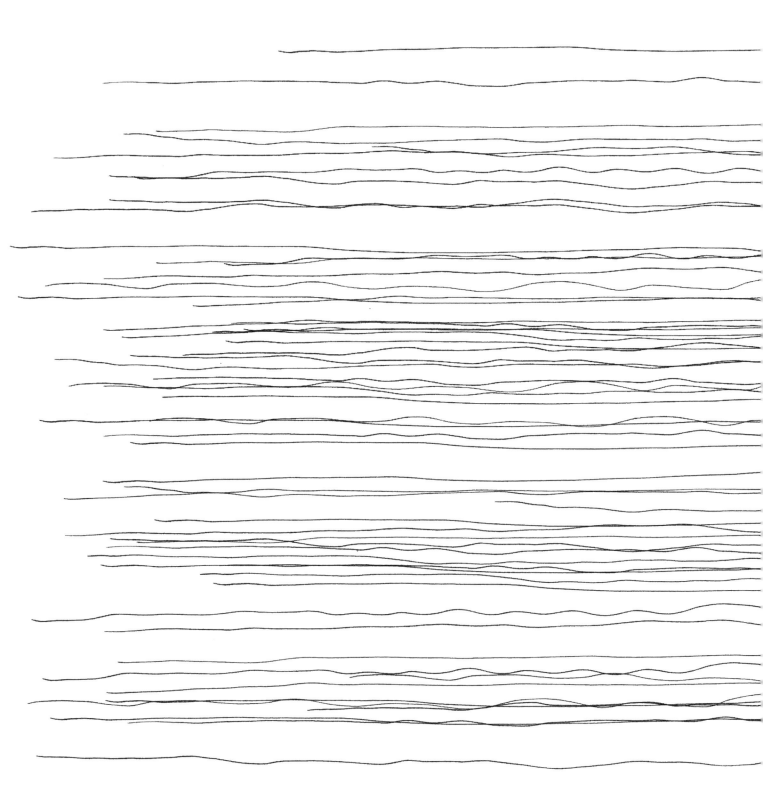

NOTES ON WOLVES AND RUIN, III

STORY AND ART BY CHRISTINE HAMM

1. The first time I kill my husband, I stab him in the chest thirty-four times and wrap his body in our Ikea comforter. I drag him down the icy sidewalk to the abandoned brownstone, my boots slipping. I fall to my knees more than once. I push and pull him upstairs to the pink door, the room with the black pool in the center. The wolves tip their heads back and whine and yip as his body sinks. The yellow moths in the rug open their wings like worried hands.

2. The next week, I steal costume jewelry from Macy's. I want to see how it looks around the wolves' throats, in their ears. Hats, gloves, barrettes, sparkling gloves... I'm saving my money for a new tattoo on the left side of my neck. This one in color. This one after a drawing by a child. Teeth in a large lipsticked mouth. The eyebrows arched and then pointed down to show ill intent. My mom had hair like this once, the Marlo-Thomas, the That-Girl flip. Dark heavy bangs, straight across, the ends brushing her shoulders. A stiff curl where the tips of the wedge hit the collarbones. The whole thing solid, brown, plastic, a wig for a doll.

3. When I was twelve and a half, Shelly and I were still swapping beds and underwear. On the field trip to the Natural History Museum, a sleek wolf pelt hung from the wall like a lost and found jacket. A gray moon shining from the bottom of a river. I pictured Shelly in that skin—Shelly the carnivore with a Peter Pan collar and Mary Janes that had lost their shine. I told her everything as it happened— the blood on my chair during library hour, the yellow vomit on my hands on the way to the nurse's station.

Under the kitchen table after the trip, I asked Shelly if I was still considered a virgin. A bag of useless cotton in my back pack. An invisible cross of blood thumbed on my forehead. She told me, "You were never a virgin." She blushed and picked at the diamonds in the floor.

I agreed, "I'm disgusting," and smiled through the ache of new teeth. One of us: the lamb. The other: the wolf.

4. My husband's been gone for eleven months before the police come by. Our neighbors have been complaining about the noise, the howling. I answer the door barefoot and bra-less, in a soiled t-shirt and cut-off jeans. The policemen wear their black down coats and furry caps, tapping silver pens in their leather gloves. It is snowing lightly again. The streetlights highlight the nearby flakes in orange and yellow. In the doorway, I start to shiver and cross my arms over my chest. One cop asks me something about Saturday parking while the other looks towards the yelling and glass breaking three houses down. I smooth my hair through my fingers and nod. I wonder if the men can smell me, and what they think I smell like: a dungeon, a bullet casing, a butcher?

5. During the next summer, leaf-shadows shimmer from the ruined windows of the turret. The wolves at the bullet-pocked walls lean in towards the center. I trip over the dark carpet, but it's not a carpet—it's water. The wolves meet my eyes as I sink, scent of chlorine/coconut oil/animal urine. And here again, my dad is teaching me what happens when I try to rescue people. The wolves' ears forward, nostrils stretched and expanded, my father with his hand on the top of my head. "This is what happens if you try to save the drowning" and I, I, I, I, I am tasting the water as it burns the back of my throat. He is pushing down and I am five, in a navy and yellow striped two-piece.

6. Three years after my first blood bath (or "The Shining," as Shelly liked to call it), she and I were smoking her parents' pot as we went through the porn mags under their bed. My face burned and my clothes fell off. Then we were in the hot tub and the water wouldn't heat up, so we shivered. Someone two houses down was throwing a party—music echoed through the valley. Black Sabbath, flashing purple lights. Adults yelling and laughing. Shelly's little brother cried in the living room, watching us through the sliding glass door. It was dark where we were and light in the house. The split-level was a square yellow spaceship, tethered to the earth by invisible electric wires. I started to cry because her brother seemed so small, even smaller than Shelly, who only came up to my shoulder. I worried that he would disappear because no one loved him. I watched him wipe snot on the striped arm of his pajamas and fall onto his side. In the morning, my mother came to pick me up from the sleepover in her blue jeep, and I felt such hatred at her pink lipsticked smile.

7. Insects outside my bedroom: slow at night, but never stopping. A shrill, *wick, wick, wick*. Or *sick, sick*. After sunset, the wolves groan as they settle and scratch. In the morning, the whole back lot is filled with droppings, with tufts of harsh fur and cracked bird bones. Weeds flourish along the edges—the rest is dust and pebbles, fractured paving stones from aborted gardens. I wear a harness around my mouth when I nap. Otherwise, I chew my tongue and fingers. A mouthful of blood. My husband used to say he couldn't sleep through the noise of my tearing in the dark, the grunting. The first joint on my left pinky, already gone.

8. As a New Year's Resolution, I get a new therapist. She has a red couch like a red tongue. We discuss the couch, how she ordered it from a catalog, how she picked the color, how the movers had to disassemble it to put it on the elevator.

Sometimes the different doormen don't believe I'm a patient, and force me to call her from the house phone before I come up. But she's always in session. I can't remember how I make it to her office those days. She refuses to speak to the staff about me, shrieking, "I'm not at your beck and call," as I gallop from the room. Twice a month, she sends me a note, says she's thinking about me, all her i's dotted with hearts.

9. Once when we were in bed, my husband whispered about my maternal instincts. "That's why you kept the baby bird, even after it died," he said. "That's why you

want to convince me that I'm smart." I stuck my fists in the pillow, thought about my dead children.

Where are they buried? I asked myself while he was ignorant, sleeping, safe. A trash can, a medical waste container. In the corners of doctors' offices, a red plastic box marked "sharps" always huddled, shuddering. Behind the hospital where they kept my father in the locked ward for a month, piles of wet gauze, old blue tubes, stuffed in a ditch. Smashed in the ravine. Clear bags with skulls and crossbones. Festive orange pill bottles, contents x-ed out. Empty syringes, which I gathered in my pink cotton book bag.

10. I'm watching the nature channel show about Coy-wolves. I've taken off my mask so my skin can breathe. I've got a rash high up on my cheeks—I think it's the rubber or fake fur in the mask. Last night, no one knew me at the party, so they were friendlier. Everyone was drunk, looming and falling, laughing and falling. I got a contact high. I haven't had a drink for ten years, and that last time, I was alone.

11. Another word for "now" or "never." "Pater" and "potato." Fifteen down. What happens when I push the needle through. Not sewing, but rending. Cotton, spoon, match. The underside of my father's tongue so gray, his eyes yellow where the lower lid hits the sclera. He told me this was for my own good, that it hurt him more than it hurt me. He wouldn't look at me. He told me the neighbors could hear and that I was embarrassing him. I thought about cutting off his hands, which knife to use.

12. Two years ago today, around three a.m. On the kitchen counter, in the picture covering my husband's textbook, clouds were indicated by ragged dash marks. My husband was still sleeping. It was hard to get him to sleep—he always got up, arranged magazines in stacks, reparked his car, hopped off to work. I liked him in bed, lax. Loved to touch his sleeping chest, kiss his puffy cheeks. A body

completely mine: the never-ending dreamer. My second favorite place in the world was our mattress—I'm still there most of the time, but he is not. That night, I mixed in some NyQuil with his egg-fried rice and covered the flavor with hot sauce.

"Um, babe," he said as he ate, standing next to the TV.

"I know, I know," I said. "So you make dinner next time, Princess."

After he collapsed onto the comforter, the garden filled with wolves. They snorted and whined, dug at the gladiolas. A shell-colored female jerked as I bent down to pull a burr from her side. She leaned against me, yanked the skin on my neck with her teeth. Each nip felt sudden and dark, a door slamming on my heart. She whispered in a girlish voice, "If you would just hold still," like I said to him, like I had just said.

[SEWAGE]

STORY BY GABRIELLE JOY LESSANS • ART BY KRISTY BLACKWELL

A week gone by a week at a time. Light pink stuffed in the corner of the closet. Crumpled. A silk ball buried like the nose buried where you never said he. Could. Light cold like lace. Forbidden you. Bitten. Buried for a reason.

Lapse.

Seasons back to blank. The ease of utter lap and lap and lap around the carpet. Where was bed when you needed bed. Where was home. Swell. Bloat. Shhhh and hush and shrink and stall. Take care not to dilate. Wait.

Taste.

Saliva traced with sedative laced with ethanol chased with chilled pasta. Almond butter toast. Whatever keeps your chewing. Jawed. Whatever tames your stomach. Ached. Whatever keeps the dryer churning. Heat. Wailing what you wont. Turn.

Flat.

Curls endangered. Rims rung in kohl layered black layer blacker 'til you can't see out the corner of your eyes. Forget what's meant to leak but doesn't for a week straight of wonder where it went. Your wonder. Swallowed neat.

Sweep.

Under stitch by stich a mind dripped into Carolina potholes. Pockmarks and assholes and organs. Sacred orifices. Chest heaved. Shoved. Back to black dream. Watch where your feet. Reap. Hot tar guarded sewers save the seep. Stay the stink.

Sink.

Down onto couch. Dosed. Drought of the mouth. Coat. Your eyes over green. Smoke. Join the club. Float. Laugh it off honey. Change the channel. Pass the mug of instant coffee pass the stogy pass whatever faster pass it faster. Rap about the weather. Wrangle it together.

Stain.

Purple slowly rising from your gutter. Got it. Inner. Shades of color. Holding space in your face for what comes after. The pictures they dared. With bare teeth. Shared. Snared ass to ass. Staged. Circulate. What tarnished molten marrow steeps. Your heart now. Solid. In the center. Its nectar never reaching. Your toes.

Numb.

Flesh thinning. Midriff stolen. Something rancid growing. Rode in. Fold in. Gore corroded. Cotton absence tainting fainting raiding reeking. Ruined. Your middle.

Finger.

Can't reach what was heaved. Can't pull what was shoved. Elbows that would've been thrust. Lay lamed. Maimed. Brain portioned into morsels. Defaced. Waste. Curdled fluid stuck. Tubes struck. Eroding liner. Soiled womb of soundless muck. Rank. Blood clots set between vertebrates. Breached. Derailed all memory.

Fail.

From the inside body outside. Body. What body. Saw your body. Raw. No body taking sides & all your red. Stolen your red. Stop. All your red coalesced to black gum & rot. You're rot. You are rotting from the inside outside purple running into black gum tar oozing out your potholes. You gutter you. Rancid piece of roadkill scent exuding from the vitals never taken. The fluids never tested. The no you never got to.

Scream.

This smell is not your smell. This smell is not your. Something. Coming. Falling from your. Water. Turn it hotter make it hotter water hotter later full week later something s t a r t s   to   s l u g. Sick you. Are smut you. Are floundering in filth. Lift. Your rabid dog leg and.

Sob.

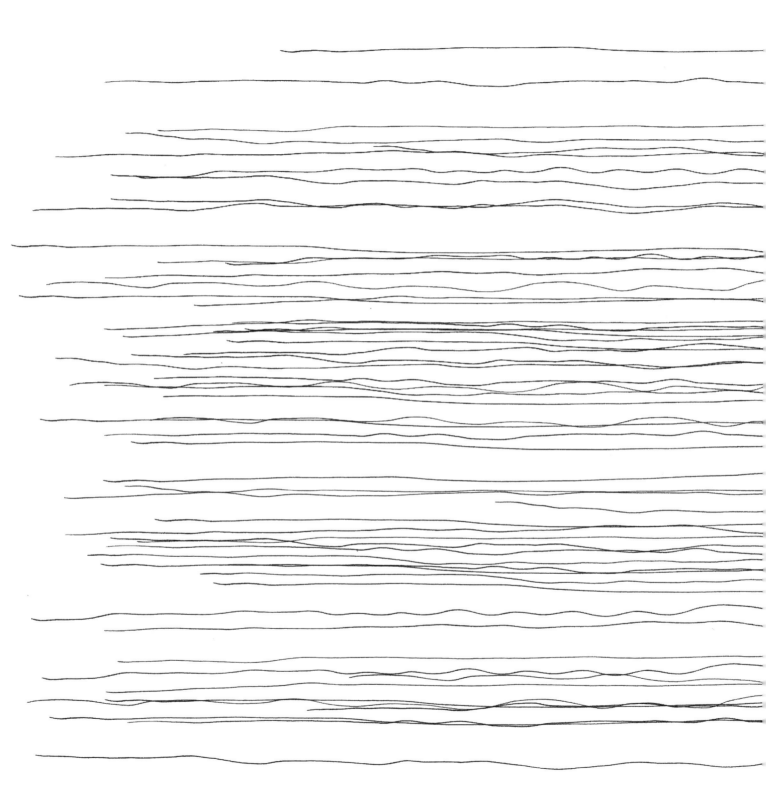

VILE GIFTS
AND WHAT THE
BODY SECRETS

THE BODY, (UN)EXAMINED

STORY BY SUBASHINI NAVARATNAM • ART BY CARABELLA SANDS

Having ensured that the door was closed, she spread her legs and tentatively pushed a finger in. Doing this always made her feel embarrassed, but an insistent beating between her legs, like a clock keeping time to her age—the one that went *get laid get laid get laid* instead of *tick tock*—always overrode the shame. She remembered Kylie Minogue's words: "I'm a red blooded woman, what's the point in hanging around"—was there a more rousing anthem in the history of pop music? That should be reason enough. She tried also to recall the you-go-girl enthusiasm of every single *Bitch* and *BUST* magazine article she had ever read: "There is nothing wrong with touching yourself! In fact, it's important for an adult woman to know her body and how to pleasure herself." Determination! She had the determination to masturbate. Now she only had to relax, and do it fast before her mother called for her.

She searched her mind for something other than her current fantasy: NCIS Special Agent Gibbs telling her she's been a bad, bad girl and in need of a good spanking. It was a good fantasy but she wasn't sure if it was okay. She was against the American police state and its imperialist foreign policy, specifically, but damn he was something else. Would she still have this fantasy if, looking as silver-haired and foxy as ever, Mark Harmon played a union organiser or a farmer instead? This is what was troubling her. That maybe the problem was that she liked the authoritarian patriarch; that was what she was getting off on. That maybe she liked a man in a suit who was a cop underneath, who would fuck her with all of his American exceptionalism built into every thrust.

Her mother would wake up from her nap soon, and then it would be time for Maya to make her a cup of tea and take it to her with some Marie biscuits on a plate. A fly buzzed around in the room. Maya was in the middle of reading a book by a German theorist about one's body as a colonial territory; the long history of subjugation and discipline, and the process of "installing dark territories, sources of terror and anxiety, in and on people's own bodies," as she recalled the words. The territories of the body that one couldn't enter, "occupied by the gods, the police, laws, Medusas, and other monsters." She thought that was a poetic—almost beautiful—way of theorising what is essentially a miserable situation. The sense of nausea and shame and desire around sex, and the fact that at thirty-three, she had yet to have it, all this was captured by the vision of her body as occupied territory. She imagined a Balkanisation of her body, its pieces distributed evenly among various "stakeholders," as the language of newspaper reporting would have it. It didn't seem fair, but here she was, with a body occupied not only by the state but seemingly her entire extended Tamil family. She couldn't even get off on Mark Harmon spanking her without wondering if her father was watching her. This was the problem with dead people. Once gone, they were everywhere.

It was the Medusas and monsters in the body that was the problem, the theorist wrote. That didn't sound so bad when she thought about it. Her monsters were different. It was the voice of every Tamil aunty she had known growing up that sometimes stopped her short. Medusa seemed benign, almost like a fairy godmother, in comparison. How bad would it be to have a snake-haired woman colonising her cunt? She would not still be a virgin if that were the case. Perhaps it was best to have the body divided into territories. Her head, once sliced off, could hang on trees, far away from here. A forest of heads, blinking and thinking.

A fly buzzed close to her face. She pulled her finger out; nothing was happening. Not while she was thinking of heads; bloodied, decaying, severed heads, sliced right across the throat. It was a hot day, right in the middle of a heat wave that made the humidity more suffocating than usual. The air hung about her face like a curtain she couldn't push through. Her back was drenched with sweat. Nothing seemed to matter. There were days when she realised she was measuring out her life in sweaty underwear. Tomorrow would be the same, and then the day after. More sweat, more laundry. On top of all of this: she couldn't get

rid of the fly. After her grandmother died, Maya's aunt, her grandmother's sole surviving child, had a theory about the fly that was always there. Her aunt was convinced that the fly was her grandmother. It accompanied her everywhere, even in airplanes and on trips abroad. Maya didn't have the heart to remind her that flies were everywhere around here, swarming around garbage made all the more putrid by the sweltering heat.

Everywhere Maya went, too, a fly buzzed around her. Sometimes it flew directly into her face, especially when she was feeling particularly low, when she felt the dark slowly enveloping her like the smog closing in on the city. She would always try to swat it away, but it would buzz close to her cheek, her lips, swoop forward with an almost painful smack and then fly away again. It was never around when she touched herself, though. It seemed to want to allow her that privacy; or maybe it was too much to bear, even for the fly, knowing what went on in her mind as she clicked through one porn video after the other, looking for that right hit.

That's when she started thinking that maybe the fly was her father.

•

After her father died, the life she lived with her mother grew smaller and smaller until she couldn't tell it apart from a speck of dust. Her elder siblings and their children lived abroad, all except for one; as the youngest she never had much to say to them, coming in last when her mother had Maya when she was forty, after everyone else was already in secondary school. It seemed a matter of course that the youngest daughter would come back to live with the mother and accompany her to every hospital visit.

Conversations between Maya and her mother were never easy; she was sure her mother was still upset that she never materialised into the accomplished, beautiful doctor that her mother had fantasised she would be. Instead, here she was: an unaccomplished, fat, unmarried daughter given to writing weird poetry that no one had read and otherwise scrounging up whatever she could make from copywriting assignments and book reviews for the local paper. It was hard for Maya to talk to the people in her mother's life, the people her family was supposed to know. There was nothing to say.

There was nothing much to be said between Maya and her mother, either. Teatime, like every other meal time, would be seen by a distant observer as a tableau of plates and cups and Maya's mother nattering on without pause and Maya thinking she might take the butter knife and drag it across her throat—would it make a clean cut, she wondered, or would it drag, a long jagged pull, tearing across her skin, the blood coming softly at first and then in great spurts—as her mother waited expectantly for Maya to chime in with an opinion about "those people" coming in to the country to rape and murder the local women, or the price of vegetables, or so-and-so's beautiful young daughter who was living in London and engaged to be married to a tall, very striking-looking white man. She tried not to but sometimes Maya imagined smashing a plate against her mother's face—and then stopped there. She couldn't go on. She hated herself because what kind of a monster, let alone a daughter, would imagine such a thing? Maya thought about those pieces of glass from the broken plate and imagined dragging it across her stomach until the flabby layers of fat oozed out, mingling with the blood. To be toned and straight as a plank: a mark of discipline. A wayward body reflected wayward thoughts. Maya as herself, fat and unwieldy, was not a body to be reckoned with. But spread across the table with her guts spilling out, the bright crimson of the blood enhancing her the earth-tones of her skin—that would be a body to be reckoned with.

•

After tea, Maya left her mother with the TV on. Someone had to talk to her mother before senility set in and became just another thing that they got used to, like a piece of new furniture they learned to move around. But Maya couldn't cope. Besides, there was so much of work to do. She did what she did most nights: she fled into her study to get some writing done.

Alone with her computer, the fly buzzed around her. It settled on her arm for a second before buzzing close to her ear and flying off. Maya's thighs stuck to the chair—the heat was like a blanket that was continuously being pulled closer around her—and her irritation with the stupid creature grew. She waved her hands about, shooing it away. The fat from the back of her arms jiggled. She pulled up the sleeves of her t-shirt to get some air on her skin but immediately felt ashamed in case her mother walked past suddenly and saw her arms for what they were: pudgy roles of dough, flesh drooping over her elbows. She hated that bit over her elbows; she scrutinised pictures of other women's arms and none of them drooped fat. They kept their fat in place. Only Maya let it hang. Her arms screamed, "Look at this fat fuck who doesn't know when to stop eating." It made the secret of her fleshiness visible. Her fat arms with their growth of hair; so hirsute as to be almost a joke, but Maya could not cope. She did not know why she had to remove the hair when it exhausted her enough to shave her armpits and her legs and tweeze, painfully, her upper lip. The rest of her face was downy. She was too ashamed to go get her face threaded like every other functioning adult woman she knew—she felt like the women would laugh, seeing her so hairy. She imagined her hair growing and growing until she was only a large hairball, shaggy, writhing around in her own fur, trapped in a laboratory and forever under observation, and stared at.

Once, in college, a guy—his skin pale and milkier than the White Rabbit candy her mother loved to eat—put his delicate, lean arm against hers and said, "Wow, you have more hair on your arm than I do!" The fact was that she had more hair than most people. Underneath her underwear where Medusa and the monsters crawled was a thicket so dense that only the most determined explorer would set forth. So far there had been a few, but getting past the gate was harder. No matter how close a cock came to her pussy the idea of letting it enter her filled her with a certain amount of anxiety. It was like letting a python slide in. She imagined that in the morning she would find the cock wrapped around her neck and she would be dead. So she always stopped just in time. Every boyfriend since her father's death—the only time she could have a boyfriend without the fear of him finding out—was stopped just in time, like a clock that had run out of battery.

Alone all the time, however, she thought about being choked by cocks, being filled by an endless line of cocks, being fucked senseless until she could barely see or hear. Being split open either with a cock or a knife until everything that was seething inside her could spill out.

The fly flew past again, near her neck. The buzzing was intolerable. She imagined smashing it with a book, its insides oozing all over her table. She wanted to retch. She thought about how it would feel to rub the sticky fly ooze all over her body, its slimy stench sticking to the hair on her face and arms and cunt, becoming so disgusting that it made sense that she was unloved, unfucked, and unseen.

•

When she got into one of these funks, it was hard for her to focus on anything. Her writing, her reading. Her mother's voice droned on and on at the dinner table. Did she notice? Can she see me dying? Maya wondered. The cleaner had been in earlier; she had prepared an unappetising spread of beetroot curry and some attempt of a dish of fish, tasting salty and sweet and similarly of nothing all at once. Desultory food for desultory people, Maya decided. In another house, perhaps, where life was detected, the cleaner might go all out in her preparations—fish cutlets coated in breadcrumbs, mutton curry, spicy fried chicken.

Maya thought of taking the plate and breaking it over her face, over and over, until tiny shards of glass pierced into her skin. She had heard of this happening to accident victims, when the glass particles of the vehicle they're in get embedded in the skin. Maya felt her skin tingle. She thought of walking around with a face of glass, knowing how precious she was even though no one could tell. Or maybe they could. Perhaps she would never stop bleeding. She would be bleeding from every pore.

Her mother continued her conversation that she had been having all by herself, stopping only once or twice to ask Maya a question, and to resume again. "Her skirt was up to her thighs and she could not even sit with her legs closed," her mother was saying. Who had worn this terrible skirt? Maya had lost track. Maya saw the edges of her thighs spill out of the seat of the chair and moved to rearrange herself in the seat, to contain herself and keep it all in. The span of her thighs in her shorts was too much, excessive, unavoidable. She thought of taking the fork and stabbing it into her eyes until her vision became clouded with dots. She would never be able to see herself whole. That seemed like the best fucking gift a person could have. She imagined NCIS Special Agent Gibbs at the kitchen counter, bending her over and taking her from behind, grasping on to her ass, her thighs, the layers of fat on her stomach, his large hands unable to grasp all of it, her fat spilling through his fingers, telling her the more of her there was, the merrier. "What kind of ideas will she give men if she dresses like that?" her mother concluded. The fly swooped in once around the food on the table, then buzzed her ear, and flew away.

•

Before bed, in her bathroom, she grabbed a fistful of hairs around her groin and wanted to tear them out. She couldn't bear to get it waxed; what if the ladies laughed or worse, exchanged looks of horror, words of horror in Tagalog and Burmese? She would lie there, face burning, pussy exposed, the fact of her shame vivid and unavoidable. Like a patient etherised upon a table, except conscious of the fact that she was being pried open for all to see. She couldn't bear to shave either because she always thought about how it would feel to run the blade over her cunt until she was dripping, literally, with blood and was slightly afraid that she might actually do it, unable to stop. How good it would feel to feel so much there until she could never feel anything there again. She grabbed a pair of scissors and squatted over the tub and snipped off huge clumps. Wiry hairs that went which and every way fell

onto the beige tub. A constellation of cunt hairs. Shedding her fur. She found one white hair and felt immensely defeated. So much for fertile abundance. Hers was headed into retirement and it didn't even try while it could. Could a pussy shut down from lack of use? A sarcophagus amidst a dense thicket of trees. She imagined Special Agent Gibbs burrowing in her forest. Would he hammer a nail into her coffin? No, she decided, he wouldn't be able to. That was a man of sparse and well-maintained nature reserves and city parks. He would not willingly, or with pleasure, venture into a moist, damp jungle. Well, not without his gun, because every jungle in the world of *NCIS* would probably harbour menace and doom, and also terrorists. And not his metaphorical gun, either. An actual gun. Maya would probably be killed for the luxuriant growth of her jungle. Special Agent Gibbs would of course take full responsibility for neutralising this threat. *We had no choice sir, we had to put it down. The threat was coming from inside the cunt.*

She thought she heard a buzz and looked up. She saw the fly perched on the edge of bathtub.

•

Maya could not sleep all night. She took off her pajama pants and then her underwear and spread her legs, running her fingers over her pussy, thinking about being spanked and then fucked hard over a table, any table. She wasn't able to get wet. She tried to recall bits of the porn videos she'd seen over the years, tits bouncing, cocks announcing themselves from within the strained confines of pants. Still nothing. Cocks distended, cocks taking a stand. On their own. A veritable garden of pussies and cocks. Every hole was a trap but it didn't matter, you could come and come and never have to feel anything else ever again. Maya felt herself nodding off, found herself in the garden of trees that were cocks. Then she saw the heads hanging, the gash that severed their necks rough and rudimentary. Someone had taken a knife across their throats and sawed through, leaving jagged bits of flesh hanging. Her father's head was blowing in the wind and he was crying out, blood coming out of his eyes like when she saw his body on that final day, trailing

down his cheeks, but Maya couldn't understand what he was saying. Maya came to with a start and felt cold all over. She wanted to feel anything but this and so started to rub herself again. Nothing was happening. She wanted to stuff anything inside her, or pull something outside of her. Just go to sleep, she told herself. But sleep brought her severed heads, as it did on some nights. Maybe she could wake up and get a snack, peanut butter on a soft slice of white bread; sweet, salty, and comforting. But she couldn't go down into the kitchen alone, not at this time of the night.

She had gone downstairs earlier for a glass of water after her mother had gone to bed and had seen them. So they were still there, and it looked as though they were here to stay. More and more, now, they were using their living room as some sort of gathering place. Maya didn't think her mother had seen them; she rarely left her bedroom after eleven. They sat on the couches, curiously well-behaved, those headless bodies. If she was honest, she had seen them sitting there, silent and cautious, practically every night for the last few months now. She had learned to recognise the cold hand running down her back, to not scream, to tell herself that this was not real. They never bothered her but the air felt dense, close around her, and her brain felt scrambled. They always sat with knives in their hands. One time one of them stood up and walked toward her in the kitchen, knife extended in her direction, like an offering. Maya had closed her eyes and pushed past, feeling nothing, just the sensation of cold hands on her body, and ran upstairs to her room. She hadn't told her mother. Maya could hear the laughter, once in a while, from inside her room. High-pitched and strange. Maybe they were laughing at her.

Since then she had just avoided being alone in the house, downstairs, after her mother had gone to sleep. It was better to stay in her room. She thought maybe they came because they knew she and her mother were always alone. She closed her eyes and tried to stay calm, breathing in and out as slowly as she could. She was not sure why she did this; it rarely made her feel better. But soon enough she felt herself slowly relaxing. She tried to think of cocks, bare buttocks grinding, men coming all over her, and put the heads out of her mind.

She felt something, and knew someone was in the room with her. Telling herself not to, she was unable to stop, and so she opened her eyes. She saw her father at the edge of her bed. He was standing but his eyes were shut. Blood was oozing from his nose, his ears, and trickling down from the sides of his mouth. He was silent and she could smell him again, the stench of death on him. The metallic tang of rotten blood. *Leave, please,* she told him. *Not like this, not like this.*

When the fly flew close this time she moved with a start. She was almost at the point of nodding off and hadn't known it was still in the room. She'd shut the windows and turned the air-conditioning on; despite this, her hair still stuck in a sweaty clump to the back of her neck. She felt the buzzing in the dark and suddenly wanted to get the fly out of the room. But the fly was on her thigh, burrowing, burrowing. She screamed, then thought of her mother in the next room and covered her mouth. The pain was sharp, like being split open by something she had never imagined before. A knife or a club or a cock. She did not know. The fly refused to leave. It thrummed against her skin, the slightest of all vibrations. She could not stop it. She did not have the strength to do it, her legs spread wide. *Just get up and swat it,* she told herself, but the pain was too intense, and she arched her back with the terror of it. Every nerve ending buzzed. She felt a slow dull ache of pleasure somewhere between her legs. The fly burrowed. She needed to stop it. Something about this was wrong but her legs stayed open. She felt herself shaking. The buzzing would not stop. She rubbed her tits, pinched her nipples. The fly stayed on her thigh. She could not seem to get up. She remembered the way he had breathed in her ear, the faint stench of garlic from his dinner, and the same terror of not wanting her mother to wake up.

•

Maya heard an insistent beeping and wanted it to stop.

She put her hand out and it continued. With a start she realised her phone alarm was ringing and she swiped at it, repeatedly, without being able to see. Her eyes were coated with gunk and her throat was dry. It felt like her head had been dunked in wet cement, allowed to dry, then repeatedly smashed with a hammer. Her entire body felt sore.

Her clothes were off and she was naked. Suddenly feeling chill, she switched off the air conditioning and looked down. There was a nasty red bump on her inner thigh. She remembered the buzzing and touched it, carefully, and it only ached slightly. She remembered the night before, the bodies seated in a circle in the living room, the visions of her father, the things she had thought about with her legs spread before the fly attacked her. Hot shame burned through her body. Between her legs she felt a slimy, cold wetness. The stench of herself filled the room.

She was afraid to look at the red bump on her thigh as she went to the bathroom for a shower. She felt it pulsing slightly, like a heartbeat. She scratched at it and it oozed a little, clear liquid. She brought her head down to her thighs, sniffing at it, and smelled the ripeness from between her legs. The red bump buzzed and hummed. She imagined her body opening up, like a flower, taking into it all that was abject and repulsive, nurturing it, letting the goodness of her nurture seep into the cracks between the atoms, like Saint Francis and the sow, how he let his love flow down the length of that unwanted creature. She knew it was coming. The red oozing skin felt vibrant, thrumming with life. The fly pushed forward and flew out.

Maya saw the fly stumbling about on the edge of the toilet seat, coated in her own blood, heavy after taking on this excess weight, this burden of her. She didn't know if she could kill it or if she should, maybe it could live on under her skin, her own minor deity, directing her over the territories of her body. Her own secret from her mother in a house where it was impossible to have anything to herself.

•

In the kitchen Maya walked slowly, worried that her mother would notice that the fly was back inside her, buzzing slightly, causing the red bump to pulse. She had tried to mop up as much of the clear ooze that ran from the wound after her shower and tried to walk without rubbing her thighs against each other, which, as always, proved difficult. In her usual daily uniform of shorts and a t-shirt, though, nothing much could be seen. She set the water boiling and heard her mother's movements as she came downstairs and went into the prayer room for her morning prayers.

The fly pulsed through her, sending jolts of a slight ache throughout her thigh, and another kind of buzzing that made her feel she had something in between her legs all the time. It was odd...and good. As she brought the butter dish out from the fridge and placed the butter knife next to it Maya thought of how it would be to drag it slowly across her mother's throat. This time she did not feel like she had to stop herself from thinking about it. It would not be such a bad thing, Maya decided. Her mother's head would always hang from the trees, eternal. And she could join the ceremony of bodies that gathered in their living room at night.

She rubbed the red bump on her thigh. It was starting to itch, just slightly.

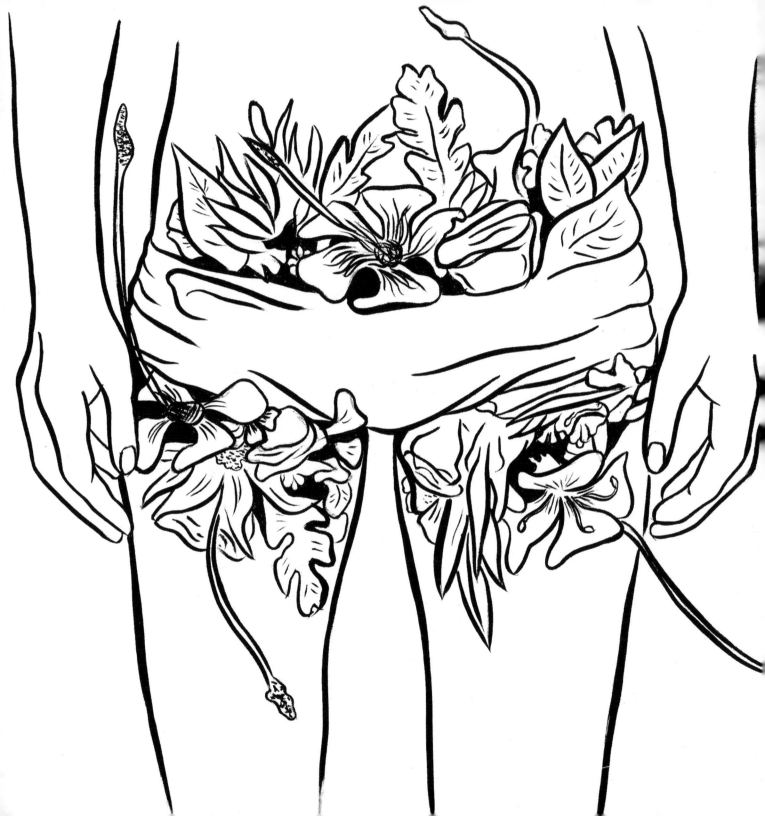

FLOOD

STORY BY T. A. STANLEY • ART BY LAURIE NASICA

Her body started producing tar. Or that was what the sludgy clumps in her underwear looked like. It was black and sticky and it oozed out of her constantly. She remembered how shortly after she turned twelve—all that blood. She knew of course what periods were, but it still surprised her what her body was capable of—all that blood. They told her it wasn't actually very much. Maybe a few ounces. But she always witnessed a waterfall. Now, she was thirty-three and it had turned to tar, clumps of black and a darker red.

She knew, even before the day the dog ate an old tampon from the trash and died, that it was poisonous. She knew, instinctively, that it was trying to poison her from the inside. Her body had turned against her. She knew this like she knew her boss had no intention of giving her that promotion, like she knew men would always be more interested in her sister than her. Or maybe it was just the blood.

It was tired of being stopped up with cotton, tired of being controlled by pills, tired of her shame for it. When she was younger it had battled against these forces by kicking out below her stomach. She interpreted these forceful attempts at escape as cramps, never paying attention to what the blood really wanted. It was only allowed out once a month, and by then she had done everything in her power to keep it close, hidden.

She had hated to see it, and she hated more the idea that anyone else might see it. The constant dread that a visible spot was forming on her pants; that a man might see the stain on her sheets. She was constantly washing it out with cold water, throwing out pairs of underwear that were beyond redemption. But the blood had had enough. So it decided to kill the source of its captivity, kill the body and flow out from it. It just wouldn't stand the barricades anymore.

Her hair began to fall out in clumps, her skin was yellowed and dried out. Friends suggested various medications, doctors, and natural remedies as the poisonous blood made its way through the rest of her body, her heart unknowingly pumping it into her liver, kidneys, and lungs. But rather than take her friends' advice, she preferred to watch the havoc her blood was forcing on her. She had never allowed herself this freedom before, the freedom to destroy, to let go of constant, vigilant maintenance. And she was tired of it all anyway. It hadn't gotten her anywhere in her life to hold onto it. She found pleasure in witnessing its darkened, unstoppable power. Knowing she couldn't control it gave her a sort of peace. It no longer came just once a month. It flowed out of her constantly—black and steady, slow. It stuck to everything and covered her in itself. She tried to wash it off, but it merely clung to the bathtub, refusing to be washed down the drain. She was living in it now and she would be, until one night it would crawl out on top of her. She would smile as she suffocated beneath it—the sticky, dark mass crawling down her throat.

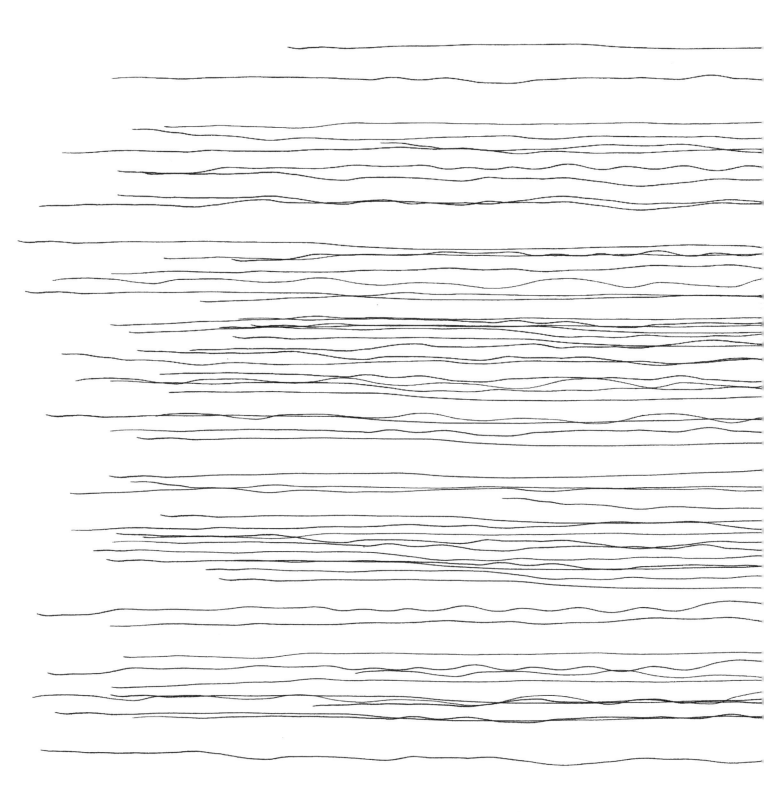

(MOTHER (WOMB (PRECIOUS (CAKE))))

STORY BY CLAIRE HERO • ART BY SOMARAMOS

the womb is like an animal within an animal
—*Aretaeus*

the child's host (some refer to them as mothers)
—*Virginia State Sen. Steve Martin*

There is another world, but it is inside this one.
—*Paul Eluard*

Once upon a time a womb was an animal. A dumb beast cached in the cave of woman. A hunted thing, a carnivore, a missing link lavish with hunger and lust. When a womb was an animal sometimes it wandered. When a womb was an animal sometimes it devoured the pale pinkly charge asleep in its hide. And sometimes, just sometimes, when a womb was an animal it fell in love with that polyp of cells and whisked her off deep in the Mother to keep. This is the story of one of those wombs. This is the story of one of those cells.

•

This bud and this bundle, this squeak of split cells: Precious, Womb named her, and precious she was, and plump as a fist. There had been others, of course. Mother had been a mother before—a real mother and a failed mother, a dreamed mother and a doomed mother. Inside Womb, cells had sparked and gone out without ever a notice from She. There would be dreams—Herself seated on a sofa with an enormous bouquet of peonies—but morning would drop the petals and that was that. Womb had never loved those previous sparks, those dim little sputters, had snuffed them or swallowed them or cast them into the zoo of Mother as she saw fit. Until now, until Precious. How could she ever give her up? *There must be a way,* Womb thought, and she thought and she thought while Precious planted and pearled and then—*a-ha!*—she had it. She would make of herself a balloon and slip away. So she untied the tubes that held her in place and sailed off deep into the dark of Mother.

•

Inside her Wombship Precious sailed through Mother, following the tides of her blood. She shunted through veins with such speed and such force that at first poor Precious was frightened, tossed on the high seas of Mother like so much flotsam. Far and farther she traveled through the body of Mother, past the slaughterhouse of the stomach and the bilge of the spleen and over the thick rollercoaster of the gut. The lungs appeared like two great oceans she sailed between, and the heart punched and punched the rafters of ribs.

They were not alone in the deep of Mother. Beneath her Wombship protozoa swam past, fanning their great wings just below the blood's surface, things with long tails and bright flashes that may have been teeth, and sometimes she could feel Womb shudder as it dragged over their rough and terrible skins.

Anchored beside the liver's still waters Precious sat down and wept.

"What is it, my Precious?" Womb purred in her ear.

"There is nowhere in Mother for me," she sobbed. "Just look," and she pointed to the pool of the liver where two flukes slipped past, red shadows in red waters.

"Whatever did you expect?"

"A Mother for my own," said Precious, "my each and very."

"A Mother is for one and all, but I am yours and you are mine. You, my pet, were made for me." And Womb swept her up with a gobble and woosh and declared, "My Precious, it is time for the Zoo."

•

Behind the smallest of doors was the Zoo of Mother. Here were her spoils and here her false starts. Here were her darlings, cellared and stashed. Here were the outcasts of Mother. Girls with one leg or three legs or more. Girls made of eyes and girls made of mouths. A Sireniform sister swimming in a sac. A bleb of a twin bundled in hair. Buddings and blunders, cankers and curls. Cage after cage after cage.

"See how I love you," Womb said to her Precious. "See how I've kept you from harm."

But Precious saw only herself in each and every: her hands and her tongue, her stump of a tail and her gash of an eye. Those girls were the Mother and the Mother was she.

Through the bars of a cage she slipped her hand, but the girl on the inside slithered away. The girl on the inside would not be pet.

"Go now," croaked the eyeless babe. "Keep your fickle Womb. The Mother is ours."

•

So they traveled the Mother, Womb and her Precious, day after day tossed on the traffic of blood, and Precious tried not to think of the others, treasured in the ever of Mother. Precious tried not to think much at all.

But Precious was growing. How was this happening? Womb wanted to know. One day Precious was a twist in the corner, and the next her shrug threatened to tip the tight ship. She was bulging and spilling. She was more than a handful.

"We must make this stop," Womb declared in a huff, and trussed poor Precious with gut. But even that would not stop the long of her thigh, would not stop the bud of her thumb from outstretching.

Womb was pushing and pressing, trying to hold Precious small, trying to wrestle her bustle of flesh into knot, when there was a rip. There was a tear. There was a cleft in Precious that looked like a smile.

"What have I done?" blubbered Womb. She tried to smush the seam closed, but it was of no use. Down the center of Precious the cleave cut clean through until there were two: Precious and more. A copy, a clone. And again Womb said, all in a whisper, "What have I done?"

Bobbing in Womb, crushed close to her bosom, the girls stretched out their hand nubs and met.

•

Now there were two girls to frolic in Mother. Now there were two girls to travel the circuit. Precious named her twin Cake—she was sweet as a crumb—and Womb said, "You better watch out I don't gobble her up," but they paid her no mind. Up a vein and down an artery the twins

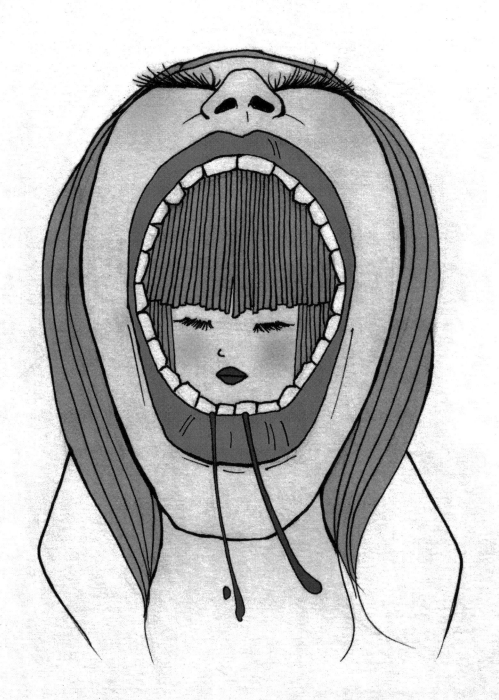

traveled in Womb, their bloated dirigible.

A Mother, Precious discovered, with Cake at her side, was a funhouse. The lungs were the same, the sluice of the kidneys, the great trampoline of the bladder, but with Cake at her side it all looked quite new.

After days of treading the soup of the Mother, her swamp and miasma, her suffer and salt, they reached the top of the Mother—the apex, the Everest, that holy of holies. They reached that lily-white door reading *Mother*.

"We're here!" Precious cried, and flapped her hands in glee. She reached for Cake, but Cake shook her head no.

"You go in alone," she said, and Womb echoed, "Yes, go," with a sly little smile.

So go in she did. Precious threw open the door, but no one was there. No one was there but her. Her stretched and her squat, her lithe and her lumpish, her doubled and trebled and her ever after refracted in glass. In this lily-white room with its gilt and its gaud there is nothing but Precious. But wait, there on the floor was the answer she sought: an envelope, creamy and thick and smelling of peonies. *To my daughter*, it read, in soft, curling letters. With her unfinished fingers Precious opened the flap and inside it read, *Get out*.

•

"There, there," Womb cooed when Precious emerged, thinking her troubled, but Precious pushed her aside. *Could this be right?* she wondered. Was it time now to leave the wilds of the Mother? But Womb would have none of it. "You don't know what's out there," she explained to the girls, and she steered them off toward the edge for a lesson.

"Put your ear there," Womb said, and they did. Through the skin of Mother they could hear the great wolfroar of the world.

"What is it, Womb?" they asked.

"A monster who waits to devour you," she answered. She told the girls about the creature made of white with flensing knives for fingers who waited at the end of Mother's Out. Of the barks she heard that nipped at Mother's ear, the teeth that shredded her fingers. Of the pearls that garrote and the ties that bind. She told them of black oil that spews up out of the sea and sun that burrows under the skin, of mouths in the sky and mouths in the cities and mouths that ate up the forests and beasts. "Everything," said Womb, "is waiting to eat you," until Precious cowered in the cuddle of Womb and did not venture too close to Mother's edge.

But Cake? Cake kept her ear to the wall of Mother and only by force could Womb drag her away.

•

Cake grew fast. Of Mother she was always eating, always pushing deeper into the forest of She.

"Do you not think," said Precious, "we should be kinder to Mother?"

But Cake, her mouth full of Mothermeat, said, "If I'm to remain trapped here in Mother I might as well play. I might as well pleasure. Come, Precious, and let's dine on her spine. Let's scup through her lung. Push on her ribs and hear how she sings." With that Cake plucked hard on Mother's gut strings and danced in the ensuing din.

She was ruthless, was Cake, and Precious was frightened, but Womb? Womb was incensed. She did not intend to den such wild beasts. For a few days she tried to throw her weight around, to knock a little sense into Cake's fontanelle, but no such luck.

And then, one morning, Precious awoke to find Cake gone.

•

There are many places in Mother a Cake might hide. Mother is made of niche and ditch, and where there is a wall there is a way. A tooth will do. A toenail. Gash a gap in Mother and slip inside. Cyst and stay alive, rocking out the years of Mother huddled in a cave. Precious had seen such things in her travels: muscles marbled by beasts, something all mouth floating by in red cells. "However will we find her?" Precious moaned.

But Womb had no intention of looking for Cake. "Good riddance," she said. "I should have known she was a bad seed, a dud cell. Should have declared her invalid the second she split from your side." And with that Womb scooped up Precious in her jaws.

Deeper and deeper in she dragged her Precious, down ducts and strange chutes into realms they had never yet reached in their circuit.

"Where are you taking me?" she asked, and when Womb opened her mouth to reply—for how could she resist her anything—she fell out into the blood of Mother and rushed away on her pulse. At first Womb rushed after, but Precious was faster. She dove into a capillary and dodged her.

For days Precious rode the current of Mother, calling for Cake. There was an emptiness in Precious, a hollow like a cave all hieroglyphed with Cake. Each time she called for Cake she felt an echoing ache, as though the scar from where they split was singing out an answer.

Cake may not have heard her, but something did. Soon, all the creatures of Mother, all the ears in her blood—macrophage and microworm and polyhedral virus—alighted upon her. They alighted upon her, with their mouths and their hunger, until she grew bulbous with bodies, a flailing, tailing ball of baby. She tried to fight them, but they were stuck fast, and all the while she was pulled closer and closer to the furnace of the heart. She could see it up ahead, that great citadel, with its spewing stacks and its door thumping open and closed.

"Cake," she cried, and "Help, please help" and then she saw something like a girl slipping through the open door; felt something like a hand, pulling her clear.

•

Precious awoke in the dim of a little red hutch to a vision of herself, or quite near. Was it the dim light that made the girl seem so unfinished? Yet as her eyes adjusted, the girl did not thicken. It was as though she could not look quite at her. Precious had to look with the corner of her eye to see her, and even then she seemed to flicker and go out.

"You're awake," said the girl, and her voice seemed viscous, congealing around a consonant and then dissipating,

evaporating, as if it never was at all.

"Cake?"

"The one and only," she said. "The doppel to your gänger. And you found me, or I you. I've been waiting."

"Where are we?" Precious looked around, taking in the greasy hides painted red that closed them in, the rough bed on which she lay, and, in the center of the room, a table upon which sat a little oven, like a toy, over which Cake huddled.

Cake ignored the question, and when, a moment later, a timer dinged, she reached inside the oven and pulled out a little cake, hard and pink.

"This one's for you," she said. It was heavier than it looked. Resting in her palm, it seemed to press Precious so deeply into the bed that she felt she might never rise again. It felt as though her insides were slowly turning soft, as though she could feel the pinkness of her lungs and heart, and when she looked at the cake it seemed to be bleeding into her hand. She dropped it on the bed and it dissolved into a salty puddle.

"I was afraid of that," Cake said, and popped a new cake into the oven.

"Cake, where are we?"

"We, my dear sister, are in the heart of the Heart of Mother. The engine room, if you will. The cake maker. We are the center of it all."

"Is this why you left me?"

"Left you?" Cake said. "It was Womb did me in. She set to devouring me."

"She never!"

"She did," Cake said, and sat down beside Precious. "Tried to eat me right up like the Cake that she claimed. I awoke to find her suckling my toes, said she never meant for no girl like me, so when she stopped for a moment to swallow a piece I limped away off and she let me go."

"Is that why you're like this?" Precious asked, squeezing her pulpy palm. "So unformed and unfixed?" and Cake nodded yes.

"She's been lying to you," Cake said. "The Outer? It's

not as she says. I've seen."

She'd been to the Eye, she explained. Before she lived in the Heart she arrived, quite by accident, in the Eye, and there she saw all.

"Tell me," begged Precious, "oh tell me, oh tell."

So she did. She told what she'd seen through the window of Mother—all its sparkle and strange—and Precious declared they must Out.

"But how?" she wondered.

"And me?" added Cake. "How can I leave in this fish-finny state? I'm unfit for the Outer."

How indeed? The girls could not answer. Precious wanted to cry, her eyes filmy with sad, and she leaned her head onto Cake's for a friend.

"That's it!" Cake cried, and hopped into her lap. "We'll stick together."

"But she'll see. Womb will see and she'll never."

"Not inside," Cake said. "Not inside your skin. I can niche and slip by, just until we're outside. I can ride out in your hide."

"Like as if I'm your Mother!" Precious said.

"Like my own cloak of Precious," Cake said.

So Precious split open the scar in her center, and Cake, now so small and unformed, crawled deep inside to cozy in her hollow, and together they rode the slipstream of Mother back to Womb.

•

"Oh Womb," Precious cried, in her sap-sweet voice, "please let me back in—I'm afraid of the wilds of Mother."

"My treacherous Precious, is it you? I wept and I wept, naughty pet."

"Yes, dear Womb, it is naughty, naughty I. Now please let me in," and Womb relented and opened the hatch.

"How you've grown," Womb declared, fondling her hair, tugging her very ten toes. "You're hardly my pet much. You're a little Mother, another, a fright. You're no longer my bud and my bud."

It was just as they hoped, Precious and Cake: Womb started to bellow. "You'll out, you'll out," she wheezed and she squeezed until Precious threatened to pop like a plug.

"What should I do?" Precious whispered to Cake deep inside her, and Cake answered, "Run." So she dove head-first into Mother's Way Out and crawled on her limb and her limb, Womb gnashing her teeth right behind her. She crawled and she crawled toward the light and the roar and there were the flensing knives Womb had warned of, and there were the creatures in white, but it was too late, too late. Precious was Out. Precious was out in the Outer of Mother, where light stabbed her eyes and cold spanked her skin. There were four limbs and the blink of an eye. But where was Cake? Had Cake Outed too?

"I'm here, I'm here," Cake called. "I'm inside your mouth."

And so she was, a crumb of Cake fused tight to Precious. From the roof of Precious's mouth Cake dangled like an ornament, this parasitic twin.

"Is it like I said?" mumbled Cake in the mouth of Precious. "The Outer of Mother, does it sparkle?"

Precious opened her mouth to let Cake see, and what emerged was a wail.

"A healthy baby girl," the doctor said, and handed the baby over to Mother.

Oh what a thing is Mother, a heap all hirsute, all gooey and greasy, but singular, singular. There seemed nothing on Mother but skin. "All ours," Cake said, and Precious agreed. She opened her mouth and they began to feed.

PERIODS

STORY BY FLORENCE ANN MARLOWE • ART BY MISHANTHROPE

I t's going on three weeks, now."

"Mmm-hmmm. And there's no chance of you being pregnant?"

"Oh, no!" Nancy shook her head. "I haven't even been with a guy in a long time."

"Good." Doctor Mason stood up, his eyes still glued to Nancy's chart. He flashed her a quick smile. "One less thing to worry about."

Nancy nodded. "So what could it be?"

The doctor pressed the butt end of his pen to his teeth. He then quickly shifted his seat, uncrossing and re-crossing his legs. Nancy suppressed a sigh.

"I know exactly what it is," he said finally.

"Oh."

"Endometriosis." He waited to let the big technical sounding word sink in. "It's nothing serious. You have a problem with your ovaries, really. Nothing serious."

Nancy sat up quickly. "You're not going to take them out?" She could see a whole life go by without children, maybe without a husband. She was already thirty-six, but she had never ruled out the possibility of a family. "Is it—like menopause?"

Dr. Mason tapped at his incisors with his pen. "Oh, no—not at all. It's very different."

Staring at his long, pale face and long, delicate nose, Nancy realized she didn't really like this man very much. She should have gone to the GYN her sister had recommended. Watching his smug face, the tight smile was pissing her off more and more and she wanted to get out of here, go home and take a shower.

"You see, when a woman has problems with ovulation, usually caused by stress or hormone problems, she'll develop endometrial tissue on her ovaries which will cause her to menstruate constantly." Nancy's face betrayed her confusion and the doctor continued, "Your body thinks it's time to menstruate all the time. So—you do!" He spread his long hands wide and shrugged.

"So what happens now?"

"Well, we can give you hormone pills that will counterbalance the hormones that are causing you to ovulate." He pulled a small pad out of his desk drawer and took some time choosing a pen from the bouquet of writing instruments jammed into a mug.

"How long before I stop bleeding?"

The doctor sighed, "Oh, about ten days."

"Ten days?" Nancy cried. Dr. Mason looked up, his eyebrows arched. "I can't take this for another ten days!"

He stopped writing and folded his hands in front of him.

"What can't you take?" he asked.

"Ten more days of bleeding! I've been bleeding for nineteen days, dammit!"

"The pills will control that," he began calmly.

"I've gone through twelve boxes of super absorbent tampons. That's two hundred and forty tampons in less than three weeks. I'm ready to shove a friggin' rag up there."

The doctor was staring at her, his face frozen. Nancy felt her throat tighten.

"Do you fill each one to capacity?"

"What? Oh, yeah! Definitely! More than capacity. I'd get the super plus, but they don't always carry them." He was regarding her. Nancy could feel a seed of worry work its way into her brain.

"Are you serious about that or is that just a number you made up?" He took a spiral notebook out of his desk and turned the pages, searching for something.

"No, that's for real. I buy four boxes every time I go to the drug store."

He found the page he wanted, ran his finger under some important line and then slammed the book shut. "Really?"

"Actually that's almost four liters," he replied. She stared back at him and he said, "It's a lot."

"I thought it was."

The doctor had gotten up and was slowly walking towards her, prescription pad in hand, his dark eyes never leaving her face. He stopped and perched on the edge of the desk right in front of her. He smiled, a slippery thing that slid the flesh around on his thin face.

Dr. Mason crumpled up the prescription he had been writing and lightly tossed it into the wastebasket. "Well, we'll have to take care of this right away." He began a new script. "This should do it. I'd like to see you back here again in three days."

"Three days?" What happened to two weeks, call me if you have any questions? She took the prescription from him and glanced briefly at the ink scratches he had made.

He was still smiling. He looked like a sharp-beaked bird, hovering over her. His nostrils flared and quivered and Nancy thought he was sucking in some dark aroma deep into his lungs.

She shrunk back from him. "I smell, don't I?"

Mason blinked. His visage softened and he shook his head. "No, no. Well—all women are fragrant during their time of the month."

Nancy sighed and sat back in her chair. "I feel like it's all over me. In my skin, my cuticles, even my hair."

Mason stretched out a long, lean hand as if to stroke Nancy's hair. She ducked her head out of the way. She wanted sympathy, but she didn't want him touching her. She felt dirty. Not Courtney Love dirty, but rolling in a loaded dumpster in the middle of August dirty.

"It's the concentration of iron and protein in the blood," Mason said as he sat back on his perch. "It can be very aromatic at times. Which reminds me," he began to scribble on his pad again.

"I'm also giving you a prescription for high potency iron tablets; you'll need to take them three times a day."

"And I'd stock up on those super plus tampons," he said. "You'll start to bleed more at first."

Nancy moaned and dropped her arms at her sides in defeat.

"Only at first, only at first," he soothed.

Nancy trudged unhappily to the door. His chipper voice called her back.

"One other thing. Before you start taking those, I'd like you to run over to the clinic for an HIV test."

Nancy spun around. "What for?"

"It's all right, it's nothing. Just a precaution, that's all. Just to be safe." His smile was absolutely fulsome. Nancy wanted to take her bag and bash his long, white teeth in.

"I want you to take this to a Dr. Roman Haledon at the clinic. He's a friend and he'll get me the results right away. They're very discreet there. After you've had the test you can start those pills. Every six hours."

Nancy whacked the door with her fist on her way out. She trod down the corridor, prescriptions crumpled in her fist. Male doctors, she thought. They think it's all a joke. She stepped out into the waiting room. Karen, the receptionist had her ear pressed to the phone. She motioned to Nancy with one finger. "She's right here. I'll find out." Hanging up, she opened a file on her desk.

"Nancy? Are you married?"

"No."

"Living with someone?"

Nancy stared at the woman behind the counter. "No. Why?"

"Just for your records. So you live alone?"

•

Nancy shook the stout little amber bottle of pills. The name at the bottom of the label meant nothing to her. Just a long, multisyllabic word she wouldn't even attempt to pronounce. The other bottle was full of deep magenta tablets. Three times a day she was expected to swallow one of those baby torpedoes. Her throat clutched at the thought of it.

The guy at the pharmacy had given her some look. With a wad of cotton taped to her elbow and five boxes of super plus tampons under one arm, she had handed him her prescriptions. He picked up each blue and white box, reading the labels, the content, instructions whatever could have caught his eye. And what was it with those blue and white boxes? Every brand name seemed to restrict their packages to blue and white and green boxes—purposely avoiding the color red on their packaging.

Drawing a glass of water from the faucet, Nancy tossed back one of the hormone capsules. It felt dry and papery on her tongue. She swallowed some water and then wrestled with the child proof lid on the container of iron tablets.

Ten days. Maybe less. She padded into the bedroom to change her tampon. She could feel the fullness of it in her crotch. They were giving up quicker and quicker. Every two hours or so she was changing them. At the clinic she had to balance on the edge of the toilet, one foot in the air, her fingers stretching impossibly long to push the damn thing up there. Even a dog shouldn't suffer like this.

She changed her tampon four more times before going to bed. A girl in high school, Wendy, swore you could use two tampons at once on really heavy days, but Nancy thought that sounded dangerous. Could you still get Toxic Shock? She unraveled the paper from the plastic container as thick as a cigar. What if two was too much and it sucked all the moisture out of her? They could get stuck up there. She pictured herself having to go to the hospital to have them surgically removed, explaining that Wendy Pooles had told her to do it.

In her sleep, Nancy drifted in a sea of scarlet. It was cloying, the metallic smell, the sticky liquid tugging at her. She twisted only to find her face submerged in the thick red ocean. She gasped, swallowing a mouthful of the stuff. Her body convulsed, her chest hitching. The air was gone from her lungs and in its place, hot liquid rushed in.

Gasping, Nancy bolted upright. She heard a loud squish. Between her legs there was a puddle of red. Leaping from the bed, she saw an oval of blood in the center of her mauve sheets.

"Aw, shit!" she hissed and peeled the sheets off the bed. The blood had soaked through to the mattress. Nancy tossed the bloody bedding onto the floor and sprinted to the bathroom for a cold, wet towel and some liquid cleanser.

The fibers of the mattress began to fray as she worked the cleanser in and she stopped scrubbing. The dank odor of her own blood made her eyes water. A dark trickle skidded down her leg.

"Shit!" Nancy squealed and dropped her towel. Running

to the bathroom, leaving a wake of bright red, she grabbed a new box of tampons.

"Things had better improve in the next three days," she snarled as she liberated her soaked tampon. It hung by its cord like a red mouse. Nancy's mouth twitched. She dropped the offensive thing into the garbage and ripped the new box open.

•

There was no point in going to work the next morning. Nancy couldn't keep a tampon inside for more than an hour. She felt the swelling begin forty-five minutes after she'd put in a fresh one and fifteen minutes later had to rush to the bathroom before it popped out on its own. An ever-growing pile of stained clothing made her give up on wearing underpants. She felt gruesome and unclean.

By evening, her crotch was sore from the constant pushing and pulling. She could hardly sit straight in a chair. Her back and breasts had hurt for weeks, but now they felt as if they were bruised, her breasts swollen. The smell was everywhere. Every time she raised her hand to her face, she caught a whiff of metallic filth. The beds of her nails were tinted deep red and she spotted stains in the whorls of her skin. Like Lady MacBeth, she scrubbed her hands constantly.

The second day was worse. Not caring to explain her condition to her boss, Nancy told them she had chicken pox. This was going to last a while. She changed tampons nearly every half hour. They slid from her body, anxious to be free. The only comfortable position to do this was lying down. Towels covered every piece of furniture, now. She slept on a bare mattress protected by the thickness of two terry cloth towels and prayed she'd awaken before her tampon filled up.

For the sixth time in four hours, Nancy was lying down, changing her tampon when she felt something crawl out of her. It wriggled from the lips of her vulva and past her thighs making her shriek in terror. The image of some parasitic worm burrowing in her bowels tore through her brain. Throwing herself from the bed, she collided with her dresser, a shower of bottles and knickknacks cascading to the floor.

Afraid to turn around, Nancy peeked at the bed. A long dark object like a piece of liver lay on the towel in a pool of blood that was slowly sopping into the towels. Nancy moaned at the huge blood clot.

"I can't take this anymore," she whispered. Pawing through her bag, she found her address book. She dialed up Dr. Mason, but the woman who answered claimed to be the service. He wouldn't be in until tomorrow, did Nancy have a message?

"I've got a message," she growled as she slammed the receiver down. Tears burned in her eyes. This wasn't fair, she thought. Her crotch felt hot and full, and she buried her hands in the damp, bloody hair. One more day and then she was going to give it to that doctor. He had some nerve subjecting her to this.

•

Again she was floating in red. The liquid seeped into her mouth and she was suddenly heavy, bloated. Her body sank. Her nose, her eyes filled with blood. She could smell it, taste it, clawing at her throat. Her arms beat at the rich redness as she swam, frog-like through the river of gore. Nancy couldn't tell which way was up or down. She could smell the coppery odor, strong in her nostrils. Why didn't she die, she thought, as she treaded the red waters. A pale figure seemed to be moving towards her. Nancy floated, expectation rising in her chest. The figure had a face, a keen oval of whiteness. It seemed to speed towards her, its body undulating rapidly like some blanched flagellum. Nancy felt an urgent need to flee, but she was dead weight, drifting. It darted towards her, the pallid face growing closer, until its eyes met her own.

She jerked from her sleep. There was a hot, thickness trying to escape her crotch and she fished the swollen tampon out. A ribbon of blood sprayed the mattress. Nancy felt an animal sound gurgle up in her throat when the phone rang.

She flicked the tampon into a plastic bag she had left

lying on the floor near the bed. It landed with a splat next to its spent brothers. Hooking the phone with two fingers, Nancy threw herself back on the soiled mattress.

It was Dr. Mason's receptionist, Karen with the results of HIV test.

"I can't stop bleeding," Nancy said into the phone.

"The doctor said you'd be bleeding a bit more at first."

"It's not just a bit more." Nancy shouted. "It's twice as much. Ten times as much! I sit on the toilet and it just pours out!" She began to sob. "I can't stand it anymore."

"Just one more day," the receptionist chirped. "We'll see you tomorrow at seven."

The receiver went dead in her hands and Nancy felt a shriek of outrage boil up inside her. She bashed the phone down and jumped off the bed, ready to dial back the doctor's office. A rush of liquid shot out from between her legs, running down her thighs. She stared down her legs, watching droplets of blood spatter on the floor. They were everywhere, she thought. Little circles of brownish red sprinkled in the bathroom, out in the hall, on her sheets. She sat down with a wet squish. Her face puckered up and she began to cry.

•

She had finally conceded to Wendy Pooles' double tampon theory and she walked like a cowboy. Dr. Mason's office was empty. Karen wasn't even at her desk. For Nancy, sitting was a new adventure in pain. Gingerly, she eased her butt onto the vinyl-cushioned chair. The familiar sting raced up her spine into her teeth. Please, God, she thought, let it be over soon.

She was about to grab a copy of *People* magazine when the inner office door opened and Dr. Mason poked his head out. His nostrils looked huge as he took a deep breath.

"Good, you're here." He flashed her that huge smile. "We'll be ready for you in a minute." Before she could reply he ducked back out of sight.

Nancy grabbed the magazine and started flipping through it. How could a man understand what women suffered? She turned the pages, fiercely. If Mason didn't

do something to relieve her from all this bleeding she was out of here and into another doctor's office, pronto.

The door clicked open and Dr. Mason motioned her in. Nancy got up too quickly, forgetting her sore bottom and she cringed. The doctor smiled as she hobbled carefully into his private office.

"So how are we feeling today?" he said as he closed the door behind him.

"I don't know about you, but I feel lousy." Nancy gently settled into a chair. "I can't even keep a tampon in me. I've got two stuck up there now."

The doctor shocked her by laughing. Nancy saw a slight movement out of the corner of her eye and realized that Karen, the receptionist was standing in the corner. The young woman was flicking a plastic syringe with one finger. She smiled brightly at Nancy.

"Have you been taking the iron?" Mason asked. He sat on the edge of his desk, his former roost, and shrugged out of his lab coat.

"Yeah," Nancy said. She watched Karen prepare a cotton ball with alcohol. "Am I getting a needle?"

"Yes, you are," Mason answered promptly.

Karen brought the injection over and handed it to the doctor. He studied the gauge.

"Did you call the office?"

Karen nodded, "Yes, I did."

"And?"

"No problem. She called in sick two days ago."

"I thought she would." He smiled at Nancy.

"What's that for?" Nancy unbuttoned her sleeve. Mason approached her, needle in position.

"Let's just say," the doctor smiled. "You're going to need it."

The injection was cold and Nancy's arm immediately went numb. "Is this going to stop the bleeding?"

"Oh, no," he answered, handing the syringe back to Karen.

"What do you mean, 'oh, no'?" Nancy's tongue felt thick. "You've got to do something. I can't keep bleeding."

Mason pulled out his notebook. He quickly jotted something down.

"Can you smell it?" It took Nancy a moment to realize he wasn't speaking to her.

Karen nodded, smiling at Nancy as her vision softened. "It's strong."

Mason was undoing his tie, "And did you set up a room for her?"

"All set." Karen flopped down in the chair behind Mason's desk.

"Did you call Roman?"

"Done."

Nancy's eyes felt heavy in her head. They felt like they might just roll out of her skull and drop to the floor. Mason looked up at her for a moment and then returned to his notebook.

"Get me some tape" was the last thing she heard before she surrendered to blackness.

•

When she first began to regain consciousness Nancy thought her mouth was full of blood. She gagged, bucking wildly only to find her arms restrained. Her eyes were misty and she struggled to see straight. Her mouth moved, but no words came. Her lips felt as if they'd been erased from her mouth.

Mason stood by a small cart. She could hear something bubbling, like coffee. There was an odor, dark and distasteful, so familiar. She attempted to move but her arms were fastened to metal poles that stuck out on either side of her. She tried to pull them free. A painful pinch of the skin cautioned her and she gave up the fight. Silver tape strapped her arms down. The same pinch tugged at the corners of her mouth. Looking cross-eyed she could see a plastic tube extending from her mouth, curling over her head. More silver tape held the tube in place. Above her, hung a bag of pulpy, brown liquid. A thick moan escaped her throat.

"Hi," Mason said casually. He smiled and walked towards her. "Just relax."

Nancy's eyes snapped open. She shifted her legs and noted that her feet were taped to the legs of the chair. But it wasn't quite a chair...

"I know this isn't pleasant, but it could be worse." His lips slid back from his teeth. He looked positively carnivorous. "Trust me. It could be much worse."

Nancy felt weak. A nylon harness dug into her flesh. Cold metal rings and chains were lying against her naked skin. This was no medical facility. Her head dropped forward. She fought a wave of nausea. She could see her bare legs. The chair she sat on was made of wood, a hole cut out beneath her bottom. The soreness was still there only now accompanied by a burning sensation further up her crotch. Her eyes strained to see what was there. More tubes projected from below leading away to several different machines. One tube was filled with a pale yellow liquid, the other was filled with what looked like red ink.

Mason juggled a few bottles from the cart and chose an empty one. He glanced up at her amiably.

"This won't be so bad, Nancy. I've had great success with this process before." He strode over to one of the machines Nancy was hooked up to and checked the gauges.

"It's really worked out well for us." He looked back at her. "For me and others like me."

Tapping a few buttons on the machine, he set the glass under a nozzle.

The machine made a loud fizzling sound and a squirt of crimson drained into the empty glass.

"Over the years we've found it more and more difficult to find what we need to survive. You can't count on superstitious villagers any more. The police hunt you down so efficiently nowadays."

About two inches of the red stuff filled the glass before the machine became silent. Mason picked up the container and held it to the light for scrutiny.

"And everything is so modernized. It's amazing what technology can teach you. Things like filtering, homogenizing and pasteurization for instance." He jiggled the contents of the glass and smiled. "The resources you find online would amaze you."

The impossibly red fluid swirled in its receptacle and Mason shook his head. "Your blood—menstrual blood—is so rich. It's heavy with proteins and iron, stripped from the deepest inner parts of your body. The bits needed to create life—all concentrated in a capsule of red nectar." He glanced up at her and winked. "Kind of like a shot of the best espresso."

The door opened and Karen stepped in. She barely glanced at Nancy. Turning to Mason she said, "Who says you get the first taste?"

He grinned back at her. "I always get the first taste." With that he brought the glass to his lips and sipped.

Karen watched.

"Well?"

The doctor licked his lips and nodded. "Good. Sweet."

Nancy felt her vision slip. The croaking sound she made in her throat caused Karen to step forward and check the tubes sticking out of her mouth.

Mason continued. "As you can see, we'll feed you and look after you like a vascular cow." He gestured at the tubing. "The restraints, unfortunately, are necessary, but you'll get used to it after a while. And if you want, we could sedate you, although I'd rather not." He held up his glass. "It does involve another step in the purification process. Gets a bit expensive."

Karen was writing something on a chart. She glanced at Nancy.

"What was her name again?"

"Nancy," he answered. "I meant to put up a little sign."

Karen shrugged. "Roman and Betty are outside and a few of the others are coming. Michael can't make it. We're going to use up what we have in the fridge."

Mason drained his glass and nodded. "We should be getting a little better than a liter from her after today. I've upped the hormone shots."

The two busied themselves with cleaning up, checking the machinery and Nancy's tubes. She watched them, wild-eyed, her breathing quick and erratic. Mason checked her chart again and made a notation. From far off, Nancy heard a doorbell ring. Karen slipped out the door and a moment later, Mason followed, clicking off the overhead light without a backward glance.

Nancy sat in the dark. Voices tittered from outside. She could hear the common noises of an evening with friends. Doors opening and shutting, laughter, the tinkle of glasses. Her face felt tight. After a while, all she could hear was the hum of machinery and the dripping from her tubes.

She hoped they would realize that she would need to be sedated before the night was through.

IN THIS BREATH, A VIOLENCE

IT WAS A
PLEASURE THEN

STORY BY RACHEL MARSTON • ART BY LAURIE NASICA

She thought she would try voodoo, having grown up in the south, with the whisper of these incantations and strange and serious uses of animal blood lingering in her ears. She bought burlap, sewing each leg, each arm, each tiny stitch made with her long thin fingers. She cut a t-shirt, one left behind, gray and dingy, unwashed, even after three months because of the way it still smelled like him, made a tiny pair of pants, fitted with a small drawstring for the waist. She worried over the hair, knowing that she needed his hair, that straight and dark thatch, so wiry beneath her fingers, to really make this work. She searched her apartment, kneeling on the wood floors, peering at the floorboards, beneath her mattress, under the couch cushions, but there were no traces of him—three years, four months, and seventeen days marked now only by absence. So she cut hair from a doll she found at the downtown Deseret Industries. She took a picture of his face and carefully stitched the edges, holding it in place on the doll. Then she began.

First she took pins, the metal shiny and stiff in her fingers, held the sharp end against the kneecap, the nipple, beneath the chin, just where the ear touched the neck, at the groin, right below the testicles in the place between his legs. Then she slid the pins in, slowly, moving them through the clothes, then the burlap, deliberate and smooth, until they all held deep in the cotton filling, the substitute musculature of this man.

Appropriately pinned and held into place, she lit a candle, not to burn, but to drip the wax, hot and streaming into the ears, then the nostrils, the eyes, and the mouth, imagining each orifice filling with wax, smooth and liquid, searing those tender mucosal membranes, slowly hardening, building up, so that sound was muffled, an uncomfortable not yet silence, and the choking, an absence of air, but the sweet scent of vanilla, overwhelming in the throat and nose.

She surveyed this burlap man, so small in her hand, speared and waxy. And still she felt sad and dissatisfied with this vindictive transference of pain. She thought about outsourcing this pain, hiring fifty small children to take it on for her, working eight hour shifts each, crying and swearing and stabbing pins in dolls around the clock until it dried up, shriveled and wrinkled, like the last crabapple clinging to the tree before it fell.

She sat at her desk, staring at the doll, all those tiny stitches across its burlap skin. And she wanted to hate him. She dug her fingernails into her palms, each nail pressing deep, then deeper, trying to embed those white half-moons into her skin.

The doll had done nothing. So she took the needle and placed the tip in the flame of the candle. She threaded the eye with cream thread, just darker than the color of the skin on her forearms and stomach. The thread was fraying, so she touched the end to her tongue, moved it slowly through the hole. She double-knotted the end, careful to make the knot large enough to not pull through, but not bulky.

Then she started. She placed the needle on her arm, pushed through her skin, slowly, feeling the metal move through each dermal layer, just enough skin so the thread held, deep enough to skim the muscle, draw a bit of blood into the thread, turning it a faint shade of pink, which she hoped would wash out with showering.

She made the stitches a quarter of an inch long. She sewed deliberately, pausing to burn the tip of the needle, to brush her skin with alcohol. She worked on her left forearm first, the stitches tight, precise, knotting the thread at the end of each word, slowly sewing the narrative of this relationship into her skin. When her arm was full, she pulled up her shirt, that smooth soft flesh, so pale, started above the bone of her left hip, in the place she liked to have kissed. And the needle was a type of caress, this smooth metal so near her bone, the pull of the thread on her skin, seductive and sharp.

She sewed and sewed, those deliberate words, dipping in and out of her body, smooth lines of pain, spelled and punctuated, neatly ordered over her organs, and bones, and muscles, rising gently from her flesh.

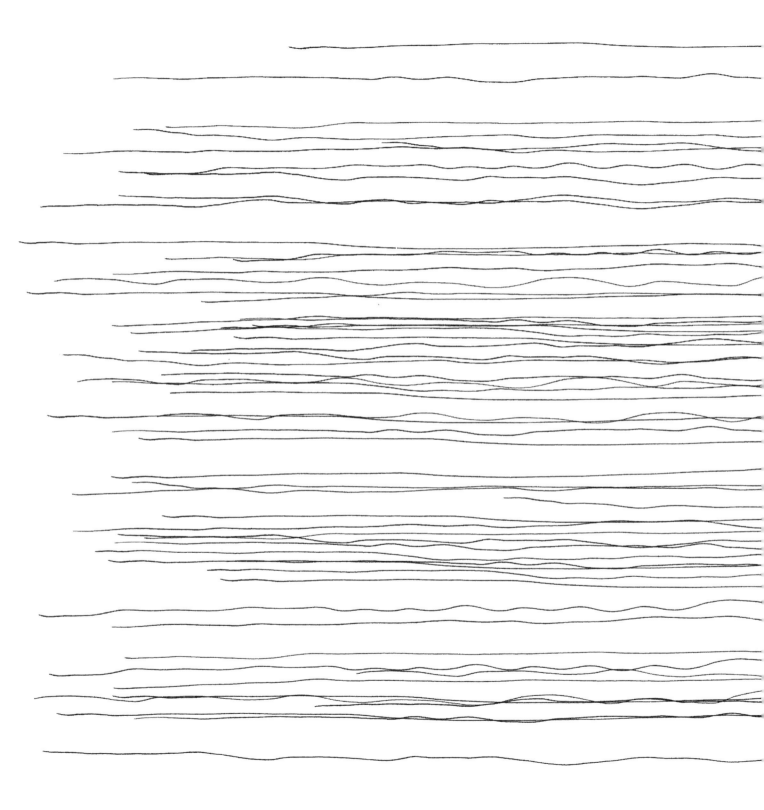

GOOD COUNTRY PEOPLE ARE HARD TO FIND

STORY BY JESSICA LANAY • ART BY JOHANNA ROSS

Today I'm dirty, tomorrow I'll just be dirt. I took my red pen and underlined the quote in the Carl Panzram biography I was reading. The sun beamed through the cracked passenger side window. The heat in my mouth turned the slushy crystals from crispy, cool sugar to mush and then liquid down my throat. I don't usually dote over benign things, but I felt satisfied. The road trip I was on was the invention of my husband who wanted to see his family in New Orleans. I felt put upon by the idea of being locked in a sedan with them for some odd thousand miles. When I told Jacob I wanted to map out the route, he grinned at me over the kitchen counter and said, "That's the spirit, Mrs. Wite."

It wasn't long before my son's pleased hums reduced to the grainy slurping sound of him dredging the bottom of the cup. I reached back and curtly snatched the cup from his hand and chucked it out of the open window. He immediately began screaming, his hands open wide, and his head tilted back, his body braced. Jacob looked over his shoulder towards our son and tried to cajole the boy by offering more candy in the near future while he flashed glares at me.

"You know you haven't been as gentle with him lately... is there something wrong?"

"Absolutely not, Mr. Wite." I said as I smacked my book against the dashboard.

I crammed my body into the backseat and patted the boy's knee as he kicked. He quieted. I sighed and watched the flat fields flash by. Elysium: expansive, faultless, breezy, no real threat or danger. It was boring, it had no sparkle, no sequin of pain in it. I heard the clicking of the MP3 player and winced. Jacob turned on the Lionel Ritchie again. I rubbed my temples, passed the boy a miniature dump truck, and wondered how I made it from day to day beset by the two of them. I climbed back into the front seat and pressed the pause button on the MP3 player's screen. Jacob's eyebrows rose and he smiled leaning towards me, nudging me with his elbow.

"Come on Mrs. Wite. Heeelllllloooo? Is it me you're looking for?"

I smiled back and then kissed him on the cheek before switching the radio on.

"Oh honey, I love the *Hello* song..." I said.

We sunk into static as the radio stations looped in and out of available signals. The radio waves double-dutched around me, encased me in a globe of white noise. Side of the road preachers melted into wives talking about their perennial gardens. Those wives became operas that eventually cycled into scandalous soap operas that sounded like the ones my mother used to listen to late at night when she thought no one was awake. The fuzziness in between these voices and the mangled order of them helped me continue reading my book. The scanning radio broke into a news broadcast. The announcer sterilely reported a rampage killer and his partner along a highway. I pressed the button to turn up the voice, and then I licked my finger and turned the page. Jacob spoke again. "Am I Karenin or Vronsky?"

I shuddered and watched him absent-mindedly lower the volume again. I had forgotten which cover I had stuck on the Carl Panzram biography I was reading, but hearing him say those names snapped me together.

"Karenin," I said.

"Oh man. The guy who gets left?"

"No, the one Anna should have stuck with."

•

I didn't connect at all to my sisters or my mother. Their presence always irked me, like the sight of a water bug crawling up a wall. My mother was jealous-hearted and ornery. Maybe because our father left her alone with us. Maybe because he left her with nothing but us. We were beaten according to how she felt each day. My sisters used her emotional instability to convince her I had done things I had not done. Sometimes my mother would sit and rock and sweat, talking to herself on the back porch.

On my sixth birthday, Mrs. Charlene, the pastor's wife, came to help set up the party outside of our house. She hot-combed my hair and then put it in a long silky ponytail down my back. I flounced my hair during the party as I ran about with the other children. I let them pet that ponytail, I pulled it and curled it over my shoulder. It was different from my usual bobbles and braids. After everyone had gone and I was in the kitchen washing out the dishes, my mother huffed in with her wide frame, grabbed some scissors and a handful of my hair and then snapped it off at the tie. She threw my ponytail into the soapy water in the tin sink like a rag that needed to be washed.

"You're too vain behind that hair," she said.

There were many broken bones and cut-off ponytails. My mother was convinced that out of all my sisters I was the strangest, perhaps because I rarely spoke. My punishments were more frequent: I was locked in closets, beat with rope, left to sleep in the chicken coop. Unless I was participating in a group response at church or a lesson during my homeschooling I simply did not have anything to say. I became unflinching and, at times, unresponsive. I figured if I were alone I would be beaten less. My sisters could not purposefully turn over the sugar bowl and then blame it on me. My sisters could not set the fringes of the curtains on fire and blame me if I was not there. My mother became suspicious and determined in her thoughts that I may have been possessed.

When I was eleven I began hunting in the pecan trees behind the house; their height and the shade of their canopies seemed safe and holy. I carried a pig sticker and carved and gutted the bark of the trees down to the white. One day I found a sparrow with a hurt wing nestled in some risen roots. While holding it in my hot palms I squeezed it. And squeezed it, until I felt the whole body pop like a tendon. That was my first experience killing anything. It must have been a symptom of my age because afterwards I would go kneel beside the creek and put my hand beneath my skirt. After touching myself I would bring my hand to my nose and smell it. It was a ritual: kill a squirrel or some infant thing that had fallen from a tree, touch myself.

One day my mother came looking for me out in the woods. I had left the house early and bunched up my bed sheets that had poppy red stains on them. It was the first time it had happened to me. When my second to youngest sister started her period she got a beating. I had sunk the sheets into the creek and the high tide had washed them away towards the main river. I didn't see her walking up to me as I squatted near the creek. I was using the water to clean my thighs. The sunlight was soft; the air was cool with coming rain. I held up my stained fingers to the light; the blood was the same color as the blood in the animals I killed. She took me by surprise and dug her meaty fingers into the roots of my hair and yanked me onto the ground. She drug me over the pine needles. I didn't make a sound, not even a whimper. She paused, her eyelids twitching with rage. She clapped her hand against my face. When she didn't hear me cry out she hit me again, harder this time. She threw me away from her, and I sat with my knees to my chest. I didn't move. I watched her with a blank expression.

I was more concerned that she would see the tiny graveyard I had made nearby, the tiny mounds of dirt over the decomposing bodies. She paced nearer to it and her foot sunk into one. Startled, she looked down at her thick, fat ankle. The bones jutted from the old grave she had stepped in. She tilted her head and examined the dismembered possum crushed under her foot. She looked back at me and I don't know why, but I was laughing.

•

I love my family—in my own way. They are proof that I am a real girl. Proof that I am not the things my mother always told me I was: worthless, dirty, that no one would ever want me. No matter how many times I've beaten the boy or neglected my husband, they always stuck by my side. Jacob knew my mother briefly and always negotiated her dislike for me as a mental sickness that went undiagnosed. And what I did to my son, well, I was careful—careful not to leave bruises.

According to the radio the two murderers were on a highway parallel to the one we were on. One highway eventually turns into the other. I traced the red line I made down the map with my index finger while listening.

Two white males, one redhead, one blonde with a baseball cap. I watched Jacob shift awkwardly in his seat out of the corner of my eye before showing him the map. "You remember that two-hundred-year-old red barn I told you about? Where I want us to take the picture?" I asked him.

"Yeah, that sounds nice as long as the owner is okay with the picture."

"It is right here." I pointed. "So in a few hours we should be there. We'll just run over and snap a few pictures, okay?"

I watched him shrug and flip the stereo back to Lionel Ritchie. The barn itself was a shady tourist site, not shady because of its age, but shady because of some missing girls found there in the 30s. It was a dumpsite for someone that was never caught. By the time they found the remains, whoever the owners were had lost ownership of the farm due to the Great Depression. Jacob was indifferent, as he usually was to any of my personal quirks. I had not allowed for the kind of relationship in which he could be interested, mostly because I needed him self-absorbed, distracted, and not under my feet.

Jacob and I continued the blooming war over the radio as the boy read aloud and stumbled over words like "of." Frustrated, I cranked up the volume on the radio and Irene Cara blared, "WHAT A FEELING! BEING'S BELIEVIN'!" Through her declaration I thought about my greenhouse back at home. How I have so much control there, how every petal is curved to my will. When a plant seems deformed to me I just stop watering it and watch it shrivel. I fantasize about my family dying down to the last stain. About coming home to find a buzzing silence with Jacob and the boy laid out underneath a blanket with blood-soaked splotches. Imagine hearing of a woman who kills her whole family only to be found sixty years later eating a ham sandwich with an entirely new family.

•

College was how I got away from my mother. Ms. Charlene covertly slipped me money from the church collection plate to pay for my applications. I was haunted by a desire to impress while simultaneously snub my mother. I decided to study biology for my bachelor's degree at a small college not too far from home. I stayed near campus underneath the excuse that it helped me to be near to the library and my teachers. It was an all girls' school in the middle of nowhere. I got a full scholarship easily. I dissected things and learned about the insides of animals, how things developed, where everything goes.

My second year of graduate school my mother called about graduation, about her coming to see me accept my diploma and then us going back home for a celebration at the church. This had more to do with her congratulating herself than honoring my decisions. She still told everyone that I was in med school even though I was studying what she called "useless" library sciences. I told her I was seeing someone seriously to end any further conversation about my personal life. The story was that he was athletic, he was Christian, and he was good to me. She would know I had been in a drug-driven roommate-on-roommate orgy with Amber and Sarah. She would know I was lying and fucking around. She would embarrass me by confronting me before the church, just this time she wouldn't be imagining things.

It was early fall when I met Jacob at a random bible study group on campus—something Baptist. I walked into the group picking loose threads from my floral print dress, hung over and raw in the throat. When I entered I held up my palm and grinned at everyone around me, "Sorry for being late." I saw Jacob right away, his biceps snugly fitted into his turquoise polo shirt, his close-cut hair, the cross dangling around his neck from a gold chain. I glanced in his direction the whole meeting until our eyes met and then he smiled. At the end of the first meeting led by a guy that reminded me a lot of Charlie Starkweather, I asked Jacob to tutor me in chemistry, which I was not taking as a class.

I had a school year to get him to propose. Jacob's family was from Chicago and well-off and Jacob was joined at the hips and heads with his mother and his sisters. I asked a lot about their routines, their likes and dislikes. I listened very closely to him speak with his family on the phone. I would discreetly lace my dressing, talking and cooking habits with those things he seemed to admire about the women in his family. But I kept my life with my roommates a secret. I didn't regale him with deep stories about my life; I just made sure he knew my mother was Southern and God-fearing. He had all the qualities I needed him to have: courteous, clean, industrious, religious and trusting to the point of naivety. He proposed by Christmas with an opal ring and my graduation party that following summer ended up also being a wedding. Jacob was not a hard sell.

•

I thought about this in the car, my head tilted to the side, my mouth slightly open. There was a danger in that old life of mine, a tightrope walk that I had abandoned in an unexplainable effort to defy and impress a person that I feared could hurt me. Now I was trapped. I could have easily become something just as forgettable as I am now, but could have had more fun. A subtle rain began to cascade down at an angle and patter against the car. Jacob wriggled in his seat as he slowed down and then turned the radio back up to the news station in hopes of a weather forecast.

"Heavy rains, thunder and lightning. So stay dry and make sure you aren't the tallest thing if you happen to be in a field somewhere." Jacob's eyebrow perked up with the last comment and he shook his head.

"They announce all the weather the same. Makes it hard to get happy about sunshine." I stared at him the way I would stare at my mother when I was younger. He glanced at me, he was laughing at his own joke.

"SUNNY!" I yelled.

"Jesus Twilla wh—"

"THUNDER!"

"Twilla, you're going to w—"

"LIGHTNING!"

Our son awoke from his nap in the backseat and began to whimper and then full out cry. I smirked before looking over my shoulder into the backseat.

"SHUT UP!"

They both fell into speechlessness. I leaned back into my seat, warming beneath Jacob's gaze, which now darted between the rainy highway and me.

"Mommy is sorry. Mommy was only telling a really bad joke." I sat facing forward and placed my hand on Jacob's thigh. "You know how awkward I am at jokes."

Another news report began, a follow-up on the murderous duo raging down the highways. My fingers twitched to turn the volume up again, but our son had already been lulled back into sleep by the movement of the car. Only the day before they had gone into a mom and pop side-of-the-road store, shot the pop and raped the mom before taking some goods they needed and left. The day before that they had kidnapped a young girl who had been found on the Missouri-Kentucky border. The reporter described her as "practically cut in half."

"I wonder what kind of people get a thrill out of that. Hurting others," Jacob said.

Half of my mouth upturned at the corner, more a twinge than an actual smirk and I mumbled, "Yeah I wonder."

Through the window the black-eyed Susans bobbed their heads in time to the pelting rain. I thought about my little graveyard in the woods. My ceremony. When dissecting an animal I would cut it from its throat to its groin, cut the skin at the ankles and wrists and then peel the flesh away. I would skin the animal alive if I could. I thought about the men whose biographies I read, the women with all those dead children and husbands. I thought about how female serial killers were much lesser known and disrespected. Perhaps killing was like everything else, when a man does it well it is an art, when a woman does it bad or good—it is simply craft.

•

Jacob was so proud to coast into the driveway of the two-story mock-Victorian house he'd bought as a wedding present for us. I sat in the passenger seat and cried when we arrived. It was pale pink with white trim hanging from the awnings. It was an oversized dollhouse, a pre-packaged dream. He had reached across and embraced me around the shoulders, his eyes welling up as well as he kissed my cheek. "I love you so much," he had said. I was crying for other reasons, I didn't want this, any of it. I didn't want pink with white trim, I didn't want to make him dinner every night and breakfast every morning. I didn't want his weight, his sex, I didn't want this life. The lawn stretched out like green silk; all of the other houses were placed far enough away for privacy, but were close enough that you had to think of your neighbors. It was a very-Jacob, perfection, picturesque scene.

I began noticing during the first six months of our marriage when I would go to mixers with Jacob's stockbroker friends that he would whisper directives to me: Do you have to laugh so loud? You have lipstick on your teeth. You should talk to Veronica about where she shops for her clothes. It was whittling away at me. But I also admired him for his narcissism. At the last company picnic he waved at me from across the park and then made a motion with his lips to tell me to fix my lipstick.

I drug my loafer-clad feet into the house. There wasn't much furniture yet, just some Victorian pieces his mother and sisters had chosen from a catalog they mailed to me. Everything was so pristine, nearly freeze-dried with sprinklings of high class and organization. I wasn't surprised, Jacob was the kind of man who would straighten the fringes of a rug with his shoe if they weren't lying straight. I often wondered if we were the same person. I ran up the stairs, my fingers not touching the white maple banister. I found the first bathroom and slammed the door, locking myself inside of it. I had arranged everything too perfectly: when you build your own cage you immediately and subconsciously bar all of the escape routes you would usually take. I looked at myself in the mirror. I rubbed my hands all over my skin, the tears making my face itch. Mascara smeared down my cheeks while trying to clean up. I saw her, Twilla, looking back at me with eyes crystal with an indifferent chill. I slapped myself hard. I slapped my jaw and my cheek until my face swelled. I dug my nails into my scalp until when I flicked mush from beneath my nails there was blood. Jacob sat on the small bench in the hallway, right outside the bathroom.

"I thought you would be happy," he said when I walked out of the bathroom. I paused, wondering just how swollen my face must look.

I stammered, "J-Jacob. I...I love this house, I just...don't like pink. I am. I'm happy." I deflated against him when he jumped up to embrace me, sobbing.

"Oh honey. I'll hire a painter."

Six months later I lingered after work; all of the pimply-faced circulation assistants had gone home. The lights over the stacks, thin like alleyways were dark, digesting the skin cells of the people who touched them. At the library I worked at, there were lots of homeless people and true to any inner city location, there were plenty of cameras around that couldn't actually help anyone because they did not work. The joy of the homeless, at least for me, is that they are interested in warmth, a bed and maybe a meal and they were willing to exchange many things for it. Due to budget cuts, I was the one and only person to close the library every day. I would always volunteer to run out the bums so that the young circulation assistants could leave without having to do the untidy task. As I shut down the computers I would ask if they, men or women, needed anything, anything at all. Most would say a drink. Others would stare blankly at me until I offered a series of things they couldn't refuse.

A warm bed in the basement.

Some cool water from the office cooler.

Some of my lunch that I hadn't managed to eat.

I had only managed once to lure one of the homeless into the office kitchen. Whitney had been hanging around the library until close for about a month. I began to notice that she never changed her shoes. I would see her eyes dart around over a book she would pick out, but obviously not read very much of. When a young man reported that he was missing his phone case that contained his cash and cards, I suspected that it was her. But I held onto that

information, told him that we weren't responsible and to cancel the cards as soon as he got home. It never hurts to have a little leverage. But this girl Whitney seemed brand new to this life.

I approached her at closing one evening and asked if she was hungry. We sat across from each other at the pressed wood table in the employee lounge. She used her dirty fingers to shove the food into her mouth, her thick, long, red hair becoming tangled up with the food and her saliva. I had lit a cigarette and was blowing smoke out above my head, nodding as she told me through mouthfuls of food how she had run away from home. How the world was not as bad as people may think. She hadn't been raped by the trucker, she gave it up, after all, he did drive her about three hundred miles and bought her a soda and a sandwich. When I asked her if feeling obligated could be considered rape she slowed her chewing. Her watery blue irises looked up at me as if she were a child that had to pee, a quiet panic. Then, her head crashed against the table. The drug I put in the food had worked.

I heaved her to the elevator that lead to the basement, took her down and laid her body on a cot I had prepared. I tried to flay a little skin from her calf. Her flesh was spotless, smooth and pale as white quartz. I cut down into the meat of her shoulder until I was scraping the bone. The amount of blood was unexpected and was the reason I stopped. Her breathing turned so shallow that I did not know if she was dead or not. I slapped her cheek, thinking I had overdosed her. While she was still out I grabbed a rag and wiped her down with a little bleach and water. I struggled with her weight, but managed to abandon her outside in the alleyway.

I came to work shaking the next day expecting the police to be there to ask questions. I forgot to put books away, forgot meetings and forgot to make phone calls. I would trail off in mid-sentence to people I was helping every time the door chimed cause someone was entering the library. By the end of the day, no police had arrived. Whitney did not return. At the end of my shift on my way

to my car, I exited the back door so I could pass where I left her the night before. I glanced at where her body should have been but continued walking. There was never any investigation. No one came searching for her. Had she died? Or did she wake up and run away with the knowledge that the world is just as bad as people think?

•

We were close. My eyes eagerly switched between the roadside exits and the map that I had marked in a long red thread of ink. In the backseat the boy was making his tiny metal dump truck crash with an action figure in dull explosions that shot spit from his mouth.

"Thunder man! I'll save you!" And he dropped the dump truck and in flew another scantily clad hero to help the last one. He placed their stiff plastic arms around each other and they embraced. I imagined them pulling each other's primary-colored speedos down to fuck. I pinched my lips before pointing to the exit.

"Right there, Jacob, take this exit." His large hand rotated the wheel and we pulled off onto another road completely flanked with tall staffs of corn stalk. The green of the flags of leaves was so dense that it cast a blue reflection of shadow onto the road. The barn sat far back from the road and a ways off from an abandoned house that was attached to the same property. We drove down the overgrown lane that lead up to the house and I asked Jacob to park around back just in case someone came by to check the property. When we exited the car, he unbuckled the boy and sat him on his feet. The house was windowless, the wood hanging in tatters from parts of its frame. The wind, wet with impending rain, made the house caterwaul over the unbroken cropland. The house clapped and begged towards us. Jacob had hoisted the boy onto his shoulders and was waiting for me.

"I have to grab something out of the trunk first. The camera and the tripod. You take him ahead and I'll meet up with you." I paused as he nodded and turned his back and then started marching in a silly exaggerated manner towards the barn. The barn did not, from a distance, seem

as haggard and broken as the house. The paint on the barn was still succulently red, a constant alarm marking the distance. The sky was cut with flashes of white blade, it vibrated with thunder even though the clouds had not overcast the sun. The dry plants rose higher, almost up to my knees and I pushed forward with a long tripod and camera bag I had pulled from the trunk. I could see the spots of their bodies appear, the barn's shape framing them. They stood in front doing muscle poses. The boy laughed before waving towards me.

"Momma, can we go in after the picture?"

"Yes, honey." I set the timer on our camera and I ran to Jacob and tucked myself under his arm and he grabbed our son and balanced him on his hip. We smiled. The camera snapped three perfect pictures just as the drops began to mist. I motioned for him to take the boy inside the barn and I grabbed the tripod with the camera still attached and the bag. Once inside, the boy was already playing in a dried-up bale of hay and Jacob stood with his arms crossed over his chest, laughing at him. I reached into the tripod bag and took out the axe.

I was tired.

How long can you dream of escape? How long can you be afraid of the shame that comes with actually succeeding in escaping? You can only avoid shame, if you kill the thing that can appear later to shame you. I swung in a full circle. I saw a glint of light flash off the sharp edge of the axe before it butterflied Jacob's body, a straight mark down the back of his head, the nape of his neck and his upper back. He didn't even make a sound. I wrenched the axe loose with a turn and pull. His body slumped down to its knees and without waiting I hefted the axe across the back of his neck. Not fully severing his head, but it was enough, he tumbled apart before me. The boy started crying. I mimicked his cries louder than he was crying. I motioned for him to come and he shook his head.

"I said come here, now!" He whimpered as he left the hay. He inched towards me until he was in arm's reach. I had done this before, come to my mother knowing full well what she intended to do to me. "Turn around." I ordered and he turned his back. I inhaled, the weight of the axe becoming a little much for my frame. I exhaled and swung high for momentum and let the tool cleft into the boy's head.

The rain was in a torrent, a sheer curtain blurring everything together into impressionist scenery. I walked away from them and into the rain where I stood in the cold shower, watching the blood feed the grass at my feet. You don't know—you'll never know, what freedom feels like.

•

My mother had died around the time that my son was born. Jacob had not met her more than twice. The first was when I brought him home after we were married for Christmas. She loved that he was a budding physician with Christian roots and a penchant for listening to mother figures. She asked after him often when she called me to see if I was pregnant and she would give me instructions on how to make him happy.

Her cancer had been lurking for some time. I began calling more than once a week for updates, every juicy progression and ripe detail. I imagined tiny white hemlock, their heads hanging like worn-out bells from her organs, their fresh green roots twisting about inside of her like garden snakes. I never denied her anything; I took pleasure in seeing her slowly suffer. Jacob did his duty as he was always expected to do and sent down thousands of dollars to my mother with favors from cancer specialists he knew in the area. But I continued to imagine those flowers popping like lovely whiteheads from her organs. When I called and she was tired, when I called and I could hear her vomiting up blood from the chemo, I felt a rush.

I knew that she was dead. I had been calling for an entire four days with no response. Then someone called me. Mother had missed her Bible studies and a family friend had found her face down in a puddle of her own bloody disgorge. I paused on the other end of the phone, feeling the corner of my mouth spasm, a tiny tear inked from my eye and tumbled over my cheek. I exhaled some long restrained breath I had been carrying around like a bag of sand inside of me. I threw my head back and released another breath.

The family friend said into the phone, "Don't cry baby, it is going to be all right."

I was holding back bouquets of laughter, ballets of joy, operatic relief.

I was happy to descend home in a flurry of perceived shock and willingness to help. I sat with the church elders and calmly and quietly listened to their affirmations of my mother being a good woman and a good caretaker. I thought of which wood I would choose to bury her in, thought of the plot behind the church where she would be buried on top of some equally long suffering and lied-about stranger. While at the house I picked through her jewelry and old photographs, which there weren't many of. I found the purple cloths she would bring to church and lavishly place over our knees to attest to our modesty. Those were the only things that I kept of hers, that and a single photo that I took of her while she was in her coffin.

We dressed her in a pillbox hat with thin white lace covering her grayish-skinned face. Her dress was also an ivory color with gold buttons creeping down the front. I put the white gloves she always wore on Sunday on her stiff hands. Her shoes were simple black patent leather and even though this was my final opportunity to shame her, I did not leave her without stockings. I sat between my husband and son; Jacob draped his strong arm protectively about me. I could feel the nodding of approval behind my back. The service ended and my husband carried the coffin to the cemetery with distant cousins and an uncle as I held my son's hand. He was a filthy little thing, his handprint appearing greasily in the palm of my white glove. I slid my hand away eventually once his father returned to take over the handholding. As they submerged her in the earth I tossed in some red roses; I had once seen her counting a dozen that had been sent to her when I was a teenager. She counted them over and over again until they shriveled, turned rust-colored, and died.

I told Jacob there were some things I wanted to pick up at the house alone. The trees crept upwards in their ashen bark, their tips sticking into the sky like lightning. The earth crunched beneath my flats, and bugs that were already drying up scuttled beneath the layers of leaves that had formed a comforter of brown against the dying grass. The roadside was bare, just a few inches after a white line. The roads had been paved anew, but as a child they were packed clay. I walked by the old houses with their wide front windows and crouching porches, wondering if the families who avoided us for going to the church we went to still lived there.

When it was dark enough I returned to the house. In the pocket of my dress I carried a pack of matches. Our house stood singularly, like a bird absent its flock in the middle of an acre of land. Fallen, lightning-eaten in the front was a massive ash tree. At night when the wind combed over it you could hear the arms and legs on the tree creek. Sometimes the limbs were flexible enough to collide with one another and the tree would make sounds like a giant wind chime. Part of the tree sagged limp and heavy into the earth like a torso sliced in half. The house I grew up in sat just beyond that, its wood withering and softened. Behind the house some thirty yards were the remains of the original house on the land. The bricks from the chimney and mantle were still in their rightful place. It was dry enough. The wind was just right. I pulled those matches out of my pocket as I stood out there dressed in black. I struck the red-tipped leg of the match and I crouched down next to a gathering of dry leaves and in no time they began to disintegrate under the flame's dire need for oxygen.

By morning there was nothing left. No one had called the cops. The nearest neighbors were about a mile off and would have seen the flames, but a lot of people burned garbage. The fire department sheriff had found the atomized house in withers in the morning. But he didn't investigate. The house stood like a collapsed mouth, the hinges of its jaw upturned by the fire, the wood wheezing to keep itself alight. The big, yellow bulldozer crept over the scoured ground and scraped up the toothy remains, exhaling smoke towards the sky.

JACK SPRAT

STORY BY CHELSEA LAINE WELLS • ART BY VANESSA MARTINEZ

"I found something in the creek bed."

John Paul is kneeling in the shade of his side yard, within clear sight of his mother as he was instructed, using a piece of broken broom handle to stab a funnel-shaped hole into the soft dirt. Lizzie always appears suddenly, uncomfortably close. He looks sideways at her round, moon-white stomach an inch away from his ear, jutting over the waistband of a pair of pink shorts streaked with mud. At the center of her stomach is a tight whorl of bellybutton like the tied end of a balloon.

"Last week," she says. "I didn't show anybody. Do you want to see?"

He glances up to Lizzie's face. A breeze stirs the branches of the catalpa tree that overhangs his house and the sun hits his eyes full and stinging like water. He squints. She is shadowed and scowling, the way she always is.

"What is it?" he asks. Lizzie lives across the street and therefore sometimes winds up in his yard, steadfastly oblivious to the fact that she is unwelcome there. He doesn't like to be seen with her. He is nine and she is barely seven, and anyway, childhood politics dictate that he is not supposed to play with girls. Especially an exile like Lizzie.

"You have to come see." She isn't moving. John Paul takes a few more half-hearted swipes at his hole and drops the piece of splintered wood. He stands and looks down at her. She is much shorter than he is and he catches sight of a tiny, pale spider scrabbling among the limp blonde hair at her crooked part. He chooses not to tell her.

"This better be good," he says, trying to sound threatening. He glances back at the window, knowing he should tell his mother he's going down the block, but it will make him look weak. Lizzie is already headed towards the line of trees at the end of Laurel Street. So he follows her, past the big two-story houses of their neighborhood, the green crew-cut lawns, the mannerly disorder of bicycles toppled against porch railings and basketballs idle in driveways. The day was deserted, eerily quiet. But it was summer, the middle of June. School was a comfortable distance away. Surely someone else would wander out.

They pass the tree line. The hair on John Paul's arms prickles in the dense shade of what everyone calls the forest, even though it isn't. A highway and two main roads run along the far edges of it, ribbons of asphalt belting nature into a clean square mile. His older brother told him when he was much younger that werewolves lived among the trees. At nine, he knows this is untrue, that werewolves are made-up and not even the scariest made-up monster his brother could have chosen. Nevertheless, he steers clear of the forest. Most of the neighborhood kids do, under threat of their parents.

Not Lizzie. She plunges ahead as though there is a clear path that he cannot see. He trudges after her, inexplicably nervous now but unwilling to turn back and lay himself open to her ridicule. Branches move overhead, their leaves murmuring like voices in the next room. Lizzie's hands trail over the trunks of trees. The seat of her shorts is black with dirt and a heart-shaped leaf clings to the back of her too-small, faded Care Bears t-shirt. Lionheart is on the front, with his stupid brave smile. John Paul rolls his eyes.

They come upon a little ravine, a gouge carved out of the earth, where a creek ran years ago. Lizzie hop-skips down the bank and out of sight, her hands held aloft to steady herself. John Paul drags his feet. It is important to appear bored. Whatever she's found is undoubtedly not worth his time. He imagines a flattened hornets' nest, a corroded car battery. Maybe something as interesting as a dead squirrel, but surely girls don't like dead things.

At the crest of the ravine, his tennis shoes planted apart in a posture of impatience adopted from his brother, John Paul looks down and sees Lizzie seated astride the lower body of a decayed human corpse.

He goes still everywhere, heart-still, his arms frozen at his sides. His face and body are numb, stunned cold. He stares at the blackened rubber soles of Lizzie's sandals, her grimy toes curled over the ends, her fat legs grub-white against the ground. She is straddling the thing's thighs. It still wears pants—tattered cloth gone colorless

and oily, fragile as burned paper breaking apart to expose dull yellow-grey bone like unhealthy teeth. She is stroking it, tenderly, petting it like a cat right where the skeleton's private parts would have been. It makes John Paul feel strange and sick, like the time he accidentally walked in on his uncle in the basement bathroom at his grandparent's house in Connecticut and his uncle was touching himself.

John Paul swallows. He forces his gaze up and away. A breeze kicks to life and lifts his dark hair from his forehead. Lizzie is staring at him. Out of the corner of his eye he can see her hand still moving, a white rhythm on the black background of the thing's body. He scours the forest around her for focal points where he can hang his attention. A squirrel frozen on a branch, a bush with red berries clustered among the leaves like the wreath his mother puts on their front door for Christmas, the running-water sound of cars rushing past on the highway beyond.

"What is that?" he says, and his voice is small and dry. He knows what it is.

"Not what," Lizzie says. She shifts onto her knees and bends close over the thing, fussing with the crumbling remnant of shirt that covers the upper body. Arcs of rib-cage rise through a ragged hole. "Who."

John Paul lets out a shaking laugh that is mostly exhalation. "You're crazy," he says blindly. His eyes dart, settling on nothing. He does not want to look at the thing's face. He won't.

And then he does. The face is noseless, green-black and textured like the shell of a walnut. Panels of bone are exposed at the forehead and cheekbones. The eyes are horribly nothing, they are the funnel-shaped hole he was gouging in his side yard. The mouth gapes open. He watches Lizzie's finger trace light with worship along the broken angle of jaw. Her fingertip comes away charcoal-dark.

"This is how he lives," she says. "He catches rain and bugs in his mouth."

John Paul holds himself still with an effort.

"His name is Jack Sprat," she says. "He's my boyfriend.

I visit him every day. We're going to get married because he loves me because I helped him. Because I gave him an arm."

John Paul's eyes search out its arms. One of the sleeves ends with a bird-claw hand, pursed together at the bare fingertips like a drawstring. The other sleeve is flat and empty. Positioned parallel from the thing's shoulder is a huge tree branch—five feet long at least and ragged with dead leaves. Bark curls away like loosened black fingernails. John Paul pictures Lizzie wrestling it into place, her voice chattering constant and senseless in the muffled solitude of the forest. He wonders what happened to the original arm and imagines it still nearby, a separate, animate thing dragging itself sightless over the dry ground in dumb circles, like a wounded animal. It could be behind him right now, a bone snake twitching across the forest floor towards the back of his ankle. His foot jerks up involuntarily and he glances wildly around him.

"What's wrong with you?" Lizzie demands. "You're being rude. Come down here and shake Jack Sprat's hand."

"You have to tell somebody, Lizzie," John Paul blurts.

Lizzie turns the strange dimness of her small eyes on him. She pins him there. He forces himself to meet her blunt ugliness unflinching, tightening his shoulders against a deep shudder. She settles back on her haunches over the thing and braces her hands on the ground behind her, one on either side, splayed out like fat white starfish.

"What do you mean?" she asks. There is an adult stillness in her words that unsettles him. He thinks of the way his father's voice sounds when his mother makes him angry. The soft danger of it.

"It's a *dead body*, Lizzie," John Paul says, nearly whispering these words. "You have to tell somebody so they can find out who he is and…bury him."

Lizzie blinks at him, but it is inhuman, slow and deliberate like a lizard. John Paul swallows against the tightness of his throat. Several seconds crawl past.

Finally he says, in a last weak attempt at logic, "It was a murder, or something."

Lizzie cocks her head and then drags her gaze from John Paul down to Jack Sprat. She drifts her fingertips over the thing's clothes, traces the gathered bones of his one hand.

"He's not always here, you know," she says softly. "He walks around when he wants to. He likes windows. He likes to watch people sleeping." Every hair on the back of John Paul's neck bristles. "He's very quiet. You won't notice him, not right away."

"Dead bodies can't walk around," John Paul says. There is a tremor in his voice that he is unable to control.

"What do you know?" Lizzie counters, her words still calm in that adult way, and John Paul understands with a bleak sinking sensation that he knows nothing.

Lizzie rocks onto to all fours over the thing and turns her head to lower her ear over the yawning mouth. John Paul watches her limp blonde hair coil against the black skin stretched over Jack Sprat's cheek, watches the rim of her ear move closer and closer to the lightless hole, imagines a faint gust of breath pushing from the hollow of his chest through his dry throat and onto the peach fuzz of Lizzie's face. He feels it on his own ear like an unseen fingertip and stumbles sharply backwards. Lizzie giggles.

"He likes you, John Paul," she says, brightly. "He wants to know which window is yours." She leans down and speaks directly into the void of Jack Sprat's mouth. "It's the house with the—"

"Stop," John Paul barks. His whole body is crawling, ants swarming his skin, crowding into his ears, his eyes. "Don't. I promise I won't tell anyone. I promise."

Lizzie sits back on her heels and rests her hands, crossed primly one over the other, on Jack Sprat's long-gone private parts. She gazes calmly up at him. John Paul imagines that spider he saw in her hair eating a hole into her soft scalp, gnawing through skull, tunneling down into the bad meat of her brain like a termite. Something is wrong inside her.

"Your bedroom is on the second floor, isn't it?" she asks. "Don't worry. He's a good climber."

John Paul's body turns itself and hurtles back towards the neighborhood before he realizes he is moving. The ribbon of her clear singsong voice trails after him.

"Jack Sprat will see you soon, John Paul, Jack Sprat will see you soon."

John Paul hits the side entrance of his house at a dead run. He stands frozen with his back against the door for more than a minute before his mother hears his ragged breathing.

"What in the world?" she says, frowning. She combs his hair away from his forehead and it stays that way, clammy with sweat. Her hands are cool on his flushed face. Her fingers find the divots behind his ears and hold him there. John Paul wraps his arms around her waist and presses his head into her side. He keeps his eyes stark wide open. Lemon-yellow linoleum, the hum and tick of the dryer, his mother's cleaning-day smell, her warm body. It isn't real, what happened in the forest. *This* is real. Lizzie is lonely and crazy and everybody knows that her parents don't really love her.

"Are you okay, Jay?"

He nods against her.

"Do you want lunch?"

He nods again. But he finds he can't eat the sandwich she makes him.

And later he finds he can't force his eyes from the strip of his darkened bedroom window visible where the curtains don't quite close. Outside the branches toss and click against the glass like fingernails in the high wind of a gathering summer storm. He hears the halting drag of Jack Sprat wandering up the middle of Laurel Street towards his house, his legs swinging stiffly, jaw dangling against his empty chest like a broken hinged door, the monstrous branch arm scraping behind him. Searching for John Paul with the sucking holes of his eyes.

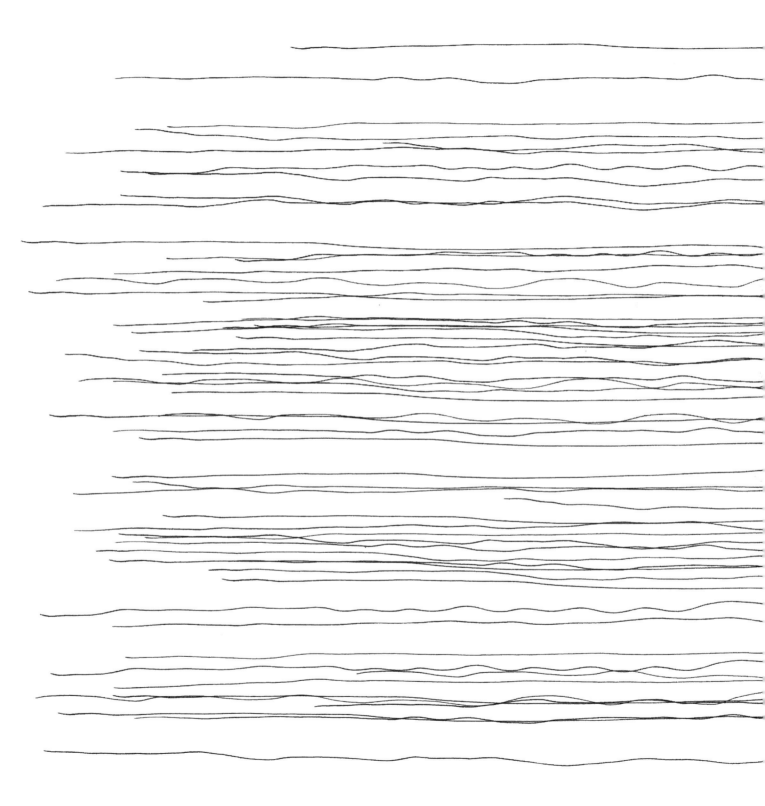

HUNGER

STORY BY JENNIFER MANALILI • ART BY SOMARAMOS

The slit of Chen's eye is puffed like a grape, open, dripping ruby red juice onto the edge of her kitchen table.

He's babbling, half-formed sentences trying to woo her into feeling guilty, remorseful—but she is not generous.

She is hungry.

He's screaming. "What will my mom and dad think? They'll be wondering where I am! You'll never get away with this! You stupid bitch! You'll never—"

And when she moves, it renders him speechless. He flinches back when she stands, the angle of her hip pushing the table towards him as she gets to her feet. Straining away from her only pulls the rope around his wrists tighter against the handles of the chair. He's shaking.

She almost laughs.

She'll save his hands for last. She always loved how delicate they appeared, cuffs always folded neatly above his wrists, and long fingers, tapered like the branches on a tree. At least she will still be able to look at them.

His breaths are like ghosts, puffs filling the space between them in the room, and for once she's thankful for how cold the winters in the countryside are. The lights of Seoul after midnight stare back at her from miles and miles ahead. She imagines the noise of the karaoke bars and nightclubs, and arcade rooms she was never invited to. The smell of fried fish cakes bathed in spicy red ddeokbokki sauce sold on the street, the fried chicken with peanuts and spicy japchae noodles she took comfort in until she came home, wearing their condensation on her clothes, the smell of sesame oil like it was a second skin.

The last bus that Chen could have taken back home to the city would have left by now. Her father's village is all darkness and space, sleeping. Even if someone were able to hear Chen's cries, she's sure they would be too old and tired and cold to come outside and seek it.

Time passes. She listens.

His silence lingers between them like a heavy weight, only hindered by the sound of his breathing when he begins to hyperventilate, until finally—

He croaks out, "I'm sorry," he tells her, as if it will save him. "I'm so sorry. Jin-woo. For everything."

Her hand stops abruptly around a bottle of soy and garlic in the cabinet.

Pathetic.

She remembers how he looked the first time she saw him, on the afternoon he walked into her life. The edges of his uniform crisp, tight around his shoulders. A red tie had been pushed into the center of his jacket.

He looked like a Christmas present brought to life. Tendrils of black hair tucked behind his ears, some pieces falling in front of his eyes, his eyelashes. The curve of his bottom lip caught between his teeth. He was beautiful. Watching him walk into the room, it was like staring into the sun.

And then she got too close—he opened his mouth. She burned. Her self-esteem reduced to ashes between his fingers.

He hadn't said anything at first.

Then, he only laughed.

And her shoulders had stiffened, as they always did, and as they would grow accustomed to. Tradition. Year after year.

"Pig!" he hurled next. "Look at this fucking pig eat."

His friends, seven or eight boys in matching uniforms behind him, stared back at her. She dropped her lunch, a fluffy white sandwich filled with creamy, yellow salad—her mother's favorite recipe. She stared back at them, watching them watch her and wincing back tears, daring them to choose a different option.

Cowards! They glanced back at Chen, looking for reassurance and he smirked, staring right back at them. It was all the coaxing they needed.

And like a pool of water sat in front of them, they leaped in too.

"Fat bitch," one cursed.

"Disgusting."

"Enough for two."

"Three."

"More!"

Year after year it went on. Picking apart her clothes, her face, her weight. Chen coaxing more people into doing the same thing like it was an initiation, until it felt like an entire cafeteria room hated the way she took up so much space.

Chen and that mouth, his lip caught between his teeth. Chen and that hair. He was so beautiful; she thought sometimes it balanced out his cruelty. It made sense this way, for someone so beautiful to be so horrible.

Year after year it went on. She suffered through lunches packed and eaten in the bathroom stalls to avoid the laughter in the cafeteria. It's been years, hating the elastic on her skirts, the buttons on her shirts flimsily trying to stay shut. Years of squeezing into spaces and sitting in classrooms and desks next to Chen, trying to make herself smaller. Wishing for it. Praying for it.

And months of planning this.

She lured him away from Seoul by walking home alone.

Between every insult, every time he'd made it hard for her to want to live, she'd gotten to know him. She knew he would follow her, wanting to make it a point again. Poor Chen, always desperate to have the last laugh. Poor Chen.

And she imagines how she must have looked to him that day, her hair blowing in the wind, sweating inside her best pink winter coat—all plump and warm and soft and ready to squeal.

He should be the one afraid. If only he had known.

Pressing the cloth of chemicals against his mouth was the first time she'd ever been able to touch him. And his perfect mouth had felt just as beautiful as she always imagined, all smooth and soft beneath her hand as she tackled him to the ground. But the best part had been watching his eyes go wild first, pupils blown wide.

The second best part had been dragging him inside of the house, pooling blood across the tiles of her kitchen floor like spilled paint. The weight of him between her hands.

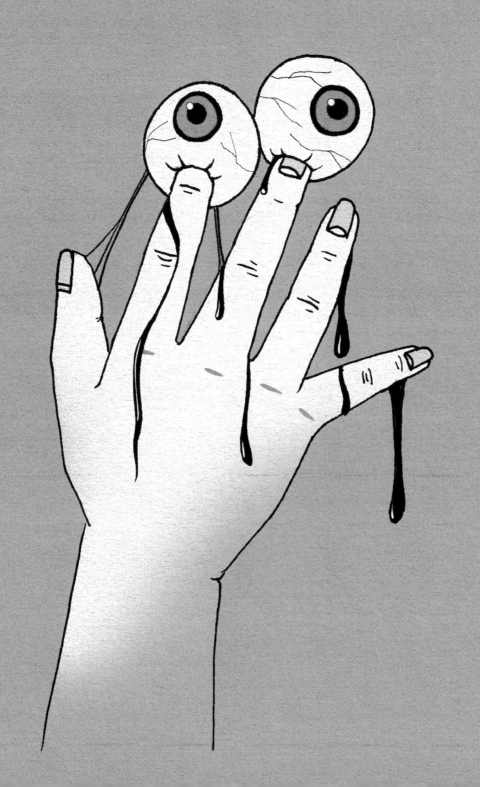

The third was when he finally stopped screaming. When acceptance had dawned on him like a weight and rendered him silent, immobile. It was like that day in the cafeteria all over again, only now he was the one speechless and afraid.

His eyes go wild again the first time she presses a blade against a vein and blood oozes out. She watches, head tilted to the side, fascinated. It reminds her of the caramel center of a piece of chocolate cut in half. It paints her in red, her white blouse, the uniform of her skirt. It sinks under her fingernails and between her hands. She can't help but smear some of the blood from her hands across her mouth like lipstick, tasting him.

"Bitch! Bitch! You crazy fucking bitch!" Chen starts to cry, broken and hopeless, helpless sobs. She watches the panic seize his body, inch by inch until it reaches his face, seems to shake the roots of his hair as he twists in the chair fighting the urge to vomit.

His pupils so wide now there's barely any room left for the hazel color of his irises. She can see herself smiling back in the reflections of the fear gripping his face.

She cuts out his lips, because they are her favorite thing about him beside his hands. She traces the lines of his hands with a knife, pulls out each of his nails with a pair of tweezers and places them in a jar next to her bed with locks of his hair. She'll keep these forever, the parts of him that will never perish.

His hair and scalp peeled off, the top of his skull broken, she stands back and marvels at the cloudy, pink wrinkles that made him cruel and insufferable. She takes a melon baller to his brains, working methodically, spooning out individual portions. Because he's so pretty he should be savored. For seconds and leftovers. His liver inside creamy fillings of chocolate cake. Spooned over ice-cream for dessert. Eyes sucked between her teeth. It makes her happy that the inside of her mouth is the last thing they will ever see.

She'll drain his blood into an ice cube tray, let it simmer in brown gravy with fried pork cutlet for katsu curry, portion it out with kimbap rolls for lunch. He'll taste delicious sandwiched between portions of rice, cheese and egg, and wrapped in seaweed.

She imagines how she'll pack a roll for Jessica, Chen's girlfriend. How the ever-popular girl will be hesitant at first, of course, but how she'll wilt beneath the offer of free food and the audience of the cafeteria.

Their favorite boy.

Now they can each have half.

Now they can finally share.

When he is packed away into different freezer bags and boxes inside of her fridge, Jin-woo will sigh, stare back at his face. She watches the light setting on his nose, his rude tongue, his perfect mouth, as she closes the refrigerator door.

She'll shower. The ruby red of him, the fact that he was here, really here, in her house, pooling into the bathtub and down the drain.

She won't brush her teeth, wanting to savor the taste of him still inside of her. Some part of her maybe always wanted to have him inside of her, and this, this will have to do.

She pulls the top of the duvet up higher until it reaches her neck. And tongue still laving against the inside of her cheek, like she hasn't gotten a fill of her taste of him yet, she will sleep.

Until she wakes up, hungry again.

CHEWING BEDLAM AND THE BITE OF BECOMING

THE FEMALE OF THE SPECIES

STORY BY HANNA TAWATER • ART BY LAURA GWYNNE

We crack the mirror in the bathroom. Maybe it was already cracked—I'm pretty sure it was already cracked, this place is a dump—but there's definitely newly-shattered glass that hits the floor when I slam backwards. I lost a button from my blouse, anyways, so something broke.

His breath is too wet on my neck, his grunts too self-indulgent, but he's strong, has no problem lifting my dense frame onto the sink, has no problem ripping through my stockings, no problem following me into the bathroom after our fourth round of well-whiskey shots.

He grinds into me like he works a slaughterhouse. I don't get off. I never get off. I read once that female komodo dragons who were deemed "receptive to mating" would yet violently attack the males who'd win the dominance display for those mating rights, so the male would have to counter-attack and fully restrain the female in order to copulate without injury. I read once that komodo dragons sometimes attempt to consume prey too large for their mouths and will ram the carcass against a tree to help cram it down their throats.

The violence of it is satisfying enough. It's biology, evolution, the urge to consume more than one can safely, realistically, take on, ramming carcass after carcass down my throat, lashing out claws first. All to slake some inexplicable hunger, plant seeds that will never sow. We are so driven by these hypothetical gardens, pheromones like pollen, hitching rides on bees' legs, just moving from one flowery cunt to the next so to populate the world in little purple flowers that smell like knock-off perfume. How much simpler would it be if we could just tend to our own gardens? But we're in a drought here, constantly craving. No flowers can grow in this climate, and my survival-of-the-species instinct is sometimes more than I can resist, leaving wasted seeds across three zip codes.

He pulls out and comes on the inside of my thigh. I watch it drip onto the floor with all the viscosity of a loogy hawked by a teenage boy. As he tucks in and zips up all I can think about is tearing into an undercooked steak. He leans in for a kiss and I offer my cheek. I wipe away the residual spittle and leave before he can ask my number.

The next morning there is a flaky patch of skin on my left knee.

•

There is a power in being wanted. It's those small chemical signals communicating that I am viable, the most viable in the room, even. But it's not *just* about being wanted. It's also the power of turning a person into an animal, watching that transformation like some backwards god de-evolving mankind into a collective writhing lower-functioning grunt.

I don't want to be revered or worshipped, though, mostly I just want to *exist*. I puke in my mouth a little every time I hear or see the word "goddess." I think: *predator*, and tend towards prey that has no idea it's being stalked. That's what gets me off. It is a powerplay that is distinctly feminine—that requires constant...underestimation.

Occasionally I wonder if I'm lying to myself, disguising intimacy issues as evolutionary psychoanalysis, a hyperbolic excuse to use when my mother asks why I never have a boyfriend. I went through a Darwin phase when I was ten, reading *On the Origin of the Species* like other kids read *Goosebumps*. For me the real horror stories were in being powerless to biology. I never really grew out of that phase.

•

I wake twice to turn the heat up. It's the worst time of year, when nights are frigid and the days too warm. Opening and closing windows, turning the heat up and then down, clothes on and off. It takes so much effort to thermoregulate. But I like the touch of my skin on different textures, opting for minimal clothing so as to feel surface and atmosphere. Tiny receptors still embed beneath our pores, and I like to use mine.

I sit in bed and scratch at the flakes on my knee. The skin is dry and papery and each flake I scratch off reveals another crack underneath. It reminds me of those stupid lotion commercials where they'd open with a sweeping shot over a desert and zoom in onto dried brackish terrain then back out on a cartoonish illustration of a woman's skin. My mother used to take me to the desert as a cheap excuse for our little two-person family vacation when I was a kid, said it would be good for my complexion and for my attitude. I wanted to hate it because I blanket-hated anything she made me do. But there is a static in desert air that only exists when it is so dry and the ground so hot, shooting up waves of warmth and electricity. It made me feel alive. It made me feel connected. That electricity traveled through my limbs, my core, made me believe I was so fast and strong and purposeful. I saw and felt and heard nothing but heat. There is too much disconnect when a body is shut up where air is damp and manufactured and where the only buzzing comes from light bulbs.

I've been meaning to go back, but life has a way of getting oppressively routine. I haven't stepped outside the city in twelve years. The weeks bleed together here—work, bar, take-out, sleep, work, bar, take-out, sleep. Every so often I mix it up by drinking at home, but my cave holds nothing but carrion and most nights I crave live meat.

I give up on my knee and start raking my nails gently up and down my legs, feeling my skin respond to my own touch. I imagine what it'd be like to be touched like this by someone else. I open the freezer and stick my hands in a bag of ice and just stand there, staring blankly at my reflection in the kitchen window. I look absurd, all bruised up legs and unwashed hair, my arms limply outstretched like a zombie.

When I can't feel my hands anymore I hop on the kitchen counter and start touching my legs again. My skin erupts in a chemtrail of goosebumps as my fingers barely skim the surface. I go down the outside of my thigh, circle my knee, and come back up the inside. My legs feel impossibly hot in contrast to my numb digits. I bring one hand inside the leg hole of my underwear and flinch at how cold it is before relaxing into the sharpness. I watch my reflection twist in the window, steam rising from my body. I imagine there is someone outside watching me. I imagine it's someone else touching me. I imagine I am in the desert, rubbing against hot sand, filling myself with static as I sink deeper away from the red surface of the inside of my eyelids. It is in this vast blackness that I tense and spasm and drift further into myself until I can see my own body, a solitary small twisted pink thing in a hungry void.

I finish and just lay there for a few moments, legs cocked awkwardly. My foot feels wet and I look down to see it found its way to a pot in the sink. I shake off the sludge, pull on the first skirt I find, and grab my keys.

•

The patch on my knee isn't new for me. The first time my skin changed I was thirteen.

His name was Dirk. Perhaps it was his shitty name that gave him a complex of over-compensation, but he was "cool" and therefore well-known and well-liked. He wasn't unattractive, but he was cute in that baby-face puppy kind of way that newly pubescent girls like. I was not yet newly pubescent.

School had just gotten out and I was chatting with Carla behind the bathrooms as we usually did after class. I didn't have many girlfriends, but I had this one. She went to church. I think she took pity on me.

"Hey." Dirk walked up with his stupid smile and his stupid dimples with his stupid friends.

"Hey." Carla said, posture immediately relaxed into a casual slouch. Watching her was like taking an acting class. I kept quiet and crossed my arms.

"I said, HEY." He emphasized the 'hey' and moved closer towards me. He smelled like corn nuts.

"Hey." I muttered back, trying not to gag.

"Wanna make out?"

I looked at Carla whose eyes lit up as she flashed a shy grin. "No." I rolled my eyes. She elbowed my ribs.

"C'mon, it'll be cool." That stupid fucking smile, his stupid fucking friends giggling behind him. I was over it and spun around to walk away.

With my back turned I felt the air close between us, felt his snickering exhalation, felt his arm reach out. He squeezed my ass. Hard. Not even just a quick pat, he

grabbed onto me like a toddler clutching at his mother. I spun around and punched him square in his shit-eating grin, which immediately curdled.

"Fucking slut."

Everything went red and I was on top of him, wrestling him against the hot asphalt. I felt someone pulling on my shoulders. I sprung back to loosen them off and started kicking him in the stomach as he tried unsuccessfully to curl into a defense posture. But between my friend and his they eventually restrained me. I could hear him whimpering as Carla dragged me away, her grip turning my arm white, asking over and over what the fuck was wrong with me.

"Uhm, he grabbed me? And called me a slut?"

"He *wanted* to *kiss* you." Her eyes were wide, like I was starving and Dirk had only just offered me something to eat. "No one is going to like you now. How are you ever going to get a boyfriend now? How am *I* going to get a boyfriend now?" *Unreceptive. Antagonistic. Now no one will ever want to feed you.*

I went home that afternoon and cried. I blamed it on the changing May weather, but my skin felt dry and tight. I fell asleep with a wet face, clawing at an itch on my side.

The next morning I woke up with my stomach in knots and convinced my mother to keep me home. It wasn't until I went to shower some hours later that I noticed the rough splotches and deep gashes on my side. I assumed I had a rash. My mother assumed I had a rash. The doctor assumed I had a rash.

The rash didn't go away.

Psoriasis, he eventually decreed, gave me a cream, and that was that. I went back to school not just an outcast, but a deformed outcast.

•

I've never been to this bar before. The room is a dim mahogany I scan and rescan each time I hear the door creak open. Every guy here tonight is with a girl. Every damn one. And all the mice look identical: "Undisputed" tee shirts and tribal arm bands, *they all like to think they're fighters*, tiger-stripe highlights and French tips, *they all like to think they're cats*, a glimmering yellow and brown field of Shiner Bocks for the man who tries, but not too much, a cloud of Victoria Secret body spray for the woman who has taste, but not too much. *Is this what living is like for normal people?* I order another shot.

The girl next to me keeps tapping her nails on the bar. Each click sends a vibration through my brain and I feel my eye begin to twitch. I want to grab her wrist and rip those nails off, splitting down the middle of each neatly polished one. She reeks of subservience. The Vin Diesel wannabe who's been talking at her since I sat down keeps glancing past her towards me. I don't know if it's the twitching or the fourth shot that draws his attention, but his lady friend finally catches on and turns around.

"You got a problem?"

"Yeah," I lean in to sniff her, "I wanted to get a quiet drink at a bar, but judging by the smell I seemed to have ended up in a whorehouse. Honestly, I didn't know prostitution was legal here."

It isn't as witty an insult as I hoped for, but the effect is the one intended. She throws her diet Jack n' Coke in my face.

Growing up my mother used to catch and domesticate feral cats. After enough scratches I overcame my childish desire to snuggle the furry things and turned my interest instead towards observing their behavior. You can't get cozy with something feral, but you can watch it and learn about the nature of the world. In cats the females are more hierarchical than the males. Males tend to be submissive to their housemates, but the females take longer to acclimate to each other, and even when they do there is one that is obviously always in control. They call women *catty* for a reason.

She obviously feels she's the one in control of this confrontation as she spits "miserable bitch," nods Vinny towards a vacant booth, and begins to rise. I wouldn't have minded so much if not for the taste of aspartame dripping off my face. I spend a split second to study her, make a few quick calculations, and decide she's weaker than she believes. So I'm up first, hissing.

Blonde tangles around my fingers as I grab her hair and thrust her face down against the bar. Blood spurts from her nose and swirls into the condensation rings on the shiny wood creating a pattern of nebulae and red dwarf stars. I barely have time to watch my new galaxy finish forming before her boyfriend is on me—a markedly more formidable and satiating target.

His right gets the side of my mouth before I have time to duck back. Hot copper fills the spaces between my teeth and I am in the desert. He tackles me to the ground, the weight of him pushing into my shoulders and he pulls an arm back to come down at me again. I use the brief space to tighten my stomach muscles and curl upward as much as I can so to reach his face. A chunk of his cheek comes back with me in my teeth, bitter and warm, and I use the resulting moment of confusion and pain to squirrel out from beneath him. Lightning fast, my appendages all throbbing with adrenaline, I am on his back, legs constricting his middle, one thumb digging into the new orifice I had created, the rest of my fingers snaking into other holes, looking for purchase, as I put all my weight behind ramming down his thick meaty head against the splintering floor. I am deceptively strong. I pull back on his nostrils, slide my black claws in behind his eyes, and thrust down again and again, a carcass against a tree and into some invisible throat. I can hear screaming somewhere, but the pulsing of my veins is louder.

•

Somehow my apartment door manifests itself in front of me. I twist the key into the lock and collapse it forward with the weight of my gasps. I don't remember leaving the bar, but my legs pushed me quickly through shadows and alleyways, my chest tightening with every footfall, my breath cold in my throat. I do remember coughing out something like "self defense" after he went limp. It must have happened too fast for anyone to intervene or even register, but for me it was already beginning to fade. I stumble onto the sofa, panting, the blood still warm on my face. I don't know how much of it is mine. I feel aroused and hungry, but mostly exhausted. I turn on to my side, my knees finding my chest, and I slip back into the void.

•

I didn't lose my virginity until I was nineteen. Not for lack of trying, but I was mean and most boys in school liked girls who were things like "nice" and "pretty" and "non-violent." I, however, was in and out of anger management counseling and still knew no restraint. My face has always been painted with a giant "fuck you" and I have never been told to smile. A man said once that it's in the eyebrows. I have "bitch eyebrows," whatever that means. My mother used to tell me it was in my eyes, though. That my eyes were nothing but venom and hate. She never built up a tolerance to that venom.

I've never gotten along with males, not just as an angry teenager. It rooted somewhere beyond "boys have cooties"—I got in fights with boys as early as kindergarten over things like they said something stupid, or looked at me funny, or were breathing too loudly. I hated my own father to the point he eventually stopped coming to visit by the time I was nine. I could never stand being told by him what to do. I could never stand the way he spoke or walked or smelled, like why did he get to assume all this power? Why did he get to decide when it was time to come and time to go? And I always thought my mother weak for submitting to general male apathy, jumping every time the phone rang, desperate for his affection, which made me eventually learn to hate her too. I don't think I've ever actually known anyone who I felt I could respect and coexist with. I just assume I am hardwired to be a sociopathic bitch. I've never even considered I could be any different way. We all have an ecological niche and I accept mine for what it is.

When I finally lost it, it was with a coworker at my first job. He had the kind of manicured facial hair that screams, "I don't respect women." I'd catch him staring at me with a mixture of lust and disdain, which I'd mirror back. He'd

saunter over, taking my eye-contact as an invitation to lean against my cubicle and prattle on about evo-psych and how at root women are biologically wired to be submissive, like his male superiority was supposed to turn me on, make me crave his procreation.

Beyond his unsolicited philosophies, we barely spoke to each other. A tension, however, was developing between us, thick and fetid and purely chemical. It bubbled up like heavy cream deep in my throat whenever I was near him. I fucking hated him and his stupid philosophy. I wanted to rip off his studded belt and wrap it around his skinny neck while mounting up and showing him who was really dominant.

It happened after the holiday party. Drinks were free and since I was the only underage person at the company no one bothered to card. We both stumbled outside for air at the same time and though neither of us did so with intentions of leaving, he offered to give me a ride home.

We made it three blocks before his hand was on my knee. I shifted my legs. Five and it was under my dress sandwiched in the crease where thigh folds into crotch. I crossed them. Six and his fingers were inside me. Eight and he pulled over. I feigned innocence and asked what he was doing. But I knew what all girls know, that in not immediately removing his hand five blocks ago that there was no going back—I had already implicitly agreed to his advance through my inaction. "You don't need to play dumb," he said and started unbuttoning his pants.

"No, let's not, just take me home." I smiled at him, but my eyes were still a conflicted cocktail of disgust and wanting. He yanked the top of my dress down and reached his hot mouth towards my breast. I slapped him. Hard. Harder than I expected, but not harder than I wanted. He hit back. That I did expect—men like him don't support that chivalrous "never hit a woman" bullshit, and don't take kindly to their masculinity being undermined. Not to be undermined myself—I could never stomach the idea of being controlled—I decided it was now or never, and shoved him against the driver side door, his head slamming the window. He had already pulled himself out of his pants, so I swung my leg over his lap and positioned myself on top of him. He grabbed onto me, digging his nails into the skin of my ass and using my body as leverage to push himself deeper. I bit into the part of his neck right behind his ear and he came instantly. This, I remember thinking, was control.

And that was it. The whole thing was over in less than two minutes, and I went back to the passenger seat with his "superior genes" seeping out of me and pooling into my underwear as he drove me the rest of the way home.

I stood in my bathroom and fingered the bruise forming on my right cheekbone in the mirror. I inspected the bloody half-moons on my backside. I took a shower, turning the water as hot as I could stand, my skin reddening, and brought myself to climax three times before going to bed.

The lackluster fruition of something I'd fantasized about so many times made it impossible for me to face him again. I wondered if it'd always be like this and decided that nothing ever works out like you expect. The scabs he left on my ass never went away. It was the first of many jobs I'd have to quit.

•

I wake up sticky, my hair crunching with dried blood. I reach up to start working the tangles out and notice a new patch of scales decorating the top of my right forearm.

This one is unlike the others that have formed. Where the other collections of dried skin on my body are grey and papery, this one is bright red and harder, like painted fingernails. I hold it up to the light and it shimmers. I rake my fingertips back and forth over it for the duration of a small eternity. It feels slightly cool to the touch and the plates gently pull with elasticity in the direction I sweep.

•

My car makes it through most of the mountains, but finally overheats at the base of the valley. In addition to what few articles of clean clothes I could find in my sudden "oh-shit-did-I-just-kill-a-dude-I-gotta-get-out-of-town panic," I managed to also shove a bottle of bourbon into a backpack, but didn't think to bring any water. I left behind my phone, ID, computer—everything but a few necessities. Except water.

I wander up the road a little way and squint into the distance, seeing only heat lines and dirt and asphalt. I must be miles from any kind of establishment. But the air feels good, dry and hot on my skin. So I walk back to my car off the side of the road and lay an old towel on the hood, spreading myself on top of it, knees at a ninety degree angle, white floral dress gathering around the base of my thighs, arms stretched outward across the metal, breathing in the sun. I probably shouldn't draw so much attention to myself, but it feels too good, and before long a truck pulls off and parks twenty feet in front of me. My body is buzzing and electric as I prop myself up on my elbows. I can shoot lightning from my fingers if I want and my skin absolutely aches.

He walks up and asks if I need help. He is not my usual speed—older, tired, nothing left to prove to anyone. I open my legs a little, revealing only skin between, and explain that my car overheated, that I was waiting for it to cool down, but it's just *so hot* out here.

I smile, not breaking eye contact on his face, not even to blink. I still have dried blood under my fingernails and a new kind of hunger rising in me.

He reddens, his eyes glued to my crotch as he stammers out something about calling for a tow.

"Or you could just fuck me." His face morphs between excitement and disbelief as he processes the suggestion. I watch him calculating, replaying my words, analyzing.

"Umm, h-here? N-n-now?" He wants to—I can smell his arousal, but his stammering does nothing for my own. So seldom do our fantasies turn out the way we expect. I am already a violent current, though, ready to spark in all directions. I tug at his jeans and pull his mouth towards mine, biting down on one of our tongues, I'm not sure whose, until my mouth fills with blood. "Shouldn't we get inside the car at least?" I tear open his zipper and slide myself down the hood and onto him, legs wrapped around his waist, the metal burning my bare skin, but I don't care.

I feel the inside of my leg brush against something leather. He is asking my name, my age, what I do for work. My silence is discomforting him—he starts to soften. "What's a wild and pretty thing like you doing in the middle of the damn desert anyways?"

"Shut. Up." I squeeze my legs tighter around his waist and thrust myself harder, placing his hand on my breast, to try and bring him back.

It works. He seems to have stopped caring about being out in the open as he squints his eyes shut and grunts into me at an awkward tempo. I watch a few beads of sweat on his forehead gather together and roll down the tip of his nose to splash against my chest. I am surprised he's lasting longer than most, but it gives me time.

I reach down and loosen his bowie from its sheathe and scrape the cool metal across the outside of my thigh a few times. He hasn't noticed. I use the strength of my legs to flip him around so that he's on the car and I am on top. He puts meaty hands around my waist and I wonder if he can hear the blade in my fist clinking against the hood like I can. It's all I can hear. I hone in and lock onto that frequency of metal against metal. I thrust down over and over until I feel him start to coil, the hood denting and buckling under my knees. He opens his eyes and meets my gaze, cracking a shy smile. For a moment I hesitate, almost feeling—something. But when his head tilts back and he grabs my hips to still me I know he's there and the moment is gone. I reach up with both hands to shove the knife with all my force down through the center of his neck.

It doesn't go in as smoothly as I thought it would. Either time has slowed or my senses have quickened because I can feel it push against the skin before puncturing through it, then the fat, then muscle, each layer until I hear cracking and crunching through cartilage and vertebrae. It catches at the end as I try to pull it back out, tugging the skin of his neck up with it before gurgling free. When it releases it does so with an arc of red into the air

that splashes across my chest and covers my dress.

His body hasn't quite caught up to its death yet—he is still hard so I keep grinding as his eyes gape into some emptiness visible only to him. The blood continues to gush out and over me. I close my eyes and clutch onto my chest, the blood warm and slick against my skin, as my body tenses. All I see is red. No man has ever felt this good before.

•

When I finish I drag his carcass behind his truck so that he's concealed from the road. My car finally starts and I drive on. I rub his blood into my skin like a warm and sticky lotion and feel temporarily satisfied, connected, purposeful. Up ahead there is a small shack off the side of the road with a large buzzing generator and a chipped piece of wood with the words "ice cold beer" painted on it. I pull up next to two other cars in the makeshift dirt lot to the side of the building and sit there for a while, letting the engine run.

Every molecule in my body twitches and trembles. I can feel the blood moving through my arms, my legs, circling in and out of my heart. Over the sound of the engine I can hear it beating. I close my eyes and feel the tug of the blackness receding and wafting into red fractals. When I open them again the landscape flattens out into a two-dimensional image, like a movie backdrop and I'm the only real thing on the set. I can see the atoms of oxygen in the air and start to lose track of where my own atoms end. I let out a long slow exhalation through my mouth.

I finally come down from the high and realize my skin is tight and itchy again. Not just itchy, it itches with *agony*. I start clawing at all my rough patches, which are now not fully covering, but plentiful enough, and more of the shimmering red starts to sneak through. I writhe against the seat, tugging and pulling at the dead skin until it all crumbles off like ashes revealing burning embers underneath.

The itching finally subsides. I sit in a pile of skin flakes with beautiful patterns of red and gold on my left knee, right forearm, right half of my torso, left side of my neck, left outside thigh, right calf and foot, and a very small delicate spot on my right cheekbone. I am fast and strong and purposeful. I sense every body, both live and dead, for miles around me. I hear every chirp and insect buzz. I hear the bottom of a bottle connect with wood as it is set down inside the shack. I smell someone who smells like me. I smell death. There is only one person inside, despite the fact there are two cars next to mine.

My skin feels clean though my dress is beginning to harden from the drying fluids. I walk into the bar and sit down next to her. There is no one behind the counter and the air smells like metal and decay. I stick my tongue out to taste it and turn towards her. She is wearing a slightly too big tan Stetson over long brown and sun-washed hair. She returns my gaze, her eyes an impossible poisonous green with elongated pupils. Her mouth stretches too far across her face, but her smile is sharp and beautiful. She reaches out to touch the spot on my cheek, her middle finger lingering against the smoothness of it before trickling down the hollow of my cheekbone and lightly drawing back. It feels like I am being touched for the first time. I realize now that I could smell her as soon as I crested the mountains, in the air and heat as I played possum, over the sweat and blood and sex. It is a smell that is both wholly new and somehow familiar, pheromones like pollen pulling us towards each other.

•

I always liked the part in *Jurassic Park* when Jeff Goldblum figures out that the supposedly all-female dinosaurs are able to procreate because of the amphibian DNA they are spliced with. *Life finds a way,* I think to myself as I slide into her passenger seat. I don't care where she's taking me, but I do wonder if there are more of us. I roll down the window to scan for them, my sisters, my lovers. I can almost taste them far off, waking up, clawing out of their holes to bask, and for the first time I feel peace. I relax my head into her strong shoulder, my body humming at a cozy frequency complementing her

own, the landscape morphing into organic patterns of orange, red, and purple ahead of us. At what point does the mutation become the standard? At what point do we win? As our surroundings change, so must we change with them, adapting and evolving, fighting constantly to advance the species, surviving any way we can, searching for dominance. The desert here is in full bloom, the air choked with wildflowers.

THE OTHER HALF

STORY AND ART BY MADELINE GOBBO

They were riding the subway gingerly together when Margarita asked, "Why don't you take those off?" The husband was still wearing the sunglasses with polarized lenses that transformed his sockets into flat black rectangles and absorbed all light. He leaned in to kiss her as he often did for a change of topic. She couldn't stand the way the cold frames embossed her skin. She begged him again to take them off. He did, but kept his eyes shut or hidden most of the rest of the way. He refused to lift his lids even when the subway dancers invaded their car with a scratched boombox. Finally the train came to their stop and Margarita stood up first, watching him. There was no way for the husband to navigate to the train door blind without her help. His eyes opened—a green flash—and Margarita crowed, "Aha!" like a French detective. The husband's eyes were dear to Margarita. Light in color and very soft, like the eyes of a dog who has run all day in search of you, his eyes were the ones she loved, and they were not green.

"Where did you get those eyes?" she cried, shaking him by the arm. People in the subway station ignored them. In a peevish mood once, she had dismissed his eyes as womanish, but now, looking closely at the strange replacements, it was undeniable that they actually did belong to a woman. The neat parting at their corners, the graceful sweep of their lashes, the flecks of gold or orange around the pupils, the thin gleam of sororal familiarity that held none of the swooning power of the husband's gaze, suggested that until recently the eyes had been in service to a female brain.

"Whose are they?" she asked again. It was not about jealousy. The man, shamefaced but with eyes staunchly gleaming, explained that these were his wife's eyes, that he had woken up with them that morning, and she with his. What they saw through the eyes was still processed by the original brain, and, as outward appearance tritely suggested, they had switched perspectives.

"Since the break-in I haven't slept," said the husband. "My wife insisted we screw constantly. Sideways, backwards, suspended from doorways. As though otherwise she could not be sure. I thought I would go mad from fucking. Then, I couldn't get it up because of the apparitions of the ghost dog. The living one barked at it. The two of them would fall silent and look at me as if to say, 'Who is to blame?' Last night I took one of her pills from the vial above the sink. It was only supposed to help me sleep. She took one of mine, for other reasons…"

Margarita knew of their trouble. The husband's mother ferreted out the truth of his unorthodox marriage. She disowned him over Easter dinner. An aunt, thinking she could hasten karma, tracked down the wife's volatile ex and told him where they were living. The couple withstood a succession of threatening letters, then late-night ringing of the doorbell and taps at the windows, a flaming heart set in their small garden, the disembowelment of one of their beloved dogs (though it was not clear whether the dog was his victim or the unlucky prey of a rapacious hawk), until finally the ex-lover broke in and threatened the husband with a Japanese sword. The husband declined to tell Margarita what his wife had done to persuade him to spare her husband's life.

"The eyes are too much," said Margarita. "Will you offer your ears or toes instead? Those I could stand. As long as you keep your eyes, your hands and your mouth. I can't share those. I don't want her watching while we fool around. She probably won't enjoy it either. Go. Make a different deal. She ought to be reasonable."

The man was silent, no doubt viewing the atrocities his wife was up to far away. Margarita understood the issue was not up for debate.

"You know, even though all the time I said I was happy with our arrangement, I was always wishing you weren't married. Not that you were divorced, or that your wife had died, but that you had actually never met her, because then I would know who you really are. It's not fair! Even the fantasy fails to satisfy, because maybe then you'd never meet me either, or you'd be a totally different person, one I would hate, or you'd wander in front of a bus on what would've been your day of meeting, I worry about this constantly—you're always gazing up at the buildings when you cross the street!—and there's no controlling how a selfish wish will turn out. So I told myself I was happy with the arrangement, because it only had one variable. Your wife."

Margarita was speaking more directly to her than to him. She trembled at the boldness of her words. The eyes appraised her without desire. On the beach, a black dog spooked three ravens. The birds rose into the air like wet umbrellas and flapped a curve back over the dunes. Every least motion was an omen.

"Look, I'll take you to the doctor. I'm sure we can work out a new arrangement, something that will be satisfactory to all of us."

Margarita hurried him along by his elbow, ignoring the wry cast to his face. Of course there could be no satisfactory arrangement. But she was in love, and she had no choice. There was a doctor in the northern quarter with whom she was friendly, a bridge partner of her grandmother's. They tried two dentist's offices under similar names before finding his practice, Sunset Strip Surgery (the same block hosted S&S Strip Surgery, Sunset on the Strip Surgeries, and Sunrise Sunset Surgeons on the Strip). The doctor was indistinguishable from other underground peddlers of artificial enhancements, a crablike figure hiding a paunch who shilled his product well below the beautiful people's line of sight. Margarita's grandmother had complained to her of the doctor's ceaseless cheating. He kept a duplicate set of cards tucked in the hem of his trousers, she alleged, to spice up dull hands. Margarita took this as a sign that the man could handle the fantastic, and burst in without introduction.

The doctor took stock of the situation, examining the husband closely with a strange pointed implement with a light at the tip that resembled the head of an inquisitive lizard. The husband's wife's pupils were dilated, and jets of air shot into them. They blinked rapidly while tears formed at the corners.

"My tears," said the husband. "She's happy that they

distort her view. I want nothing more than to gaze at you, but she says she is fed up and she cannot look at your face for one more second. She says you have an unnerving number of moles."

"In my opinion," the doctor chimed in—he had a voice like a peeper frog—"this condition will only worsen. If you see something you like now—" he gestured to the man's graceful hands and pianist's fingers, "better to cut it off and hide it in a strongbox somewhere known only to you."

"But whatever piece I take will die, eventually, separated from the whole. I can forget about almost anything. Once I left a lizard in the sun for six hours. When I came back it was burnt to a crisp. Then when I opened the cage, a breeze carried it away."

"Can you tell us what will go first? How much longer have I got, Doc?"

"How old are you? How long married?"

"Nearly thirty-five. Married six years. Together fifteen."

The doctor punched some numbers into a clumsy calculator with large buttons that clicked at each decimal. Around them, televisions perched on rickety wall mounts expounded the benefits of buttock enlargement, calf engorgement, breast ballooning, gelatinized lips, eyelid inflation, cheek flaps smoothed over plump scoops of collagen. The cold capture of flaws on tape. Margarita and the wife's eyes stared in fright at the bone saws and rotating drills engaged to computer-simulated bone. Brightly colored pumps sucked up reserves of yellow fat from the belly and thighs and, chugging, deposited them at alien sites. Margarita felt the urge to bolt stronger than ever before, but held fast to the husband's hand and so remained. For if she were to leave, she knew the wife's love would immediately rise up and fill the hole and smooth the edges over as though it had never been.

"The locus of decay remains elusive," said the doctor. "But I am confident that you have, at the very least, until Tuesday afternoon." It was Sunday.

"Oh, stay with me, please!" Margarita cried, beating at the husband's breast. "Let me stand by you to the end! You'll have each other forever after."

As they left the doctor's office, Margarita watched the husband's skin mottle and his freckles wash away, replaced by the bronze radiance of the wife's tan. They were walking through the park on the way to her little house when his legs gave way, in fact disappeared entirely as if they had fallen through a burrow in the floor of reality—he was always clumsy, but Margarita suspected that this time, he actually meant to fall. Determined, Margarita gathered up his torso and lolling head and carried him home on her back. She could feel his lungs inflating and deflating against her spine. She pictured them in his broad chest as voluminous sea creatures, their purplish fans unfurling to catch the bounty borne on his breath's tide. His exhalations whistled past her left ear as she climbed the stairs to her door.

She rang her doorbell to make the visitor's presence known throughout the empty house. Treat him kindly, she thought to herself. Make him comfortable. Force him to live in the present.

He finally fit on her small bed. The places where his legs had been were smooth, featureless, like sandstone eroded by the wind. She remembered an old fantasy, before the dawn of sex, where she had wandered through a ballroom filled with ambulant, torsoless hips and legs. At the stroke of midnight, the leg-people shed their tights and in synchronized formation, launched into the Rockettes' signature eye-high can-can. Margarita twirled helplessly down the chorus line of faceless genitalia. In her child's bed, its frame painted like a lion with the mattress set in its belly, her body swooned.

Margarita slotted in behind him. Never would she cease to marvel at the desire tall men have to be held by small women, irrepressible as dogs climbing into laps they have outgrown.

"Can I get you anything?"

"A vodka seltzer. Raspberry-lime. No. Jameson on the rocks. Soft music on the stereo. My hands in your hair. To look at you with my own eyes."

The doorbell rang again as Margarita was putting the kettle on for tea. Then came a knocking so frantic the umbrella stand toppled and crashed into the arrangement of dried flowers Margarita kept in the entryway. She rose reluctantly and peeked around the jamb, trying to ascertain whether the visitor was any of the bill collectors she'd slept with for amnesty.

The wife stood in the doorway with the husband's eyes in her hand. Margarita had met her only once before, at a party. They shook hands without making eye contact. They had already been intimate in other ways. The wife could smell Margarita on her sheets. Margarita could pick the wife's words from the husband's mouth.

"I have no obligation to be *reasonable*," the wife spat, breathing hard through her nose. Her eye sockets were flat and empty. Margarita noticed the creep of freckles over her prominent collarbone. A hint of red stubble. Fog was rushing over the hill. "I'm not. According to my own mother, on the phone this morning, I'm difficult. I'm untrustworthy, I've lost my darling figure, and I don't give a fuck. I pick fights at gas stations. I stole my dog's Xanax. 'Reason and love keep little company,' even the fairies know that. What you understand"—she let the eyes drop—"could fill an Oriental vase. Love! Love is everything else. What would a girl like you do with romance—stash it in your hollow leg?"

The wife collapsed into a pile of attributes on her doorstep. A Mrs. Potato Head from which the potato has been removed. Margarita ran after the husband's left eye, which was rolling around behind her aloe. She brushed it off on her blouse and put it in her breast pocket. The other eye she set in the pendant of her necklace. It rested against her skin like cold marble. Inside, the teakettle screamed.

"Well, how did it go?" he asked. Margarita pressed the eye into his palms.

"You won a medal."

"Best Rat in a Maze. America's Next Top Fraud."

The subsequent hours passed in a white haze. They put mushrooms in the tea so that the husband's dissolution didn't seem so out of place. They tried to have sex but he couldn't get hard. Margarita searched the corners for ghosts. He shut his wife's eyes, held up his own between thumb and forefinger and shot long tracking shots across Margarita's breasts. She rolled him over and massaged his back.

He murmured into the pillow. "I dreamed I was looking at photographs of you walking over an iron bridge with some man I didn't recognize. When I woke up I went online to see if they were real, but I had invented them. This jealousy is new for me."

Things fell to hell on Monday night. The wife's hands crawled in from the garden and smashed all of Margarita's dishes. The husband's heart and magnificent lungs shrunk, leaving him gasping. Occasionally the wife's voice would issue from his throat. "I won't cook up a fucking roast! Or grandkids either!" He grew legs again but they were hers and refused to stand for it.

"I know what we can do to keep from forgetting."

"I'll do anything."

Margarita plucked the eye from his hand and popped it into her mouth. It had a glutinous texture, like rice dough, and tasted of oil. She took the last of her silver soupspoons to her left socket. It wasn't much more painful than taking out a contact lens. Winking, she placed her eye on his tongue like a pastille.

"Swallow it whole."

They held each other and watched their slow progress through each other's interior.

On Tuesday morning she found a pile of Mr. Potato Head parts on the mattress next to her. She dumped them in a hope chest with the wife's parts and threw away the key. Safely forgotten, away from the wind.

She had the doctor fit her with a glass eye. If this was the price of love, she wanted none of it. Again and again, she took hot showers and felt each cell of her surface area scream.

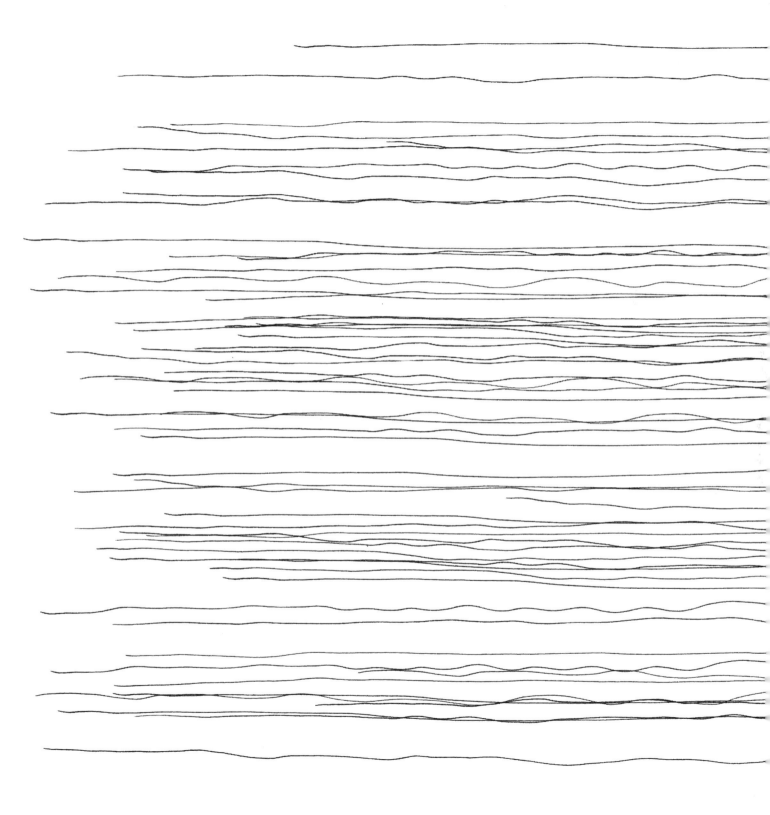

SWEET

STORY BY RACHEL BUSNARDO · ART BY VANESSA MARTINEZ

Long after the remaining secondhand smoke dissipated, Hank could still be heard passive-aggressively coughing from all the way inside Marcy's kitchen. Hank was Marcy's neighbor, though Marcy didn't know a thing about him other than he hated cigarettes and loved his lawn.

Marcy nestled into her couch and turned on the television. The stink snaking its way in from the kitchen was really getting out of control, but she'd take care of it tomorrow. It was only a problem if she wanted it to be. Besides, only a few short hours remained of Sunday and she didn't want to waste a single moment of it.

The sun was setting when Marcy heard a knock at the door. Probably one of Hank's hellions—his children had no concept of space.

When Marcy opened the door, she was struck by the sweet smell of cotton candy, which mixed with the unfortunate odor harmonizing in her living room. Like someone had rubbed her face in her own filth then tried to cover up their crime.

And under her feet stood a small, green *thing*. The thing was round with a pale green candy shell. Chocolate kisses acted as eyeholes and the mouth shaped like a scream. It came inside the house.

Marcy always was weak in her senses. She swallowed back the bile pooling under her tongue. The thing was twisted, unnatural. It plopped itself on the couch.

•

At her ordinary office job, Marcy was the pariah. Between her scent (the cigarettes), her constant vomiting, and her definite dislike of teamwork, people just didn't get on with her and Marcy was totally okay with that. Especially if it separated her from her project manager, Gale, and her daily chitchats about her children's mediocre successes, her newest gaudy hair clip, her surface-level politics, her paleo diet...

The thing had white, puffy hands and feet, but thick, black lines for limbs, like one of the many bendable toys in Gale's cubicle. They hated each other, Marcy and the thing—but Marcy and Gale too—and they both knew it the first time they saw each other. Marcy considered dialing 911, but figured the police wouldn't believe her anyway. The gun was out of ammunition so that wouldn't kill it. Setting it on fire was tempting, but not practical. She decided it was only a problem if she wanted it to be.

The thing followed her to her room. It watched her undress even when she tried to hide behind a screen. It was just there, everywhere she turned, making the air sweet. Mouth shaped like a scream.

•

After some pills, Marcy fell asleep while it watched. Like most days, she figured everything would be better in the morning.

She dreamt she was in an ordinary meeting and Bill, her boss, was assigning her to Gale's project team, which brought about a hurricane of heavy sighing. Bill said: I know, I know, but she's all we got. Marcy then went to her team meeting where first Gale said they were right on target to finish two weeks past the deadline and then Carl said he could use some overtime and offered to stay late, which caused Tiffany to protest having to stay late before anyone even asked her to, and then Gale looked to Marcy, that haystack of hair threatening to shed in Marcy's mouth at any moment, and asked if Marcy had anything productive to add to the conversation, in which Marcy replied no, letting the *o* sound sing out just a little longer than comfortable.

•

In the morning, Marcy could feel her uterus fist-bumping through her abdomen. She would have wondered if seeing the thing was a hormone-induced vision—because Tiffany at work apparently got them all the time—except that when Marcy woke up the thing was curled up next to her. She peeled her thighs off its candy sticky surface. This was when she realized there was something off about her flow. Nothing she could describe, but sort of a general knowledge that something was wrong. To confirm her suspicions, she took a little of her menstrual blood and rubbed it between her fingers. It was stickier than it

should have been. She sniffed it: sweeter than it should have been too. Upon tasting it, she knew; it wasn't blood at all, it was strawberry jam.

•

For the two-block walk to the bus station, the four-mile bus ride, and the three more blocks walking it took to get to Marcy's office, the thing followed and other people saw it. They did nothing. Marcy wondered if she was the only person who could see it and if that made the situation better or worse. In the foyer of her office building, Marcy was turning to look behind her to see if the thing made it through the revolving doors at the same time Bill was checking his stocks on his phone as he walked to the elevator. They collided, hard, but not hard enough to fall over. Marcy could see the anger pulsing through Bill's face, but he smiled and it appeared to be genuine. For the first time since she'd known him, Bill told Marcy she looked nice. He asked what new scent she was wearing. He said it reminded him of something from his childhood that he couldn't quite place.

The thing made it through the revolving doors and stood beside Bill's leg. Marcy thanked Bill for the compliment and told him she was wearing Chanel because that's all she could think of to say.

But the whole office seemed strange and not so ordinary as it normally was. People were telling Marcy hello. They stood very close to her when they spoke. In just one morning three people even thanked Marcy for always being so sweet.

It turned out all of Marcy's officemates were heading out for a Monday happy hour that night and they asked her to come. Normally, Marcy dreaded these kinds of invitations, but since they'd never asked before, she wasn't prepared with a ready-made excuse. She said she'd love to, and figured she could come up with something she forgot she needed to do after work before lunchtime.

But she wasn't really able to think about much since everyone kept coming up to her desk to be nice to her. The thing just sat on her desk, feet swinging; no one said a word about it. Marcy stayed in the office for lunch for fear of having to eat with any of her newfound fans. She was hungry, but she valued being alone much higher than being filled. Right as the others were returning, Marcy started to feel a strange pain in her shoulder. When she investigated, she felt what looked like the beginnings of some kind of cyst. As she investigated further, she found more, less painful cysts of various sizes springing up all over her body, even one on her face. The strange pustules were growing at an alarming rate. Marcy removed herself from her desk and headed to the restroom.

The thing followed.

The cysts began to sprout big purple heads like bruised nipples throbbing on her face. She did the only thing she could do. Marcy took a finger from both hands and squeezed the pustule on her face until it gave way. What erupted from the break was a thick, syrupy purple liquid. She tasted her finger: liquid grape candy.

While in the restroom, she checked to make sure her menstrual blood was still something it shouldn't have been. She reconfirmed the presence of strawberry jam. That's when Marcy looked at the thing, sitting on the sink. It was a mystery how it got up to high places; Marcy never saw it jump.

In the bathroom, Marcy lost it. She crumbled up a napkin from the automatic dispenser and threw it at the thing. Then another one. Then threw a small trashcan. The thing had no reaction. It just swung its feet; mouth shaped like a scream. I hate you! Marcy yelled. She paced back and forth feverishly. I hate you! What do you want from me? Why won't you leave me alone? What have you done to me? She yelled all these things loudly, not worrying about whether or not anyone could hear her. Or perhaps she just forgot anyone else was around. Or perhaps she was too preoccupied to consider her actions and their consequences because when several minutes later Tiffany came in, Marcy was immediately ashamed for acting crazy.

Tiffany's face conveyed concern. She asked Marcy what was wrong and Marcy told her she was sick. She told her she was really, really sick and she just didn't know how to tell anyone. Tiffany asked Marcy if she was going to die and Marcy said she didn't know. She lied, but the essence of the lie was so close to the truth it wasn't much of a lie at all.

Tiffany embraced Marcy. She stroked the back of Marcy's hair and told her to hush. Tiffany said she was there for her and not to worry. She would talk to Bill about getting Marcy some time off to get better.

•

A half an hour later Bill sent Marcy an email asking her to come to his office. When Marcy arrived, Gale was there too. She was sitting in one of the chairs where clients sat and Bill was leaning up against the front of his desk. When Marcy walked in, Bill said he was so sorry to hear that she was sick and asked if there was anything he could do to help beyond giving her some time off. Gale echoed his sentiments.

Marcy started crying again, which caused her to vomit just a little bit into her own mouth. She swallowed it back down. Bill hugged her and said there, there, it's okay. Gale got out of her chair and stroked the back of Marcy's hair, like Tiffany had done earlier, except Gale's large, inexpensive rings kept snagging on tiny strands making the motion choppy and painful.

You smell so good, Bill said. Gale agreed. Mmm, she said and then refused to believe the scent was Chanel. Marcy stopped sobbing as her two coworkers orbited around her body, sniffing the air as they went. The circus, Bill said at last. You smell like a circus. I think she smells like the snack shack at my son's little league games, Gale said.

Do you mind? Bill asked, moving his face towards Marcy's neck. He brushed her hair away from her shoulder.

This was when Marcy looked over Bill's shoulder and saw the thing sitting on Bill's desk. Its mouth shaped like a laugh. This was when Bill cupped his mouth over a seeping wound on Marcy's neck. And it was there he suckled.

This is delicious; you are DELICIOUS, he said wagging his tongue. Marcy could feel Gale lapping up a section of skin on her arm, like an animal taking a drink. I really shouldn't, Gale said. How many calories are you, do you think? Marcy didn't want to talk about it. All she wanted was to get home and wash the spit off her skin. She felt a hair in her mouth and, inexplicably, it was one of Gale's.

It would be better tomorrow. It would be better tomorrow. It would get better.

Marcy spat as she got off the elevator. There you are, Carl said. He was standing in the building's foyer. Are you coming to grab a drink with us? I sure hope so, Carl said in a wolfish voice. He playfully kept stepping in front of Marcy's pathway, which kept her from getting to the door. So she pushed him. He fell, not hard, but still he fell and he wasn't happy about it. Everyone says you're a sweet girl, he said as he stood and dusted himself off, but you're really just a sour bitch, aren't you?

Marcy ran. She ran the three blocks to the bus station, where luckily the bus was stopped, and then she ran the two blocks home. Her sweat smelled like honey, very sweet up front and a musky smell in the back.

Hank was, of course, out watering his lawn while his two little girls ran around the yard screaming in circles. Go get her! Hank yelled and the two little girls, ribbons streaming in their hair, ran towards Marcy, who was very tired by this point. Each girl grabbed a leg and held on tight while Marcy tried, as best she could, to move forward. You taste like candy! They both screamed. Candy! Candy Candy! Don't spoil your dinner! Hank called back to them. Off! Marcy yelled, but the girls kept licking. I said, Off! But they just suckled her kneecaps comparing the different flavors of her body. This one tastes like cherry! This one tastes like pineapple! She finally removed them both by their hair, which caused them to cry and run home screaming Daddy! Daddy!

When Marcy opened her front door, the thing was standing in the middle of the living room. It seemed satisfied with itself and Marcy asked it if it was. What do you want? She begged. Tell me what you want! She embraced the thing's rounded body with her arms like she was hugging a small car. I'll do anything, she said. Just tell me what you want from me! The thing didn't say a word. Marcy wondered if it even could.

She fell to her knees and began to cry. This was when her phone rang. Hello, she said. It was Bill. She could hear voices and the tings of cups and plates in the background. Bill's words were slurred as he said, we're over here at happy hour and I just want to say we all agree you should get a promotion starting immediately. He ended by thanking her for all the hard work she'd done around the office and saying this promotion was long overdue.

Marcy did what anyone would do. She accepted the promotion and said thank you. Meanwhile the thing stared, its mouth shaped like nothing. Marcy's tears were lemon-flavored and stung the sores on her face.

•

A short while later, there was a knock at the door, but Marcy found herself unable to move. The thing answered the door instead, stretching its bendable arm up to the knob.

Hank looked furious on the other side of the door. You hurt my daughters, he said. How dare you. Get up, he commanded. But Marcy couldn't get up even if she wanted to. The truth was she was melting. Her skin was no longer a solid and her insides were starting to bleed out. Strawberry jam leaked all over the area rug.

What's wrong with you? Hank asked, confused. Actually he wondered how he hadn't noticed Marcy's misshapen body before. Help me, Marcy said through corn syrup saliva. Hank agreed, reluctantly. I'll get help, he said, and disappeared from the doorway.

The thing shrugged and then checked its watch. It gave a little wave goodbye and left. Somehow Marcy knew she'd never see it again, and though she was thankful for that, she also knew the reason why.

•

She vomited, but this time she didn't hold it in. She

let it come out and spill over her remaining form. Warm banana ice cream sat on top of the jam. Everything felt soft and sticky until Marcy felt nothing at all. All of her senses vanished except one. Her sense of taste. All of her flavors pooled on her tongue and poured down what remained of her throat. She could taste everything, all of her sweetness, all of it at once, and it was drowning her.

It was then that she floated outside of her body. Marcy never thought it was true, that the near-dead could see themselves from above, but she did.

She watched as the front door swung open. She watched as her living room flooded with first responders led by Hank. Is this her? A paramedic asked pointing at the puddle. That's her all right, Hank replied.

What is this stuff? Another paramedic asked scooping up a pile of gelatinous sweet stuff with a spade. I haven't smelled anything like this since I was a boy, he said.

It reminds me of the candy store I take my kids to over on Maple Street, the other paramedic said.

This takes me back, a firefighter said, my grandma used to always make strawberry preserves when I was a boy.

Cherry pie, a police officer said wagging his finger in the air. Just like my wife makes for my birthday every year.

This is the sweetest thing I've ever smelled, an EMT said kneeling over the puddle that was once Marcy, reminds me of a girl I liked in fifth grade. He took the tip of his finger and swirled it around in the muck. Once his finger was good and coated, he stuck his finger into his mouth. You've got to try this, he said. The paramedics, the firefighters, the police, all circled around, taking handfuls of Marcy's body and putting it into their mouths and, with only one taste, they too were hooked.

SECOND LEGS

STORY BY JOANNA ROYE • ART BY CHRISTINA COLLINS

When I was a child, growing up in Dardanelle, Arkansas, my shinbones sprouted out of my legs and rolled away. It's a thing I watched happen to my own body. I felt it from the inside out. My second legs were a part of me—a precious, sweet, strange part of me. And then they left me over the course of a night spent sweating on the bathroom floor.

It was the summer when I was ten. Despite being a healthy child, I complained every day about the ache in my legs. My mother told me it was just "growing pains." My father told me what I'd get if I kept up my whining. As it was explained to me at the time, amid the clink of wet china and the slop of frothy dishwater, growing pains are what happen when the bones in a child's legs grow faster than the meat around them.

"When will it stop?" I asked, hearing myself begin to whine. My voice quieted as my shame rose.

My mother paused to push a strand of hair behind one ear with her wrist. Haloed in the rising mist and the sickly light above the sink, the line that pressed deep between her eyebrows seemed to gouge further.

"Honey, I don't know," she sighed, and turned her exhausted eyes away from me.

The school year was finishing up and the other kids got growing pains too. They told me it hurt them in the front of their thighs. Mine hurt in my shins. All I got was passing looks of confusion when I told them this. None of the other kids got growing pains in their shins.

Sometimes I'd get home and find my mother in the sitting room that was for company only. There she'd be, alone and silent in the wing-backed chair, smoking and looking out the window at the McArry's barking dog. The sitting room was the last place I looked for her, and I was surprised each time I discovered her. I knew I was intruding when I'd come to her, little kid tears leaking out of the corners of my eyes, and tell her how much my legs hurt. My throat dried up when I broke into whatever clandestine things she was thinking as she gathered ash into an empty whiskey tumbler.

My mother would exhale a cloud and walk graceless to the refrigerator. She'd take a bag of frozen peas out, wrap it in a dishcloth, and slap it on one of my legs. The cold distracted me and numbed the pain for a while. She'd pause for a moment, watching me until I'd stopped sniffling, then go back to the sitting room and close the door.

After thirty minutes, the pain would come back. I'd knock on the door and complain again, and my mother would grouse at me for complaining when the peas had obviously helped my legs for the past half hour. I would chew on my lips, trying to untangle how the peas had indeed numbed me for a while, but hadn't actually cured the aching. She'd sigh and look out the window. The sound of the barking dog would fill up the emptiness. When my mother finally spoke, it was softly, and to banish me to my room. I used to lay on my bedspread on those afternoons, curled up on my side like a dying squirrel, and try to ride through the misery.

One day when I was massaging the growing pains, I noticed bumps about a third of the way down toward my ankles. They felt like BBs lodged beneath the skin, one for each shin. I knew how embedded BBs worked thanks to my sadistic brother, Otto, but these didn't shift when I touched them. Instead, they caused excruciating spasms to ripple up over my knees to my thighs. After a few days, I adjusted and the agony faded into curiosity. I would press and prod them, exploring and wondering what they could be.

Then while I was sitting up in the cloistered fragrant shadows of the magnolia tree, it hit me: maybe my legs were broken. Maybe the nubs were bits of bones that had shattered off, or maybe the tips of my shinbones themselves. One part of me said, How could you have climbed almost to the top of the magnolia tree if your legs are broke? But another whispered What if they are? What if there's something wrong and you don't know it?

I got nervous, so I showed my mother the bumps. She poked and prodded at them herself. Tears streamed down my cheeks.

"Good Lord, I told him if he ever shot you with BBs again..." my mother muttered. Her call for Otto pealed through the house like a rifle shot. When she found him, he was sentenced to his room for three days.

Later that night, I heard the door creak. I saw Otto's shadow there. Closing the door quietly behind him, he stepped over the squeaking floorboards to my bed. I saw the broom handle in his fist. He cracked it across my legs. The thin summer sheets didn't cushion against it. He whispered, "If you cry out or scream or even whimper, I'll put it somewhere else."

Somehow, something mysterious and unseen protected me. It kept the broom handle from striking the nubs. The next day my shins were black and green and blue. I wore my long church skirt to hide them from my mother.

The nubs grew. In a week they were an inch long. Once while I was studying them and playing with them in the bathroom, the thought occurred to me that perhaps my legs were like the roots of a mangrove tree. I'd read about the mangrove swamps down in Florida, and the branching protrusions of my shins seemed to follow the form of a reaching root. I couldn't imagine why my skeleton would be seeking to plant an extra limb to the ground, but it wasn't keeping me from walking. In fact, I'd become more graceful out of the practice of avoiding coffee tables, corners, ottomans.

It was a Saturday when my skin split. It looked like someone had taken my father's razor blade and sliced down the front of each of my shins. The shoots of bone that'd been growing so diligently had finally burst through. It happened in the night, while I was asleep. I remember waking just before dawn, groping to understand the pain in the half-darkness. I remember throwing the sheet off me and seeing my flesh spreading open, revealing the pale yellow stalks. The nubs had leaked a clear liquid and soaked my sheets and mattress.

The next morning, I dressed quickly to hide my disfigurement. It was excruciating to pull my bobby socks up over the bones. I didn't fold them down and they looked strange coming all the way up to the knee. The quarter-sized bows that usually looked so pretty on the outside were now cramped under the fabric and left their own mysterious lumps. Bows and bones, hidden under the dingy cotton.

After breakfast, my mother discovered my bed. She paddled me for a crime I thought I'd left behind by the age of six. I whimpered at the humiliation. In my squirming, I knocked my right shin bone into her leg. She froze, spoon raised in the June heat, and ordered me to take off my shoes and roll down my socks. There was a quick sip of breath, the wrinkles of her face ironing out in astonishment when she laid eyes on my splits. Her cheeks pale, she took me and dabbed Mercurochrome into the wounds. The angry pink of the gashes was covered over by the bright red-orange of the medicine.

When my father got home, he grabbed Otto by the collar and dragged him to the lawnmower shed for a spectacular beating. My mother dutifully put Mercurochrome on him too. Dinner was conducted in silence. Every time I heard Otto sniff under his bruising eyes, I heard a crack of that broom handle, as if each stroke had been written down in a ledger.

Amid the screeching sound of silverware on plates, and the burping, chewing, popping noises of my family's mouths, I felt something shift. It was as if the world around me became a vast, uncanny, and unpredictable place. A place full of wonderful surprises. Excitement tingled in my belly. I couldn't wait for my second legs to finish growing.

Two weeks went by. I learned how to dab Mercurochrome and how to apply bandages. My mother stopped doing it for me after the second dressing. She'd kept swallowing, as if something were stuck in her throat and she was trying to wash it down. Then, all of a sudden, she threw down the roll of bandaging tape and said she'd be right back. I didn't knock on the sitting room door. I learned to take care of myself.

One night, my legs woke me up.

I hobbled to the bathroom, swallowing my lips as I limped past windows of moonlight. I didn't dare cry out and wake the rest of the house. Once in the safety of the bathroom, I quietly closed the door and leaned over the sink, crying until saliva dripped from my open mouth. It was a while before I got up the courage to unbandage my legs. With the exception of a small patch of tile around the shower, our bathroom was carpeted. I sat down on that musty mauve-colored carpet, tailbone going numb, writhing slowly and wordlessly as I unwrapped the gauze that bound my calves.

With each pass, the sensation shifted. My mind whispered hysterically as it began to imagine what I'd find underneath. Maybe my second legs had branched, dividing over and over like those mangrove roots. Maybe they had fragmented and a shattered mush would fall heavy to the carpet with the wrappings. Maybe something more than just bone was growing there, and I'd see red tendrils dipping in and out of the tips of the bones like hummingbird tongues. Even though the pain lessened with each loop, my dread expanded, not wanting to see.

It turns out, the pain was being caused by the bandages themselves. They'd been putting pressure on my second legs, trying to squeeze them back into line with my normal ones. I gulped in a single deep breath and rested my head back against the wall for a moment. Now that the bandages were off, I could see my precious bones. They rose out at an angle like toy battleship guns sighting a target. As they slowly relaxed into their natural position, I saw they were four inches long now.

I cried with relief. The pain moved in my mind into something manageable, the pall of fear and confusion dissolving away, leaving only the burning ache of physicality. I sat there for a long time, looking down at those two pale parts of me. I pulled a towel over and used it to soak up the liquid that had begun to trickle from the second legs down my calves and over my ankles. For the first time, I just existed with my second legs bare in the timeless late-night light of the bathroom, private and unashamed. I fell asleep like that, sitting against the wall across from the sink.

The most excruciating pain I've ever felt woke me. I cupped my hands under my knees and looked. My second legs were working their way out. I watched them shift side to side. I thought of a snail's eyes, slimy stalks moving and rocking. They were six inches long now and steadily extending. Something in me wanted to cry out, but I couldn't manage a sound. I gazed at my second legs as they struggled to get free of my body.

Then the right one popped. It separated wetly but definitely, like when my father twisted off the Thanksgiving turkey's drumsticks. It fell to the floor, leaving a dappling of bright red blood on the dull carpet. The asymmetry hurt me then. There was a hollow hole on the right, a still-writhing bone on the left. My mind felt funny, pulled thin and in odd directions. In the haze, my mouth dry, the left one went.

I cried and reached for one. Something tickled the right side of my face, and I realized I was soaked in sweat. That's when the second legs began to roll. As if they were blown by some secret wind, they unstuck themselves from the bloodstains and the carpet fibers and rolled. Like my brother's broom handle, like my mother's loose cigarettes, they rolled across the floor, escaping. They slipped between the carpet and the cheap wood of the door and disappeared.

I was left there with my single pair of legs. I put my fingers into my wounds and hurt myself, looking for another set of nubs, hoping the process would begin again. Praying I wasn't alone now.

The next morning my mother found me bunched up behind the door. My shins were already beginning to heal, pulling themselves back together, covering up. My mother looked at my legs, that line in her head deepening. She smoked at the breakfast table for the first time that day, the filter wrinkling with orange juice.

A month later, when it was time for school to start again, my mother went to clean out my brother's closet. In the back corner, under socks and worn-out shirts, she discovered two dirty magazines and a pile of bones. Most were animal bones. I got a chance to spy on them when she went storming through the house calling for Otto, clutching the stiff, water-damaged magazines. In the bone pile there were chipmunk skulls and rib cages from roasted chickens.

And, in the center, I saw my second legs! They must have found this nest of their kin after they abandoned me. Just then, my mother returned, red-faced, with a brush and dustpan. She slapped the bones out of my hands and screamed at me to play outside.

I spun on the tire swing and the scars on my shins itched. Soon, my father came home. Dinner was conducted in silence. The smell of Mercurochrome hung in the air.

As I scraped the dinner plates into the trash, I saw my second legs for the last time. My mother had just dumped them in the garbage. Even among the potato peels and ripped magazine pages and ash from the whiskey tumbler, my bones still looked beautiful. They reminded me of piano keys or a fine Chinese flute. My mother's voice snapped across the kitchen; her words stung the back of my neck.

I brought her the plates. I didn't speak when my mother told Otto to take out the trash. I didn't speak when she told me to go to bed. I lay awake all night. I scratched my shins. When dawn gave definition to the room, I heard the roaring and hissing of the early morning garbage truck. I heard the men call to each other as they slung the contents of our trashcan into the back. I listened as its rumbles faded to the next house and the next house and the next. I didn't speak when my mother gave me breakfast in the morning.

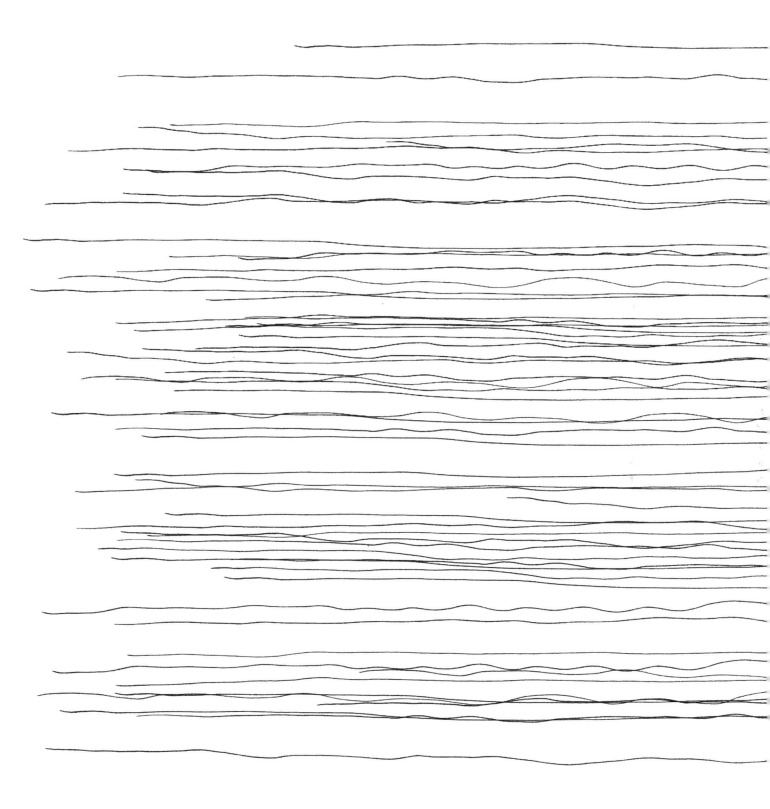

BELLY-FULL & TENDER LOINS

STORY BY CHRISTINA LYDIA • ART BY LAURA GWYNNE

Ashes soft on bare skin, cold from the night's fire pit. Gentle for her scars. Embedded memories each deeply marked with varying lengths. Chinchillas move like her, squirming in the snow dirt ash, blood mingling in her hairy armpits, ice crystals sticking to her toenails. She takes a handful, swipes horizontal left-right swishes, softening long stretch marks on her abdomen with a bony forefinger. She smiles. Her body in a thick layer. Swollen curves, sore back and feet. She adds more to soften the skin all around. Closes her eyes.

A week after the blizzard had settled, her father took her hunting to the last known source for fresh venison. The sun, its shine irregular. A leftover frosty breeze, dry moisture from her breath. Although barren of things crawling but for imprinted hooves pockmarked in the freshly poured snow, it was a peaceful place. Green grass and brown weeds grew in patches surrounding a stain of mangled elm trees. Snow melted in small puddles. She imagined birds drinking, bathing. Living.

Her father told her to wait for his signal—a low whistle like a stream of air blown from soft lips into a wooden flute. E sharp. F. She found refuge behind one of those mangled trees for what at first seemed like hours but was only a few minutes by the sun's count. Heat rose from the ground in slow circles, mixing with the air above like a half-formed torrent failing to become a full-fledged adult. She closed her eyes and breathed in the smell of earth. She savored the few moments of solitude by sitting underneath wasted branches and on newly formed mulch.

Sunshine reflected in steady twirls, her gut hook knife expertly handled in a rhythmic tempo, sharp end pointed to sky then snow, her heartbeat the metronome. Her eyes landed on two ravens by a splintered tree trunk. Big birds. Almost the size of eagles. One was larger than the other, its beak sharper. They fought each other, claws outstretched, bodies partway in flight, for a small chunk of rotten meat. It looked like rabbit. Tar feathers littered the snow like scraps of blown tire rubber. Claws hooked each other's wings, noisy shrieks momentarily filled the air with life. They were too large to take both out. Too sharp their claws for use with a knife unintended for this type of kill. Unfortunate.

The ravens fought like gods, their attention elsewhere. She leered at their forms. Their twigged wings lifted the snow as they circled the air in full whirls. They did not notice when her hand, knife outstretched, also aimed for the chunk. Slowly, she sat on her heels, belly to knees in a low squat, and squirmed her way with a left foot shimmy and then a right foot shimmy. Left and right. It became her mating song, she with the knife for that small chunk of meat. She needed that meat.

The wind picked up its pace, her cheekbones deep grooves like on a sports car. They made her movements faster, slicker. Aimed her foot to balance her weight, she leaned in, off-center from the fight—her left hand hovered with the knife, her right gripped a tree branch. She paused to feel the wind move her like a leaf. Some would have called it hesitation. She called it timing. She felt it rising— a knowing. A feeling more than the sum of *go* or *now*. Primal. Deep. Understood as words unsaid. Leaned in, knife leading body, breath inhaled slowly. Then exhaled. Through her exhale, she aimed her knife and picked. The chunk stuck. Slowly, she retracted her body, coiling like a snake around a branch. Without much thought, she returned to her original spot, her feet leading her along a freshly worn path. She sifted through the chunk, squished the few maggots it had and took a bite.

Sunsets no longer held that magical quality of hope for a new day. Its light was permanently hazed within clouds of ash booming from distant fires whose daily excess covered everything in a fine layer. She imagined a sky once blended with reds and oranges, tones of purple within the blue. She imagined warm summers, long beaches, stretches of endless water lapping effortlessly onto the sand in a hypnotic, rhythmic tempo.

Her father's soft signal came when it turned dark. Eight hours, by her count, did she walk among remaining limbs of mangled elm trees. She saw a low light, the beginnings of a fire, loom not too far from where she was. She walked toward it.

The soon-to-be barbecued meat was a heavenly urge too hard for her to keep in. She cleared her throat when she approached him.

"It took longer this time."

His eyes flicked to hers as he cleaned his knife on a rag. They lingered on her belly. "The deer are less now. But I got this girl right here." He pointed with his knife. "Come check her out."

In the middle of a snowy meadow lay a twitchy deer, large in belly. Red flowed into the snow. It slowly pumped from a slit in her throat. The heart did all the work. This one needed a meat hook, higher elevation. Gravity. But the slit would do. The puddle reached her shoes. She eyed the deer's belly and felt her own. It was all too messy, too big. Would attract too much attention from bigger things.

"Weren't there others? Smaller maybe? Less messy."

His tongue roved across his upper lip in a soft, languid motion.

"No. But this one's special right here." His eyes met hers as he smiled coyly. "Double prize."

She smiled back and took a breath, calmed her pounding heart. Gripped her knife. The night always played tricks with her. Thoughts of dinner on oak tables. Pots on electric stoves. Television. Beer. Former luxuries that were all too comforting. Too alluring. Once, when she was nine, she and her classmates stood in a choir room, voices in tune to "Wade In The Water." Singing was a comfort she would never disregard. It was her clutch but it gave her strength. The song and its doleful melody was a reminder of present times. She cleared her thoughts with it. Took hold of her knife. She waded into that blood water with her Moses-led shoes, blood soaking up her once white shirt and blue pants like—

"God's gonna trouble the water..."

The deer moved her big eyes as she approached. Mouth opened, closed as if to say she understood what was going on. With the blade hooked under skin, she pulled her knife roughly upwards like if shearing leather fibers or a corn husk. Blood stained her hands and stuck to the handle. She stood back to observe her choppy lines. The deer's legs were twitchy, squirmy. She would be quick.

Belly-full and tender loins some would have called it. She called it fawn venison. Infant so tender the flesh fell off the bones when cooked over a spit. Mother nature meat. The juicy fat dripped up her elbow and mixed with dried blood. She cleaned her fingers on her shirt. Tossed the bones into the fire pit. Watched the fire swell slightly as if acknowledging an offering before quieting down again. She leaned back onto her elbows. Stretched her legs. She glanced at her small growing belly. Felt it warm for the first time. Tender. Full. She looked at her father. Steady eyes met hers, watched her movements. He scooted closer.

The fire, warm. The food, filling. The blood, intoxicating. Leaned in, she nestled her forehead against his shoulder. Smelled his fatherly smell. She imagined a strong tenor singing her lullabies, prickly cheeks against her own, soft touches on her skin. She traced his bottom lip with her finger. Felt him quiver. The wind was a playful breeze, the fire a low ember. Dazed were his eyes. She met them back with her own.

Pressed lips. Soft whimpers. Quiet moans. Leg twitchy squirms and pleasurable caresses. She murmured love things, dirty things to his ears. The air cool against her back, his body warm against her. Sweat shimmying stickiness between her swollen breasts. Her breath a rhythmic puff in the moonlight. Never did she imagine the warmth of an older man and his ever-familiar comfort to be more fulfilling than any other boy she ever had.

Afterwards, they lay bare in tattered blankets, his form a silhouette against the moonlight. The cool air gently hardened her nipples. With her body temporarily sated in hunger and desire, she caressed her abdomen. Her thoughts lingered at the large pack that was once a mother deer. It was a chopped carcass awaiting its journey as their food for a few weeks. "The deer are less now," her father had told her. Perhaps this once-mother deer was

the only choice. The surest for survival. Her finger traced newly formed stretch marks against her small bump. A barren land full of mangled elm trees, tar feathered snow, maggot filled meat. She imagined her belly, round and full of life. An eventual infant. She inhaled, exhaled slowly. Perhaps they made the land forever barren.

She closed her eyes, dreamed of God and ash, scars deeply embedded with carnivore succulent desires. She dreamed her father was daddy and she was daughter and they were family once again. She saw blood and hunger, a belly-full of meat sliced in horizontal left-right swishes, snow dirt ash mingling to her skin. Flaws so morbid she zipped them up lengthwise, her hardened guts and damaged heart rotting away inside.

He was gone in the morning, looking for a new place to sleep. Something he always did after they lay. Her hand moved to her scars. A fine layer of freshly powdered ash covered the fire pit. Slowly she crawled to it, the left-over blood in the snow smearing on her knees, the snow and the dirt beneath rising with each shuffle she made. Her swollen curves became heavier with every passing moment.

She saw the bones she tossed in, remembered the fire's slight swell, the accepted offering. She paused. Felt it rising—a knowing. She grabbed a handful of ash and smeared it against her body. She lay on the snow and dug her fingers in the dirt underneath. Its warmth radiated to her hands, her body craving its energy. She took a deep breath, stretched her legs, and closed her eyes.

POSTLUDE

GRAVEYARD SHIFTS

STORY BY BRENDA SIECZKOWSKI • ART BY WILHELMINA BONES

My job: to snuff any fitful buried—in graveyard parlance, "scrabblers."

To rattle the rails of burial ladders or seal off moss-domed escape hatches. Plaster over glassy-eyed periscope lenses. Muffle the vexatious chorus of gravel-throated casket bells coughing under the evergreens. Under inexorable erasure.

What a stiff nuisance, inhumation: a clamoring for locked coffins, imprisoning crypts! And yet hardly a corpse is buried but a skeleton key is sewed into the hem of its shroud. How much more natural to lay out cadavers in cradles of combed grass—at nightfall, the graveyard transformed to a votive garden of flickering corpse lights.

The fine print of my funerary apprenticeship, as the years rolled over, dissolved to the grainy pollen of a weathered epitaph. Yet one vital provision remained deeply engraved in my brain: should I prove proficient in discharging the above duties, at the expiration of a fixed period I might entertain hopes of ascending to floating groundskeeper and thence, perhaps, to associate spiritual landscaper—positions more palatable to my vegetative ambitions.

The tedious nature of my duties, however, necessitated the introduction of a number of expedient methods of my own devising were I to preserve sufficient leisure for horticultural study.

The casket bells, for example.

Whether their sporadic tollings were indeed effected by the shifting of a corpse as it frothed under bloat and blowfly, or by the spasmatic quaking of a body escaping its cataleptic swoon, I was never under great pains to discover. Rather, I carried a pair of pruning shears on my person at all times, with which I was easily and irrevocably able to sever the attached cords.

Other facets of my environment proved more agreeable. The copper umbels attached to subterranean ventilation tubes served efficaciously to conduct certain odorous gases—cadaverine, purtrescine—whose detection ensured I need trouble myself with monitoring a particular plot no more. And, naturally, my sphere of employ provided ample granite slabs indispensable for pressing and preserving sprays of freckled stargazers, gold-bladed chrysanthemums, white camellias plucked from virginal burial mounds.

The sarcophagus of M.—, a mausoleum resident of long tenancy, served passably as a table upon which I could spread open my much-thumbed copy of Linnaeus's *Species Plantarum*. On propitious nights, I potted what botanical cuttings I could salvage from the funerary carnage on its marble lid.

Most flowers, once lopped, are fated to irrevocable decay. But the roses—these it was possible to propagate, resurrect, while the leaves were yet filled with green sugar, the corolla bright as blood. Each night in my sepulchre, I wormed a finger into urns of freshly turned earth, positioned rose slips, and tamped down dirt. Harbored the cuttings in scoured honey jars. Soon, my gardening closet overflowed with rose shoots respiring in glass globes, licking into root.

I took to injecting the honey, as neighboring beehives swarmed the peak of harvest, down the breathing tubes' black maws.

So that the dead might rest embalmed in sweetness, so that the dead lie enduringly still, lulled by the hum of blue lividity softening to wax.

Though, Reader, I did not.

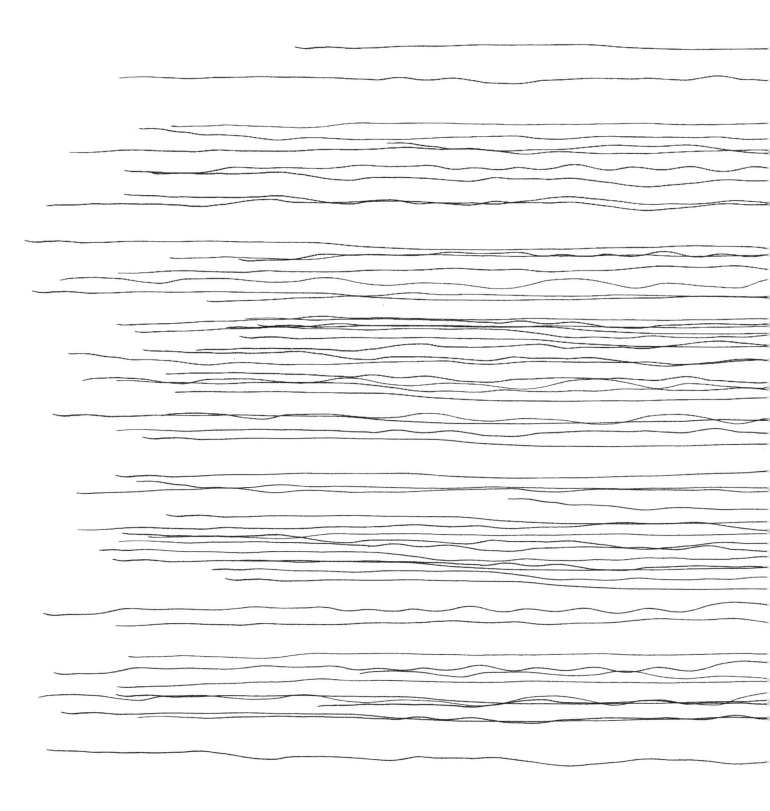

CONTRIBUTORS

Bonnie Alexander is a freelance writer from San Diego. She is a graduate of Northwestern University and currently resides in Israel with her partner.

For **Kristy Blackwell**, figurative work creates a space in which both the artist and the viewer may experience self exploration. The surface upon which she paints is the meeting place between the artist, the subject, and the viewer through a shared human experience. Trained in fine art and, thereafter, in computer animation, Kristy has had an accomplished career as a digital matte painter and compositor on over 50 feature films. But Kristy's first love is fine art and her experience creating photo-real digital images has inspired her to experiment with various traditional techniques and materials to both create and deconstruct reality on canvas or other supports. Kristy was raised in small town Manitoba and Ontario and has spent the last seventeen years living and working in Toronto with her husband and two daughters.

wilhelmina bones is a digital artist. she likes some video games, most chocolate cakes, and all cats.

Colleen Burner is a writer and artist, co-editor of *Shirley Magazine*, and Oregon Literary Women Writer's Fellowship recipient. Her work has appeared in *Quaint Magazine* and *Permafrost*. She lives in Portland, Oregon.

Rachel Busnardo received her MFA from the University of Colorado at Boulder where she now teaches creative writing. Her work has appeared in *Bone Bouquet*, *Dreginald*, *deComp*, *Madhat Lit* and and other places. She currently lives in Boulder, CO where she spends a lot of time in her garden.

Cait Cole is a writer and artist from New York. Her work has appeared in *Bitterzoet Magazine*, *Slink Chunk Press*, *The Strangelet*, and others. She is also the creator of the Pacific Northwest zine *Witch Crafts*. She studies creative writing and visual arts at The Evergreen State College in Olympia, Washington, where she resides with her husband and dog.

Christina Collins is a visual artist, writer, editor, and musician. She currently lives in Minneapolis.

Jennifer D. Corley is a writer, editor, and storytelling coach in Southern California. Works can be found in *Hobart*, *Queen Mob's Tea House*, *States of Terror Vol. III*, *More Monologues For Women, By Women*, and elsewhere. She is a recipient of a Community Voices Fellowship in Playwriting from The Old Globe in San Diego, and a recent participant of Tin House's Summer Workshop for short fiction.

Mary Crosbie is a writer and performer who lives in New York. She has so many cats! Cats, cats, cats! Visit: www.marycrosbie.com

Sarah Girdzius is a Chicago born artist making stuff in San Diego.

Madeline Gobbo's illustrations have appeared in *Full Stop Quarterly*, *Meridian*, and *Queen Mob's Tea House*, and are forthcoming in the erotic fanfiction anthology *Loose Lips*. Her collaborative fiction with Miles Klee has appeared in *McSweeney's Internet Tendency*, *Territory*, *Hexus*, *Funhouse*, *Joyland*, *Another Chicago*, and *Wigleaf*. She lives in Davis, California.

Melissa Gutierrez is an artist and writer living and working in Northern California. Find her on Twitter @mmgutz.

Laura Gwynne says *"Black Candies por vida."*

Christine Hamm has a PhD in American Poetics, and is an editor for Ping*Pong Press. She is currently an MFA poetry student at Columbia University. Her poetry has been published in *Orbis, Nat Brut, BODY, Poetry Midwest, Rattle, Dark Sky*, and many others. She has been nominated five times for a Pushcart Prize, and she teaches English at Pace. Echo Park, her third book of poems, came out from Blazevox in the fall of 2011. The New Orleans Review published Christine's chapbook, *A is for Afterimage,* and nominated her work for a Pushcart in 2014, and in 2017, Ghostbird Press is publishing an excerpt from her ongoing manuscript, *Notes on Wolves and Ruin.*

Rayna Hernandez is a South Dakota native. She recently received her bachelor's degree at the University of South Dakota in both English and Art. Her work reflects upon intersectionality and her hybridized identity.

Claire Hero is the author of *Sing, Mongrel*. Her poetry and prose has appeared or is forthcoming in *Bennington Review, Black Warrior Review, Cincinnati Review, Handsome, Lady Churchill's Rosebud Wristlet*, and elsewhere.

Lily Hoang is the author of five books, including *A Bestiary* (winner of the inaugural Cleveland State University Poetry Center's Nonfiction Contest) and *Changing* (recipient of a PEN Open Books Award). With Joshua Marie Wilkinson, she edited the anthology *The Force of What's Possible: Writers on Accessibility and the Avant-Garde.* She is Director of the MFA program at New Mexico State University. She serves as Editor at Puerto del Sol and for Jaded Ibis Press.

Carrie Anne Hudson is a visual artist from San Diego, California. As an illustrator and painter with a natural fascination for all things strange and spooky, she hopes to open the darker doors of the imagination.

Jessica Lanay is currently an MFA candidate in the poetry program at the University of Pittsburgh where she also is the Graduate Student Assistant at the Center for African American Poetry and Poetics. Originally from Key West, Florida, she arrived to Pittsburgh by way of New York. Most recently she worked at *Poets & Writers Magazine*. Lanay received her MA in Latin American, Caribbean and Iberian Studies with focuses in Art History and African Diasporan History. She received her BA in Art History from Agnes Scott College. She is a Callaloo and Cave Canem Fellow. Lanay is a short fiction and poetry writer; her work has been published in *Acentos Review, Crab Fat Magazine, Five Quarterly, Sugar House Review, Salt Hill Review*, and others. She has work forthcoming in *Tinderbox Poetry Journal*, and *TAYO*.

Gabrielle Joy Lessans lives in Colorado, writing, teaching, doing yoga & playing with her cat.

A graduate of San Diego State University, **Christina Lydia** holds a Master of Arts degree in Rhetoric and Writing as well as a Bachelor of Arts degree in English and in Social Science. She is a writer of all forms and classifications that involve the written word as its primary source of communication and/or art. She is the Founder, Administrator, and Creative Deviser for a humble online interdisciplinary journal called *The Black Lion*. When she is not being quirky or laughing at her own jokes, she is often found ruffling through her bookshelf or writing. You can find her on twitter @cina_lydia and @TBLJournal.

Jennifer Manalili is an aspiring Filipino writer. Raised on Star Trek reruns, she is passionate about science-fiction and horror, feminism, and spreading the word about being body positive. She can often be found drinking iced coffee, listening to Beyoncé, or watching a whole lot of Food Network.

Since 2008, **Florence Ann Marlowe** has been published by e-magazines and hard copy publications such as *Macabre Cadaver, Demon Minds, Pseudopod, 69 Flavors of Paranoia, Dedman's Tome, Death Head Grin, Fantastic Horror and Wiley Writers.* Her stories have also appeared in the anthologies *Reflux, Peep Show Volume 2, The Pulpateers, Fantastic Horror's Temptations and Other Sins, Fear's Accomplice* and *Fear's Accomplice: Halloween, Terror at the Beach* and the upcoming issue of *Ladies and Gentleman of Horror.* She has just finished her first novel titled *The Bitter Dead* and is looking for a publisher. Originally from Hoboken, Florence has lived from one end of New Jersey to the other and currently lives on a small farm in southern New Jersey. Her closest neighbor happens to be the Jersey Devil.

Rachel Marston lives in central Minnesota, where she has been introduced to the wonderful world of the hot dish, below zero temperatures, and meat raffles. She is an Assistant Professor of English at the College of Saint Benedict and Saint John's University in Minnesota. Her fiction and nonfiction have appeared in *Shimmer, Event,* and *The Collagist,* among other journals.

Vanessa Martinez lives in San Diego and sometimes draws as an attempt to make porous the surfaces with which we define our universe and give form to the sludge that lies beneath.

Kayla Miller is John Wayne as a queer gal with an MFA. She was born and raised in Jonesboro, Georgia, and currently lives in the Wild West of Las Vegas with her dog. She has won a Talbot International Award for her writing and will be headlining the 2017 Agnes Scott College Writers' Festival alongside Claudia Rankine and Mat Johnson. Her work has appeared or is forthcoming in

the journals *Tahoma Literary Review, hold: a journal,* and *Profane.* She writes about ugly folks doing ugly things.

San Diego illustrator **Mishanthrope** specializes in fine line, black & white art. Her focus on the female figure, body horror & depressing themes form a body of work that's described as "beautifully grotesque." For updates on new work & upcoming exhibitions, visit www.mishanthrope.com or instagram.com/mishanthropeart.

Laurie Nasica is a French born illustrator, artist, and educator just hoping for the best.

Subashini Navaratnam lives in Selangor, Malaysia and has published poetry and prose in *Quarterly Literary Review Singapore, Mascara Literary Review, Aesthetix, Sein und Werden, minor literature[s], Anak Sastra, Jaggery, Halo Literary Magazine, Liminality: A Magazine of Speculative Poetry,* and *Dead King.* Her writings on books have appeared in *The Star* (Malaysia), *Pop Matters, 3:AM Magazine* and *Full Stop* and she has published nonfiction in MPH's anthology, *Sini Sana* and fiction in *KL Noir: Yellow.* She tweets at @SubaBat.

Marie Johnson Parrish is a writer with roots all over the United States, most recently the Mountain West. She holds an MFA from Southern Illinois University Carbondale and hopes someday to live in a Victorian mansion with a bad reputation and bats in the attic. Her previous work has been published in *Gingerbread House Literary Magazine.*

Danielle Renino has a minor in Creative Writing and an affinity for things that go bump in the night. When she isn't reading or writing, she can be found exploring her favorite abandoned asylum. Want to go on a ghost hunt? You don't need to ask her twice!

Johanna Ross is a fiction writer, memoirist, painter and salvage artist who lives in the stunningly inspirational high desert of Joshua Tree, California. She likes to hug trees and giant rabbits.

Joanna Roye lives in the hills south of Blacksburg, Virginia with her husband, daughter, and lots of bloodthirsty cats. She loves gimlets, opossums, and weird stories from around the world. She considers horror an exercise in building empathy. "Second Legs" is her first published work.

This is the first fictional work **Jeanette Sanchez-Izenman** has shown anyone she is not related to. She lives in Tacoma, WA with her amazing husband, a tiny cuddly dog and an evil cat. She does theatre in her spare time.

Carabella Sands enjoys free food.

Brenda Sieczkowski's poems and creative essays have appeared widely in print and on-line journals, including *The Colorado Review, Versa, The New England Review, Poetry Daily, Verse Daily, Diagram, The Florida Review, Bone Bouquet, The Seneca Review, Western Humanities Review, Gulf Coast, Dusie, Sidebrow, and Subtropics* among others. Her essays have won awards from both *Writers at Work* and *Knee-Jerk Magazine*. She has published two chapbooks, *Wonder Girl in Monster Land* (dancing girl press, 2012) and *Fallout & Flotation Devices* (Little Red Leaves Textile Series, 2014). *Like Oysters Observing the Sun,* her full-length poetry collection, was published by Black Lawrence Press in 2014.

T.A. Stanley lives in Brooklyn. She writes and does other things. Her work has appeared in *The Atlas Review, Belleville Park Pages, Crack the Spine Literary Journal,* among others and is forthcoming in *Paper Darts*. Follow her on twitter @ladytstanz

Hanna Tawater completed her MFA in writing, with an emphasis in poetry, at UC San Diego in 2014. Some of her work can be found in *Dirty Chai, New Delta Review, White Stag, The Radvocate, States of Terror vols. 1 & 2,* and *Amor Forense: Birds in Shorts City*—an anthology of border-region translations, as well as various online collaborative projects on *Entropy* and elsewhere. She cohabitates in California with two cats, a snake, and a man.

Rachel Lee Taylor is a whey-faced, egg sucking, trash-bandit. She is also a graduate of UC San Diego's MFA in Creative Writing, and her work can be found in *States of Terror Vol. 1* (Ayahuasca Publishing) and *Beyond the Taboo* (White Stag Press). Follow Rachel on twitter @HagBeast.

Chelsea Laine Wells has been published in *Hobart, The Collapsar, New South, The Butter, Third Point Press, The Other Stories, PANK,* and *Heavy Feather,* among others, and has work forthcoming from *Paper Darts*. She is managing and fiction editor of *Hypertext Magazine* and founding editor of *Hypernova Lit* (a journal publishing the work of teenagers), as well as a high school librarian and creative writing teacher. Her work is represented by Maria Massie of Lippincott Massie McQuilken. Find out more about her at www.chelsealainewells.com and follow her on Twitter at @chelsea_l_w.

EDITORIAL STAFF

GUEST EDITOR

Natanya Ann Pulley is Diné (Navajo) and writes fiction and non-fiction with outbreaks in poetry and collage. She has published work in numerous journals including *Waxwing*, *As/Us*, *The Collagist*, *The Toast*, and *McSweeney's Open Letters*. She has been an editor for *Quarterly West* and *South Dakota Review* and is currently an Assistant Professor at Colorado College. She teaches creative writing, Native American literature, and experimental/innovative fiction. Natanya spends her time thinking about monsters, societal fears and abjection, how time shapes narrative, liminal voices and broken forms, how the body is made weird by expectations of normalcy, and graphic novels. She and her husband and two dogs love living near the Rockies.

EDITOR

Julia Dixon Evans is author of the novel *Other Burning Places*, forthcoming from Dzanc Books. Her fiction can be found or is forthcoming in *Hobart, Monkeybicycle, Paper Darts, Black Candies,* and elsewhere. Her non-fiction work can be found or is forthcoming in *Barrelhouse* and *Like the Wind*. She works on programming, publishing, education, and production for So Say We All in San Diego, and has taught creative writing for many non-profit and education institutions. She was a PEN in the Community Resident in 2014 and received a Poets & Writers Grant in 2015. Her editing credits include *Incoming* and *The Radvocate*. Twitter: @juliadixonevans.

BOOK DESIGNER

Carolyn Ramos is a graphic designer who pushed pixels for an ad agency in Guam, nightlife moguls in Vegas, and junior apparel in downtown Los Angeles, just to find her way back to San Diego. She's currently the art director at the alt-weekly *San Diego CityBeat* and draws pictures as **somaramos**. Her illustrations have found homes for mostly independent projects including Tight Songs for Fresh Selects in Portland, music 14KT in Los Angeles and M Restaurants in London. She enjoys breakfast at night, whiskey, palindromes and a trusty alter ego. You can see more of her work at somaramos.com. Instagram: @somaramos.

FOUNDING EDITOR

Ryan Bradford is author of *Horror Business* and the founder of *Black Candies*.

ACKNOWLEDGMENTS

First, all of my appreciation to the contributors to this journal. Your words and stories have run through my own self—mind, bones, and veins—for many woke and dreaming hours now. This issue would not be possible without your efforts, patience, and attentiveness, and, of course, your talents, wisdom, and originality. I'm in awe of each of you.

A robust "Thank you!" to So Say We All and all that have supported *Black Candies* now and in the past. Much appreciation for sharing links and spreading the word, for building spaces for community and art without hesitation and always with such vim!

Thank you to my JP and to all my family and friends for listening and cheering.

Thank you, Dr. Angela Marie Smith. Without your Horror and Gender course and your support at the University of Utah, I would have never known how to listen to these voices and stories. I wouldn't have known what that delightfully gruesome throbbing was within each of these selections and this issue simply wouldn't exist.

Always love and glee for the singular Ryan Bradford and his brainchild *Black Candies*. I remember the first inklings of this journal and the DIY stapled copies we squealed about many years ago. Thank you for inviting me into this beautiful monster of yours and for clearing a space for the kind of horror that makes a home in our spines. Thank you for committing to this special issue and handing over the reins with so much trust. And you have my sincere love and appreciation for stepping back when I wanted to trust you more than I wanted to trust myself.

Lastly and with all my heart, thank you Julia Evans for not just being an amazingly badass hummingbird hawkmoth assistant editor and facilitator of all things admin on this project, but for your wise, funny, sharp, sensible, dreamy, and encouraging support and friendship. You're a treasure and everyone who works with you should know this (and tell you everyday).

Natanya Ann Pulley
2016

Made in the USA
Middletown, DE
18 December 2016